# TOSS THE BOUQUET

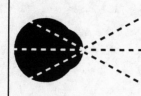

This Large Print Book carries the
Seal of Approval of N.A.V.H.

# TOSS THE BOUQUET

## THREE SPRING LOVE STORIES

## RUTH LOGAN HERNE, AMY MATAYO, JANICE THOMPSON

**THORNDIKE PRESS**
*A part of Gale, Cengage Learning*

GALE
CENGAGE Learning·

Farmington Hills, Mich • San Francisco • New York • Waterville, Maine
Meriden, Conn • Mason, Ohio • Chicago

**GALE**
CENGAGE Learning·

Thorndike Press® Large Print Christian Romance.
The text of this Large Print edition is unabridged.
Other aspects of the book may vary from the original edition.
Set in 16 pt. Plantin.

**LIBRARY OF CONGRESS CATALOGING-IN-PUBLICATION DATA**

Names: Herne, Ruth Logan. All dressed up in love. | Matayo, Amy. In tune with
  love. | Thompson, Janice A. Never a bridesmaid.
Title: Toss the bouquet : three spring love stories / Ruth Logan Herne, Amy
  Matayo, Janice Thompson.
Description: Large print edition. | Waterville, Maine : Thorndike Press, 2016. |
  © 2015 | Series: Thorndike Press large print Christian romance
Identifiers: LCCN 2016005730 | ISBN 9781410488268 (hardback) | ISBN 1410488268
  (hardcover)
Subjects: LCSH: Christian fiction, American. | Romance fiction, American. |
  Weddings—Fiction. | Large type books. | BISAC: FICTION / Christian / Romance.
Classification: LCC PS648.C43 T67 2016b | DDC 813/.01083823—dc23
LC record available at http://lccn.loc.gov/2016005730

Published in 2016 by arrangement with The Zondervan Corporation,
LLC, a subsidiary of HarperCollins Christian Publishing, Inc.

Printed in Mexico
1 2 3 4 5 6 7 20 19 18 17 16

# CONTENTS

**ALL DRESSED UP IN LOVE** . . . . . 7

**IN TUNE WITH LOVE** . . . . . . . 155

**NEVER A BRIDESMAID** . . . . . . 289

■ ■ ■ ■

# ALL DRESSED UP
## IN LOVE

RUTH LOGAN HERNE

■ ■ ■ ■

*To Jean, Kathy, and Donna, who welcomed me into "Bridal Hall" and made eight years of my life so much fun! God bless you, my friends! You are beloved!*

# CHAPTER ONE

Greg Elizondo stared at the daily ledger on the front desk of his mother's bridal salon. The white leather-bound appointment book taunted him. He swallowed hard and fought the rising surge of panic.

Six appointments were due in throughout the day and no one to handle them. Six future brides, along with whatever form of friend, family, or foe they dragged through the front door with them, coming to find the dress of their dreams for that oh-so-special day. And no one but him in the store.

Panic escalated to full-bore heart attack mode.

*Call some of your mother's former employees. Someone must be able to help.*

They would, too, if only they were available. They had gathered around him at the midsummer funeral, professing their love for his mother and pledging their help. And his mother's regular employees — her

11

"bridal team," as she'd called them — had done a great job keeping things afloat all fall.

Then Donna delivered twins at Thanksgiving, and Jean needed time off unexpectedly to care for her sick father. Kathy was down with the current stomach bug, and the newest bridal consultant had called in yesterday, the last day of her vacation, to give notice, saying she was staying in Louisiana to save some fish from extinction.

Who did that kind of thing, anyway?

Maybe there was somebody else. Anybody.

His mother's 1980s Rolodex lay in the top drawer. He leafed through it, searching for familiar names. Two of them had gone south for retirement, one had passed away the previous year, and the only other name he recognized had just been put into a skilled nursing facility near Valley Forge.

*Doomed by your own ineptitude. You should have taken care of this yesterday. There is no way Kathy could or should have handled this on her own, so blaming the norovirus doesn't get you out of the hot seat. At this point, you deserve what you get.*

His fingers went numb. His head ached. He could handle boardrooms filled with Armani-clad executives. Toss him into dinner gigs staffed by tuxedo-wearing waiters who faded into the background while taking particular care to be attentive, and he'd be totally on his game.

But this?

Mermaid gowns with laser-cut lace? Dresses suited for a medieval drawing room with acres of organza? He wasn't even sure what organza was, but he was pretty sure he hated it by default.

Satin-filled walls pressed in on him as the clock ticked on.

Why did Donna Martin have to go and have twins, anyway? Wasn't the world populated enough?

With less angst than he was feeling right now, he had faced down oppositional executives and told them that his law firm was about to take over their company, slice it up, and sell it off piecemeal, like leftovers from yesterday's garage sale. Nothing fazed him. Nothing but . . . well, but this.

The bridal team hadn't listed phone numbers next to the names in the appointment ledger. If they had, he'd call these women, apologize profusely, and lock the doors on Elena's Bridal forever. Except that doing so would break his heart.

If he had a heart . . .

He must have one somewhere, because it ached when he thought of his mother, the time he missed, the long weeks he barely saw her, even though they lived in the same quadrant of the city. His corporate ladder-climbing kept him forward focused, but now she was gone, unexpectedly, and there was no more time.

There were no more chances. He was surrounded by the business she spent thirty years developing after his father took off with a long-legged blonde. From three days shy of his fourth birthday, it had been him and his mother, taking on life side by side.

And now it was just him. What could be more distressing than shutting down? How could he even consider ruining thirty years of all her hard work in six short months? He hauled in a deep breath and checked the book again.

Yup. Still six brides scheduled for their initial appointments, a day his mother referred to as "feast or famine." Shopping for a gown either brought folks together or ripped them apart.

*Great.*

He stood and squared his shoulders. He could do this. He *needed* to do this.

He didn't have to dress the women. Their friends or sisters or mothers could do that. Worst-case scenario, they could dress themselves, right? The sight of an alterations room at the end of the right-hand hallway gave him an idea. He'd call the seamstresses and see if any of them were available to help.

No one answered. He left messages for all three, hoping someone would hear his plea and take pity on him. Having one of those talented alterations women on hand would be a huge help, but if none of them came through, he needed a Plan B.

What would his mother do?

He didn't have to think twice. If Maria Elena Elizondo were here, she would do it herself. Her example had trained him to handle whatever came his way. Today was no different, but it was a whole lot lonelier.

So that was it. He would show the brides and their entourages through the store, let them pick out what they wanted to try on, then guide them through the sales process.

Could it be that simple?

Common sense said no. If selling a wedding gown were that cut and dried, why did his mother list follow-up phone calls as part of her training manual? With hundreds of gorgeous designer gowns to pick from, didn't women usually just find one that looked great, plunk down their debit card, and leave?

*Fittings and alterations. Hems. Veils. Tiaras. Jewelry. Shoes. Hosiery, hoops, petticoats . . .*

His mother's checklist went on to undergarments he didn't know existed.

The panic re-spiraled. In twenty minutes the store would open, the first January appointment would walk through the door, and he'd be toast. And once word got around that Elena's Bridal had no help, online reviews would tank and he'd be putting a For Sale sign in the front window.

So much for all his mother's hard work. Everything he needed in life — everything he *was* — had come from this shop. Parochial school. Holy Ghost Prep. The University of Pennsylvania. Harvard Law.

His mother had gone the distance for him, working night and day, never a word of complaint. Losing her suddenly was bad enough, but ruining her hard-won business because he was clueless?

That would cost a bunch of jobs. No one wanted to be jobless in Philadelphia right now. Not in today's tough economy.

*So the economy is your fault? Don't you have enough to do with the Weatherly merger? If you want a job alongside the heavy hitters in Manhattan, focus on what you do best: dissecting inept companies and selling them for parts.*

A sharp rap on the front glass snagged his attention.

16

A young woman stood there, tapping her keys against the glass. A customer? He glanced back at the book and caught a glimpse of a name: Jasmine. It had to be, right?

He stared, spellbound, wondering why she was so early. He started to point up to the clock, then realized that was a horrible way to do business and went to the door. He unlocked it, swung it open, and leaned out. "We're not open yet. Sorry. But would you like to wait inside?" He added the last as a gust of arctic-cold January wind swept down the narrow side street filled with rustic-looking shops. "It's really cold out here."

She stepped in, glanced around, then turned his way, expectant.

"Are you Jasmine?"

She frowned, shook her head, and pulled down the scarf she had tucked and wrapped around her collar. Honey-brown curls spilled forth, a lot of them, like in one of those shampoo commercials that promised the best hair ever if you bought the product. Whatever product she used, worked, because this woman had the best hair ever.

"I'm Tara. Tara Simonetti."

He frowned. There was no Tara Simonetti in the book. "Are you meeting a bride here, Miss Simonetti?"

17

She looked startled, then laughed and shrugged out of her coat. She tossed the coat and scarf on one of the chairs inside the door, turned, and stared at the bridal room beyond him.

"Whatever I do from this moment forward, please don't hold against me." Reverence marked her gaze and words as she swept the racks of gowns with a long, slow, almost comical look of appreciation. "I'm in heaven."

She moved forward, and Greg wasn't sure if he should call the police or a mental health facility. The look in her eyes said she was about to go ballistic. And if there was one thing Greg Elizondo purposely avoided, it was women who went ballistic.

*You're in a bridal store, buddy. Trust me. It happens.*

He brushed the internal warning aside and started to move forward, but then she turned, shoved her hands into her pockets, and breathed deeply. "Are you the owner?"

"Not intentionally, but yes." A jab of pain struck his mid-section. "I am. Greg Elizondo. This was my mother's shop."

"Your mother?" Tara stopped. A look of realization passed over her face, a very pretty face, alive with emotions. Bold eyebrows, strong and sharply etched. The mass

18

of hair framed a slightly squared face that seemed perfect for her. Golden-brown eyes that would have matched her hair, except for the points of ivory making them brighter. A generous mouth for her petite face, and she wasn't afraid to use just enough makeup to enhance features that didn't need embellishment.

"Is she gone?"

He nodded, still unable to say the words out loud. No one should just up and die suddenly in their midfifties, before they had the joy of retirement and the fun of bouncing a grandchild or two on their knees. But the unexpected cardiac arrest said otherwise, and the admission made his throat grow tight. "Yes. Last summer. It was sudden."

"Oh. I'm so very sorry."

She looked sorry. Her face, her gaze, the way she reached out a hand to his arm, as if his mother had meant something to her. She hadn't, of course, but still, the sincerity of the emotion seemed nice.

"Is that why you need help, Greg?"

He stared, perplexed.

She crossed to the chair and withdrew a sheet of paper from her coat pocket. Suddenly things began to look clearer. "The 'Help Wanted' flyer I posted in the commons area at Temple."

"Which has now been taken down because the minute I saw it, I knew I wanted this job."

Relief flooded him. "You've got experience in bridal, Tara?"

"Doesn't every girl?" She laughed, eyes bright. "Barbie 101. I could dress her and Ken with the best of them."

"So . . . you don't have experience." He'd been almost hopeful for just a minute.

"Not hands on, as yet. But here's hoping that will change." She flicked a sunny glance around the broad, open shop where white walls met natural wood in a calming effect of neutrality. "I've always wanted to work in a bridal shop, but I'm from a tiny northern Pennsylvania town and there was nothing like that there. I'm in my third year of law school doing work I could have completed my second year without breaking a sweat, and my student loans and grants have been sliced and diced by federal budget cuts. On top of that, I have a great appreciation for regular meals. Working here will give me the taste of bridal I crave, the hands-on experience of working with fabric, and the added bonus of food money. Total win, right?"

It was so far from a "win" that Greg had to choke back the first thoughts that came to mind. "Tara, I appreciate your enthusiasm, but the bridal industry isn't like anything else in retail."

"And you're an expert on retail and bridal?"

Her cool rebuff put him on guard. "Not an expert, but I've watched my mother and her friends run this business for years, and it requires a certain level of insider knowledge. I'm a lawyer, you're a 3-L, and we both know we don't take classes in silk and shantung in law school."

"Really?"

She hiked a brow his way, and something in that arched brow told him that if he was shooting pool with Tara Simonetti, she'd be pocketing the eight-ball before he got half his stripes played.

"Is your mother's staff here?"

He grimaced and clapped a hand to the back of his neck. "No. One has eight-week-old twins —"

"Oh, I love twins!" Tara couldn't possibly be inventing the look of joy she shot his way. "Boys, girls, or a mixed set?"

"Boys. As I was saying . . ."

"Fraternal or identical?"

He had no idea. Why would he ask that? Why would *she* ask that? He started to bring the question back around to the matter at hand, but she put up a hand to pause him. "So she's out for a while, I take it."

"Yes."

"And who else works here?"

"Jean, she's marvelous, but her father's ill and she's got to have a few weeks to take care of him. He's a great old guy." He shrugged because Jean's dad had been good to him for the twelve years she worked here. No way could he begrudge her time with him, even if it left them in a lurch.

She glanced around the roomy store, puzzled. "That's it?"

"No, of course not." Two people could never run a thriving bridal business. The idea was ridiculous. "There's Kathy, she's been the assistant manager for years. She's the greatest lady."

"Is she in the back?" Tara moved left and peeked around a corner, then turned back with a questioning gaze.

"Norovirus."

"Ouch. So she's out for —"

"A couple of days, most likely."

"Which leaves you. Unless you've got other employees?"

"We're in a bind, but honestly, Miss Simonetti . . ."

"Tara." She corrected him as she flipped her head forward and down, the mass of hair tumbling halfway to the floor. He stared as she wound it into a twist, tucked it up and under, then wove a pencil through the hair, creating an old-fashioned and very professional knot just above the nape of her neck.

And a very pretty neck it was.

"Greg, you don't know me. And I'm going to bet you don't know bridal all that well, because the minute I saw your name I recognized it. Anyone who's followed mergers and acquisitions would realize you've been too busy dissecting companies to have much wedding experience yourself."

Was that a backhanded compliment or a clever dig? He wasn't sure. "While that's true, I —"

A young woman appeared at the entrance and peered in through the glass.

Tara glanced toward the door. It was the stroke of ten, Saturday morning. The first customer had arrived.

She smiled and offered a challenge. "Let me have a try with this one. If it's a total bust, you win. I'll leave and go flip burgers to earn food money."

"And if you do well?"

"Then we settle on wages and compensation at the end of the day."

"Compensation? Don't wages qualify as

23

compensation, Tara? Because they do in the corporate world." He said it as a challenge, but he had to admire the way she tossed the barter out there, as if she had bargaining rights.

"I was thinking along the lines of a cheese-steak from Sonny's and a Rita's frozen ice. I'm planning to be hungry by five."

She turned and greeted the first bridal group as they stepped through the inner door. Taking her jacket and theirs, she hung them in the closet to the far left. She let him enter the bride's information into the computerized system while she walked around the cavernous bridal room to his right.

She slipped on a pair of dark-rimmed glasses as she surveyed the displays, and his heart about fell out of his chest.

The tucked-up hair, well-done makeup, and "I'm smarter than you thought" glasses made him draw a deep breath.

She said she was a 3-L, a third-year law student, across town at Temple. That meant she'd be leaving in a few months, going back to wherever she came from, her law degree in hand. But if looks could sell wedding gowns?

Tara Simonetti would get a solid commission check come February.

24

# CHAPTER TWO

Smokin' hot with the greatest eyes known to mankind.

The phrase summed up Greg Elizondo, with his dark, wavy hair, deep brown eyes, thick brows, and rugged jaw. At about five-ten he wasn't huge, but he carried himself huge, which explained the legal kudos surrounding his work a few blocks away in Center City.

*You're not interviewing for a date, sweetums. You want a job, and if you get the job at the end of the day? Crushing on the boss would be a stupid action on your part. Savvy?*

Tara savvied, all right, and she had a list of solid reasons to avoid ladder-climbing lawyer types, so she nudged the handsome owner into a mental closet labeled "hands off" and examined the walls of gowns surrounding her. Silk brocade, embroidered hems, Swarovski crystals, draped bodices, and ruched side-sweeps.

Tara Simonetti was pretty sure she'd died and gone to heaven.

First, Greg Elizondo's mother was pure genius at organization because each gown was tagged with a number that corresponded with area tags coded for each designer. If someone wanted a Maggie, she knew where to go. If they were after an Angelo, the chart showed Tara where to find it. If she had questions that needed to be looked up on the computer, she called on Greg to do that, and he seemed more than happy to help.

Still, by one o'clock she realized she was nearly an hour behind, and that wouldn't bode well for the later appointments. Just when she thought she'd run into major time-crunch danger zone, an older woman with a pencil stuck behind her ear marched into the bridal area as if about to lead a delegation into battle. Or — and Tara hoped this was the correct assumption — she'd come to help.

The middle-aged woman stuck out her hand to Tara. "I'm Maisy and I do alterations here. I don't want to brag, but if it's a tricky fit or sizing, I'm first to be called. Now today, for instance?" She offered a brisk smile to the customers gathered around the first dressing room. "Greg called to see if I could come in to help." She folded her hands across her ample middle, and Tara had a feeling that when Maisy meant business, she meant business. "I'm not one bit good at selling anything, but when it comes to moving gowns and dressing girls, well . . ." She clapped her hands together to show a job well done. "I can handle that with the best of them. And . . ." She stared at Tara as if groping for a name.

"Tara."

"Tara here can tell you the ins and outs."

Tara nodded agreement but then wanted to hug the older woman when she went on. "Normally we'd have a little more time to do things. We lost our owner not too long ago, so it's been a tough holiday season for the Elizondo family."

Instant sympathy marked every single face in the two groups of people.

"But with the new season on us . . ." Her tone said everyone should sit up straight and listen. They did, Tara included. "We're pulling everybody back to work, and we're determined to make this the best bridal season Elena's has ever seen."

The gathered shoppers adopted a "rally around the flag" attitude with gusto. Sisters and bridesmaids jumped in to help, and Tara became more like a sideline coach than

27

a proper bridal consultant. With Maisy's help, she locked in several sales before bride number four walked in the door at one thirty.

*Hello, Bridezilla.*

Tara recognized the symptoms from the score of magazine articles she'd read about *not* being Bridezilla. Obviously this bride — Aislynn — hadn't read the articles, or didn't care. With a single glance, Tara put a mental check mark in both columns.

"I don't do princess anything," Aislynn announced with an authority more at home in a boardroom than a bridal showcase. "And I'm not a bit froufrou. My style" — she paused with purpose, elongating the word as if it had multiple syllables while aiming a chilled look at Tara's skater skirt, loose blouse, and bolero jacket — "is Hepburn elegant splashed with Hepburn chic."

"Perfect," Tara exclaimed, ignoring the condescending once-over because she thought this outfit was super cute. *Take that, Bridezilla.* "I love both Hepburns too."

Tara's quick take on the bride's riddled request lightened Aislynn's expression, a definite plus. "Katharine's humor made her movies some of my all-time faves," Tara continued, "and Audrey's fragility?" She sighed. "Breathtaking. So why don't we start with Dona Dona's Vintage line?"

"You have the Vintage gowns in?" Aislynn appeared impressed, and Tara was willing to bet that not much impressed Aislynn. "I thought only select stores were allowed to carry that collection."

"Stores in classic, vintage, and/or historic locations got the nod for the Vintage line because the backdrop complements the gown. You won't find these in malls because Dona Dona decided a classic gown needed a similar setting and Elena's is the only shop in the greater Philadelphia area allowed to carry them."

"Aislynn, aren't you glad I made the appointment here instead of at the mall? This is perfect!" Aislynn's mother preened from the side.

"New York has plenty of shops, Mother. Well staffed with amazing designer connections." Aislynn trained an impatient look on her mother. "But I wanted you happy, so I'm spending my last free Saturday for the next month here at" — she pursed her lips as if saying the words proved distasteful — "Elena's place."

Maisy almost growled. She didn't, but Tara recognized the temptation because she felt the same way. She thrust two gowns at Maisy, excused herself, and went to the front desk to grab a new wedding folder from Greg. He angled his eyes toward the grumpy bride, then dropped his gaze to hers.

Those eyes. The kind a girl could get lost in. Lashes that should be considered wasted on a guy, but on him?

*Not wasted at all.*

Strong facial planes, a hint of dark stubble already dusking his chin, and the cleft in that chin? It matched the little wrinkle in his forehead, and they were both to die for.

"What's up with her attitude?"

His question brought her straight back to the task of the day: winning a job in this bridal shop. She scrunched her brow. "Classic 'it's all about me' type. Every bridal operation gets a few, and we treat them like we do any Very Special Customer." She drew a bright pink heart on the outside of the folder and tapped it lightly. "With lots of tender, loving care."

Greg noted the pink heart and grinned. "Great idea."

"Thank you." She took the folder back to the sales floor while Maisy pulled a few more dresses. By the time the late-afternoon appointments arrived, Tara had pulled over sixty dresses, which meant she'd re-hung almost as many.

30

Greg did the paperwork for the sales, relieving her of that task. Maisy showed her how to get accurate measurements to assess the best possible size to order, and by the time the last young woman left the shop at 5:05, she'd booked three bridesmaid parties totaling sixteen people. On top of that she'd sold three stunning wedding gowns, had info on the other three, and met Greg's grin of approval with a matching smile.

"I'm amazed," he confessed as he turned the key in the lock. "I thought we were doomed."

"Well, it wouldn't have gone so smoothly without Maisy." Tara turned and gave the older woman a spontaneous hug. "That meant everything, having you here to help get the girls dressed while I was jumping from room to room with the bridesmaids."

"Not our normal method of operation," Greg admitted. "Mom always liked each bride to feel like they had our undivided attention from start to finish. That was her hallmark, and she made it work."

"Which is fine when there's enough help on hand," Maisy reminded him, and the strength of Maisy's tone suggested she liked to speak her mind. "But we've had times in the store where folks drop in without an appointment, and your mother knew to spread

31

herself thin as needed. Sales are the bottom line, and she would have been proud of how well Tara did today. How long have you been here, dearie?"

"One day."

Maisy pretended to clean out her ears. "You don't mean that, surely. I've been off for a few weeks because December is slow. You started today?"

"On a bit of a challenge, yes." She turned back toward Greg. "So what's the verdict, boss? Did I meet the challenge? Do I have the job?"

"You crushed it." He bumped knuckles with her and handed over an old-school application. "Fill this out and we'll talk hours. Is your final semester class schedule light like it usually is for third-year law students?"

"To the point of boredom, yes, so I'll fill this out and return it on Monday. Did you book appointments for next week?" she asked. "Because this is the season for girls to be out shopping, planning summer and fall weddings. We don't want to miss the opportunity to strike while the iron's hot. Who knows how many girls found engagement rings under their Christmas trees? Bridal stores thrive on locking in those winter and spring sales."

"I did book appointments, actually, although I berated myself every time the phone rang." He tipped his head, watching her. "How do you know this stuff?"

She exchanged a look with Maisy that said all women knew this stuff, but cut him some slack because he was a guy. In Tara's book it was okay that most men didn't know this kind of thing.

On top of that, she loved weddings. She loved the gilt, glitz, and glamour right alongside the simple and the vintage and —

*Everything.*

The planning, the implementation.

She'd married off her fashion model dolls on a regular basis years ago. The advent of bridal reality shows mush-roomed her dream into something bigger and bolder. While she was busy making top grades in her law classes, her heart was planning seating charts and floral arrangements for friends.

She *loved* it. Being here, immersed in the wonderful world of weddings at Elena's Bridal, was a dream come true, but a temporary one because in four short months she'd become a law school graduate. Her duty then was to return to her hometown in upstate Pennsylvania and help serve the people of Kenneville, a pledge she made long ago.

But for now she'd revel in the joy of being Tara Simonetti, bridal consultant extraordinaire.

*An amazing woman.*

Greg wasn't thinking about Tara's looks, although they fit the bill.

And he wasn't weighing up how well she did today, bouncing from customer to customer, remembering names, occupations, wedding details, then gathering that wellspring of information into locked-in sales with a final total of over ten thousand dollars. And that was without the bridesmaids' dresses and the accessories.

What truly astounded him was her appetite.

She wolfed down a Philly cheesesteak, an order of cheese fries, and a Rita's lemon ice with barely a pause except to talk about wages and hours.

She was incredible. Focused. And hungry.

He thought back to his third year of law school and cringed. The lighter course load meant too much partying. And he'd still done well. He didn't remember being short on funds or hungry, though, which meant he should have appreciated his mother more than he already did.

"I've seen truckers eat with more finesse."

He nudged her shoulder as she finished the last bit of lemon ice and was glad when she laughed, un-insulted.

"I was hungry. I've learned to camel-pack food because when I get caught up in a project or a job, I forget to eat."

Greg couldn't imagine forgetting to eat because food was, well . . . food. And delicious. But something about Tara made him think that maybe she didn't forget food as much as she pushed the thought aside as unaffordable. That realization seemed to fit her profile. Driven. Tough. Short on funds.

But at ease with herself and her body, unlike most women he'd met lately. Tara liked herself, and that was a refreshing change.

"So what are you doing tomorrow?" She swiped a napkin across her mouth, tossed it away, and looked up at him.

"You asking me out?" He grinned because the thought appealed to him instantly.

She made a funny face that said, *Um . . . no,* and he found himself wishing she'd at least considered the idea. "Not in this lifetime. Never date the boss: sage advice from where I'm standing. But the store will be open on Sundays starting next week. It's closed tomorrow, and if I can take the afternoon to go through things, I can familiarize myself with the dresses, the manufacturers, the layout of the files. I can also see who's got spring weddings coming up, because those girls need to be reminded to make their fitting appointments, try on their veils, double check for shoes and accessories. Did you know that some of the more savvy manufacturers are designing dresses with deep pockets?"

He didn't know that and wasn't sure why it was significant. "And that's important because — ?"

"A bride needs to have things on hand on her wedding day. A purse is a terrible inconvenience. A maid of honor with an emergency bag is wonderful, but just when you need her help, she's dancing with the best man's brother, so if the bride has pockets" — she patted the right hip of her jacket — "she's got a miniature arsenal at hand. Pretty solid."

"I never would have thought of such a thing," he admitted, but the thought of a bride facing a whole long day with nowhere to put anything made her logic sensible. "I can see where it would come in handy. But I'm going to bet those mermaid dresses don't have pockets. There's barely room in them for the bride."

She made a face of agreement as they walked toward her brick apartment building. "If you're sporting the perfect hourglass shape, they rock. Right now the mermaid look has taken command of the advertising end of the industry, über-dramatic and crazy chic, but those dresses aren't comfortable, you can barely dance in them, and I've seen brides have to be lifted into limousines because they can't move their legs enough to climb into the car unassisted."

"You're kidding."

Her expression said she didn't kid about bridal, and Greg was beginning to believe it. "Glamour and comfort *can* go hand in hand. I wish more girls realized that. The way your mother's shop is laid out, I can see she understood that premise. It's not just the fashion of the moment. It's the timelessness of the fashion."

She had the common sense of an established business-woman in a fairly young package. Sure, she had to be pretty smart to get into the law school at Temple, but smart and sensible didn't always mesh. He worked with a lot of smart folks, but a fair percentage of them had trouble finding their way in out of the rain.

Based on today's observations, he was pretty sure Tara would know how to get out of the rain and equally sure that if she got wet in the meantime, she'd handle it just fine.

"Thanks for walking me, Greg." She turned her gaze to the plain front door, quite different from the colonial-style upscale row house he lived in. "Is it all right for me to check out the shop tomorrow? You don't have to hang around. I'm sure you've got other things to do."

*Football playoffs.*

His buddy Tim was having a bunch of the guys in for football and wings. He'd been an Eagles fan from the time he was a pup; he even had one of their old-style bright-green jackets to prove it. He'd played football and run track, racking up good grades and great scores.

In the end, education won. Sensibility grabbed hold and wouldn't let go, urging him to make his success on the paper-pushing side of higher education. His big self-reward on fall and winter weekends was football. "I'm tied up tomorrow, but I can let you in. Then I'll swing by later to lock up or just leave you the key and the security code."

"Perfect." She stuck out her hand.

He grabbed hold, and for the life of him, he didn't want to let go. He stood there, looking down, meeting her gaze, hands locked, and if a bus hadn't rumbled by just then, they might have become frozen in time, one of the many Philadelphia sculptures pigeons and tourists adored.

"Well, good night." She pulled her hand free as if the electricity of the moment had no effect on her, and that was just as well.

If she didn't feel it, he must have been imagining things.

*That went way beyond imagination. Admit it, she's . . . intriguing.* He shushed the internal voice as the door swung shut behind her. He turned to walk the mile and a quarter back to his place, glad he hadn't brought the car. Walking might clear his brain. Smack some sense into him.

His cell phone interrupted the moment. He grabbed it up, scanned the number, and accepted the call. "Reed, what's up in New York?"

"Two openings custom-made for you at One Financial Center," his law school buddy reported. "And like we expected, they're looking at the Philadelphia and Boston offices to fill them."

"My name's in," Greg assured him. "I forwarded my updated résumé last week." He'd applied to the New York office of his law firm when he was fresh out of law school, months before he passed the bar, but he'd been assigned to Philadelphia. In hindsight, it had worked out. He'd had the last seven years near his mother. If he'd been in the New York office, he wouldn't have seen her nearly as much.

*As much?* the voice in his head scoffed. *You might have seen her more. You might have prioritized hopping a train or grabbing a flight home. Instead, you lived six blocks away and barely saw your mother once a month.* An ache the size of the Walt Whitman Bridge yawned open inside him.

His mother had labored so hard, so long, and he'd never appreciated how crazy her life must have been until he spent today watching a much younger woman run around, dealing with people, pomp, and personalities.

All those years, often working seven days a week during the busy season, running the show, booking brides, selling, cleaning, ironing, mending. She'd done it for him, so he could be strong and successful. Never once did she make him feel guilty about it.

He felt guilty now. The thought of what she gave up, what she was willing to do —

Why would God take her at this stage? What point was there in putting a faith-filled woman through her paces, then letting her die before she ever had a chance to enjoy life? Was that how it worked? Because if it was, if there was some Supreme Being calling the shots, Greg was pretty sure he didn't call the game fairly.

"I'll be on the lookout for more info from this end," Reed told him. "I'd love to have you here. There's nothing like weekend nightlife in the Big Apple. Pretty wild, my friend."

"Keep me posted, Reed." Greg hung up the phone. Clubs. Professional sports. Upscale apartments and rooftop gardens. The chronic bustle that was Manhattan. What could be better? What more could he possibly want?

He was almost home now. He passed the Old City Mission and the quaint brick church around the corner. The sign outside gave times for services, and every Sunday morning the bells chimed a welcome, the steeple stretching up between old oaks.

And every weekend he waited them out, rolled over, and went back to sleep.

A strong wind broadsided him from the Delaware River.

His mother was gone. The days were short and dark at both ends. The coastal wind was brutal, and either snow or icy rain had pelted the city since the loneliness of the just-past holiday season. He ached for something new and different. Something vital and vibrant.

New York City was all that and more, but the thought of selling Elena's Bridal — if he could find a buyer — galled him. Could he do it?

*Hey. Life goes on. Change happens. The team knows this. They'll be okay with whatever you decide.*

He grimaced as he shut the brightly painted historic door behind him.

They'd *pretend* to be okay because they loved him. He'd been surrounded by pseudo-mothers from the time he was a little boy. Kathy, Jean, and Maisy had shared in his joys and sorrows, his successes and failures. And to pull the rug out from under Donna and those twins . . .

Where else would she find a job that understood the importance of raising her babies and earning a living?

*Not. Your. Problem,* the niggling voice inside reminded him.

Not so. It *was* his problem, and he knew it. His mother had raised him to be considerate, to put others first. But when he looked in the mirror, the image he saw was his father, Carlos Elizondo. Hard-hearted, heavy-handed, and crazy competitive, his father's legacy seemed to take hold more fiercely every day.

But in his mother's life, in her work? Kindness mattered. And he could do no less.

By the time he climbed into bed and closed his eyes, he was able to switch off some of his wandering thoughts, but two images remained. The sight of Tara Simonetti doing a slow, full-circle spin in his mother's store as if she'd just grabbed the gold ring on the carousel . . .

And the sweet rush of awareness that woke him out of a months-long funk when his hand gripped hers.

He fell asleep remembering the warmth of her hand and the true sympathy in her eyes, and for the first time since last summer, he slept soundly.

# CHAPTER THREE

She hadn't wanted to let go last night.

The grip of Greg's fingers, the touch of his hand, the strength in his gaze, had made her long to linger. She wanted to step forward. Meet his smile. Grip his hand a little tighter, longer.

So, of course, she stepped back.

Tara frowned into the mirror, remembering Greg's face, his profile, his shoulders, his . . .

Everything.

The shirt and tie. The casual sport coat that said custom designers and good taste mixed well. The black trench so typical of professional men in big cities, uniform to the max.

She saw beyond the tough negotiator and read the sorrow in his eyes. His lingering sadness melted her.

But she'd been raised in the fallout of a ladder-climbing lawyer. Her family had suffered for nearly two decades because of one man's greed. The moral of that story was that she would always tread carefully, even though she longed to stare into Greg Elizondo's big brown eyes for oh, say, forever?

She couldn't risk it.

She'd be kind, friendly, and compassionate because the guy had been through a grievous loss, but that's where she'd draw the line. Greg's professional record and competitive nature put him in the "Danger Zone" category. She glanced at the clock and hurried out the door to catch the midmorning service in the two-towered church around the corner.

*With God comes joy.*

Bells chimed happiness around the City of Brotherly Love every Sunday morning, their call a reminder of what built this great nation: the longing for religious freedom.

She slipped into the church, loving the brass-trimmed old lighting, the ornate wooden panels, and the carved balustrade wrapping the choir loft.

A blue-robed woman waved from above. Her friend Truly Dixon.

Tara waved back as the gospel group began a harmonized hum before breaking into the opening song of praise.

Tara left the church an hour later feeling

energized, ready to walk the one-point-five miles to the bridal store.

Ice-cold, wind-driven rain changed her mind. She waited in the covered entry of the church for a bus, dashed across the road when she saw it approaching, and took a full-on splash from a careless driver heading in the opposite direction.

A few minutes later Tara arrived at the store — nearly an hour before she was scheduled to meet Greg. She sighed, scanning her options. The full-frontal drenching had put a damper on her church-inspired hope.

A nearby coffee shop smelled marvelous and looked warm.

She succumbed to the temptation, grabbed a plain coffee, and doctored it up with mocha powder, cream, and a dash of vanilla. It wasn't fancy, but it was tasty and cheap, and these days, that was her rule of thumb.

The church bells woke Greg, as they always did on Sunday morning. Bright, vibrant, ringing in the new day with a gusto that should be reserved for classic movies.

*Make a joyful noise unto the Lord.*

One of Maria Elena's favorite verses nudged him. She'd have been there this morning, singing. Praising. Praying.

And he'd have rolled his eyes, turned over, and gone back to sleep. But the bell's tolling seemed even more enthusiastic than usual.

Rain drummed overhead.

Sleet beat against his back window.

Clearly the bell's excitement wasn't weather related.

*Tara.*

He jumped up, scanned the clock, and panicked. Those were the noon service bells, not the early ones. He'd promised to meet Tara at noon, and apparently he had slept through the first bells and was already late. He threw on some clothes, grabbed his coat, and jogged toward the shopping district.

The miserable weather magnified his guilt as he passed the mission and hooked a left. She was trying to do him a good turn, learn the business he was in danger of losing, and now he'd kept her waiting. Talk about a first-class jerk.

He reached the shop and headed for the door, then heard his name and turned. Tara was hailing him from the coffee shop across the street with a look of . . . welcome expectation? Her kindness pushed him undeservedly into the "hero" category.

"Good morning." Gladness brightened

her face as he crossed the road. "I got here early and grabbed coffee."

Greg tapped his watch apologetically. "Technically afternoon, my bad, and coffee sounds like an excellent idea." He grinned down at her and fought the sweet swell of emotion growing within. Her forthright smile was absolutely contagious. He eyed her empty cup. "Can I get you another?"

She shook her head.

"You might want one later, and you can't leave the store with the doors open," he reminded her. "Although you could always lock up and run over. And you had no problem making me buy you food last night," he added. "So I would think a Sunday coffee would fall within the parameters of *compensation for job well done.*"

"An excellent point, so I'll say yes."

"What kind?"

She hesitated a fraction of a second before saying, "Just straight coffee. A medium."

He watched her doctor the coffee at the fixings bar near the front window, and then he got it: she loved fancy coffees, but her budget-conscious mind didn't allow the extra expense. Instantly he felt like he'd paid too much for his shoes, his shirt was too high-end, and he should be supporting more charities.

She turned and raised the cup. "Thank you! This is perfect. Shall we go?"

"After you." He held the door open, let her pass through, then noticed the wide splotches on her pants and boots. "You're soaked."

She shrugged as she crossed the street. "I *was* soaked. I'm almost dry now. Took a wicked splash on Germantown and got the worst of the deal. No biggie."

From the look of the splash pattern it was a biggie, at least it would have been to any woman he knew.

*Which should tell you something, Einstein. Charm is deceptive and beauty fleeting . . . Come on, all those years of Christian education. You must remember something, don't you?*

He did.

And Tara Simonetti brought the sweet proverb to life with her inborn optimism. Her hopeful attitude was just what Elena's Bridal needed.

*Except she's leaving in a few months, which means your decisions have to be based on the here and now.*

Greg pushed that reminder aside for the moment. He opened the door, followed her in, then pulled out books and computer procedures for her to study while he joined his buddies at Tim's. He'd come back after the first game, lock up, then drive back to Tim's apartment in Manayunk. This way she'd have a four-hour stretch of time to familiarize herself with the store, with coffee.

"Okay, I'm good." She hung up her wet jacket, stowed her purse, turned up the heat, and was perusing the various bridesmaid gowns for color options per style. "I've got your cell number. If I need to ask you anything, I'll call."

"All right. Although Kathy knows way more than I do."

"I have her number too. Maisy gave it to me yesterday."

"Oh. Well. Good." The fact that she could call Kathy for advice instead of him didn't sit right, but that was absurd. Kathy knew the business inside out. She was the assistant manager. She'd loved his mother and she loved bridal. Why wouldn't Tara call her?

"See ya."

"Right." He walked out the door, heard her click the lock behind him, and struggled with his feelings as he trudged to the parking garage for his car.

He wanted to stay.

*You do not.*

Greg tucked his chin lower into the neck

of his jacket and recognized the silliness of his thoughts. There was nothing he could do there. He had an afternoon of football planned, and the guys were waiting. He'd anticipated this respite all week long. His fantasy team had tanked early, and his beloved Eagles had already been knocked out of the playoffs, but hey, it was football. More important than just about anything except money-making mergers.

A lone bell chimed the one o'clock hour.

A new day, a new week, a new person working in his mother's beloved store. As he climbed into his car, he realized it felt wrong to be starting out something so new with something so same old, same old, especially a game he didn't care a whole lot about.

Scowling, he put the car into gear, eased into the street, and headed to Tim's place near the banks of the Schuylkill River. He'd put in plenty of late nights this past week, nailed a lucrative takeover of a faltering fossil energy business, and had a significant promotion on the line. There was nothing wrong with taking an afternoon off to watch football with the guys.

Nothing at all.

*Don't go. Stay here and show me around. We*

51

*can talk about dresses and bridal and walks in the park and faith and babies and why Billy Joel songs are still the best.*

He left, of course.

Tara watched as he turned and headed south outside the door. She had to keep herself from chasing him down. Grabbing his hand. Gazing up into those deep, brown eyes and drawing him back inside.

She needed to get a grip. Her goal here was to learn as much about Elena's Bridal as she could. She took a deep breath, tugged her sweater closer, and studied the store from records to rooms, gauging what worked and what didn't.

By three forty-five Tara had done all she could. She texted Greg not to worry about her, closed up the store and set the alarm, and started home, thinking. The information she'd gleaned concerned her.

Maria Elena had a brilliant eye for gowns and placement, but when it came to social media and Internet presence, she'd crashed. The sales numbers for the past eighteen months had gone into a slow freefall as a result.

Tara had a love/hate relationship with numbers. She loved their objective ease, but when they added up to a serious downward trend like she saw at Elena's Bridal, she disliked them immensely. Was this the end of independent bridal salons? Had corporate-owned chains pushed everyone to big-box settings?

The rain and sleet had stopped, but the temperatures were dropping fast. She pulled her coat closer around her and walked a little faster.

A car pulled up alongside her. It wasn't dark yet, but the heavy cloud cover, coupled with the shortened days of mid-January, made it dusky. A woman alone needed to be careful. She averted her gaze and sped up even more, ready to duck into a still-open drugstore just ahead.

"Tara? Why are you walking home?"

Her heart did a quick tumble when Greg called her name, one of those crazy things that shouldn't and couldn't happen because Greg was her boss and a ladder-climbing lawyer. "You're supposed to be watching football."

He double-parked the car, got out, and met her on the sidewalk. "It's freezing out here."

"Walking warms you up." She said it with a bravado her chilled limbs didn't feel.

"Really?" His look said he wasn't buying it. "Get in, the car's warm. I'll drive you."

"No, Greg, really, I'm fine."

He made a doubtful face, took her arm, and led her across the quiet street. "Warm is better. I promise."

Warm was better. It was so much better that she could have done a little happy dance as the blast of hot air from the car heater enveloped her. She held back on the dance, but just barely.

"I went to the store and you were gone. I thought we had this all arranged."

"I texted you." She indicated the cell phone sitting between them. "Didn't you get it?"

He picked up the phone, opened it, and grimaced. "I did, but didn't realize it. Sorry."

"I decided there was no reason to interrupt your one day off with driving across the city just to make sure I locked up. It seemed wrong to interrupt a guy and his football." She kept her gaze on the street ahead, because making eye contact with Greg made it tough to maintain a keep-your-distance mind-set. "Besides, walking makes me hearty. It refreshes the soul."

Her sensible reasoning would have been great if Greg had been able to focus on football.

He hadn't.

He'd spent the afternoon wondering how she was doing. Did she need help? Did she have questions? And then the one thing she did text him about, he hadn't noticed. "I appreciate your consideration, but you've gone above and beyond trying to school yourself in a job where there's no one around to train you. I feel bad about that."

She raised her backpack and pulled out a bridal magazine. "I've been schooling myself for years."

He laughed. "That anxious to get married?" He was slightly disappointed when she shook her head.

"No, that will happen in God's time. It's the planning I love. The structure, the helpful side of making things right. Cutting costs, trimming ribbon, planning seating. I love the logistics of weddings. My own?" She shrugged. "That will take care of itself, but being of service to others to make this special day memorable and stress-free? That's my natural high."

"Then why law school?" At the red light he stopped and turned toward her, puzzled. "If you love the wedding industry, why put yourself through the rigors of that?"

"My dad."

"Ah." Greg nodded, thinking he understood. "Family law practice. I get it, a lot of

55

my pals went into law for that reason."

"My dad wasn't a lawyer."

"No?"

She shook her head, and for the first time since meeting her yesterday, he sensed trouble. "He was a laborer. He was disabled in a work-site accident twenty years ago. Back then, it was tougher to prove fault and disabilities."

Before the laws shifted gears. She was right.

"An attorney said he'd represent him, the company involved paid off the lawyer so he'd do a lousy job, my dad never got the benefits he needed, and we lost him to suicide four years later."

"He killed himself?" Greg covered her hand with his, unable to imagine the sadness of that scenario, but able to read the reality in Tara's shadowed eyes. "Tara, I'm so sorry."

"Us too. We'd prayed hard and long for him to get better, but in the end it wasn't enough."

"Because God didn't save him?" That would have ticked Greg off, but Tara's quick shake of the head disagreed.

"Dad was angry about everything, and mental health services were expensive so he wouldn't go for help. He didn't want to go to church with us, or be around happy people. He avoided everything we considered nice and normal, so it's hard to blame God when my dad refused to even try to meet him halfway. I don't think God forces his way into our hearts and souls."

She paused, thoughtful. "I think we invite him in, and my father was angry for so long that I think he forgot how to be happy. I decided I'd become an amazing lawyer. Strong. Smart. Dedicated. And when I say I'll help people, I'll do it. No matter what."

Her words hit home. Had Greg ever considered the fallout of his legal actions? The innocent people who were affected by the firm's wheeling and dealing? Did his initiatives leave other children out in the cold, scrabbling to get by? Probably. Could he afford to get sentimental over work? No. Degrees of separation were crucial in corporate law. Business was business.

*Perfect!* his conscience scoffed. *Your father would be proud. So proud.*

"We survived," Tara went on. "My mom is a wonderful person. She works two jobs, and she's always been there for me and my younger brother. We're the first to make it through college, much less law school. So my success is really her success."

Greg felt the same way about his own

mother. She had groomed him for victory, but right now he didn't feel all that victorious. A part of him felt like a little boy lost, wondering how to get home. A crazy thought, when he was on the cusp of something big. "My mom was like that too. They would have liked each other."

She nodded, started to say something, then stopped. He helped. "What's on your mind? I can tell you've got something to say and you're not sure if it's your place to do it."

She hesitated, still frowning. "I do, but it might take a little while."

"Food?"

She waved him off and looked embarrassed. "I wasn't hinting for supper, Greg."

"Well, I was." He made a quick left, then a right. "Tim had chicken wings, but I need something more substantial."

"But there's another game."

He didn't care.

That realization should have unnerved him. It didn't, because the prospect of spending time with Tara seemed better than a game. "Mexican?"

"Love it more than life itself."

He grinned at her enthusiasm and pulled into a parking space down the road from a great little Tex-Mex place that looked like a dive but had the best food around. He rounded the car just in time to open her door.

She looked up, surprised and pleased. "Thank you."

She smiled, and what he wanted to do was take her hand. Hold it. Walk with her hand clasped in his, just to see if last night's reaction was a fluke.

He didn't.

She was leaving for the valleys of northern Pennsylvania. He was destined for New York City. No sense starting something with so little time.

When the counter clerk served up their food on a burnt-orange plastic tray, he wondered if he should have taken Tara to a more upscale place. She was country at heart, but didn't a woman like Tara deserve the best?

"Oh, be still, my wedding-loving heart." She laughed when he brought the pile of food over to the table.

"You set the table." He glanced at the paper napkins and plastic silverware. "Well done."

"Doing my part." She smiled at him, then at a young couple's baby across the aisle.

The little boy promptly burst into tears — loud, yowling tears that forced his mother to get up and walk the little guy around.

"Your cheeks are red."

"I've just scared a baby, and I'm about to tell you that your bridal store needs help. And I'm not talking about another clerk on hand. Of course my face is red."

"The books have us in the black." He raised his shoulders. "And whether or not we keep it open, the black is a good place to be."

"Should I disagree now and risk the removal of my food, or wait until I've eaten?" She stared at the food with longing, as if assessing the possibilities.

"All right. Eat and talk. Your food is safe."

"Elena's is one-of-a-kind, purposely."

He nodded. His mother had seen the value of the Old City shop at a time when the historic area of Philadelphia had fallen on hard times. She'd put together the payments to buy the store with the cool cash settlement Carlos paid out when he ended their marriage. From a dream broken came a dream fulfilled, which made closing the store harder than he ever imagined.

"But . . ." She elongated the word with purpose. "It has no Internet presence, no Facebook page, no social media interaction at all, so it's become fairly invisible."

"People spend way too much time on their

computers and phones," he grumbled. But hadn't he told his mother the very same thing last year?

"The store's reputation got it listed in Philly's Five Best for ten years in a row," she continued. "It didn't make the cut last year, and it won't make it this year because we're out of date with some of the top designers for our niche clientele."

"But Mom was always on the cutting edge," he protested. "She and Kathy talked about that all the time."

Tara's face told him that was no longer the case. "I called Kathy. She said that money got tight when two corporate bridals moved into town, one in Cherry Hill and one in King of Prussia."

His mother had never breathed a word to him. Why not? He could have helped, could have gotten her marketing advice from experts in business.

"Your mother and Kathy closed ranks, keeping things more minimized than they had in the past. And then a wave of brides came in, tried dresses on, got sized, then ordered them off the Internet at a discount price."

"So the store takes the brunt of overhead cost for time, employees . . ."

"And the online site gets the sale. Pretty much."

"How can you fight that kind of thing?" He stared at Tara as the decision to close the store loomed bigger. "It's a tiny store surrounded by fire-breathing dragons. Who can win that battle?"

"How did David beat Goliath? Faith, guts, and the will to survive." She sat back as her food cooled, and she locked eyes with him. "But that's what I need to ask you. Are you in this for the long haul? Because bringing things up to par to survive takes hands-on work, sales, and energy. If you're not keeping the store, then it's probably better to liquidate what you can, give the women who worked for your mother a severance, and sell the shop."

"You discovered all this in four hours of checking bridal gowns?" Suddenly her spiel sounded a little too convenient. How did a sharp young woman like Tara Simonetti, with admittedly no experience in bridal, come up with an entire dynamic for his mother's three decades of hard work and dedication in one afternoon? Impossible.

"Who are you really, Tara?" He leaned in, delving for answers. "Who do you work for? May's? Filene's? Because no way did you walk in off the street yesterday fresh from the sticks of Pennsyl-tucky and figure this out in a few hours."

He thought to shock her into the truth. *Wrong.*

She burst out laughing and he sat up straighter, baffled and not one whit amused. "This isn't funny."

"Oh, it is." She took a sip of water, giggled, then sat back and wiped her mouth carefully. "If you could just see your face right now."

"Angry? Disappointed? Disillusioned? Take your pick."

"All three," she assured him. "First, you're being corporate lawyer silly, and it's downright preposterous but kind of cute too. In a vintage TV show kind of way. Although I prefer my alpha males to have a clue. That keeps them from jumping to conclusions that have no basis in fact."

He started to sputter and she held up a hand. "My turn." She waited for his nod, then ticked off her fingers. "You're too close to the situation to see it. You've suffered a keen loss, your heart isn't in any of this, your workers are wonderful women, or at least they sound like it from everything I've heard, but they know more about the store's bottom line than you do, and that's because they don't look at last year's numbers. They look at this year's appointments."

He hated that she made sense, but she did.

"You can't sell gowns to empty chairs, so if you're going to keep this going, we have to tempt girls in, show them the goods and convince them that first-class service reduces the stress of their wedding day, then lock in the sale."

His head went instantly to major-league-style ad campaigns. "You're talking some big expenditures," he warned.

She shook her head. "Not necessarily. I can arrange to have the website done by my friend Truly. She's a whiz at graphic design, and she'd do it for the cost of her wedding gown from stock. She's getting married next fall, and bartering is great for a bride on a budget."

"Okay . . ."

"I can put us on Facebook. We can arrange trunk shows; we can call on former brides to model for us. Nothing like having brides dressed in Elena's Bridal gowns to do impromptu appearances at area fairs and festivals. It's not just about the gown, Greg; it's the name recognition of quality and substance. Some folks will opt for cheap-as-they-can-get, then scramble to fix things when they go awry, but there's another type of shopper out there. Women who know what they want, who like the security of a good store that stands behind its work and respects the American wallet. We can be that store again, but that's really up to you."

She sat back, splayed her hands, and waited.

She wasn't pressuring him. She wasn't begging him. She was laying the cards on the table and letting him make the choice that best suited their situation.

*And she's not a shark from some other company. Come on, man, what were you thinking? Although it gave her a good laugh.*

It had, and he couldn't believe he'd gone straight to that kind of suspicion. But considering the corporate pool he swam in, it shouldn't be such a big surprise. "I need to think about this. Weigh the options."

"Understandable." She went back to eating as if she hadn't just laid two divergent paths before him. "I know being a numbers guy means you've checked out the books, the debits, credits, etc. But bridal is a year-ahead-of-the-game merchandising scheme. Last year means little if this year isn't prepping for next year."

"The sensibility behind this astounds me, and I'm still wondering how you know so much."

"When you've been broke forever, you

65

learn to examine deeply." She faced him straight on, and the soft sheen of her golden eyes made him think of long, slow sunsets and tall, waving wheat fields. A nice combination, in his book. "And I've always had this little-girl wish to have my own place, dress brides, plan weddings. So on one side of the coin I ace my law exams because our town could use a stand-up person to make sure folks are well represented when they need help."

"And the flip side?"

"I studied bridal in print, I watched every bridal reality show produced, perused bridal blogs, and drew my own conclusions about what makes a store successful. Your mother had the formula down pat until the rules of the game changed a few years ago."

Her reasoning made sense.

His mother had been a smart, industrious bundle of energy, but she'd been old-school in many ways. He could see how Tara arrived at her conclusions. But now he had some serious thinking to do.

Tara boxed the remainder of her meal in the Styrofoam carton the clerk provided and stood. "I have to get home. I need to prep for my business law clinic tomorrow."

"Of course." He stood quickly. As she moved through the door, a new wave of

66

wind-driven rain began to beat against the dark street. He touched her arm. "Let me get the car. Stay here where it's warm and dry."

"Either that or —" She reached inside the neck of her coat and tugged the hood of her fleece over her head. "We race!" She sprinted down the sidewalk ahead of him and beat him to the car, but then had to wait as he fumbled for his keys to open the electronic locks.

"You're crazy."

She climbed inside, pulled the wet hood down, and adjusted her seatbelt. "Safe is good, but sometimes life just dares you to run in the rain."

Her words made him pause. When was the last time he ran in the rain?

Undergrad. A lot of years back. He'd been a little foolish then, a little reckless. He'd had a few run-ins with bad choices, so when he decided on the straight and narrow path to the corporate top, he had hugged that path with a ferocity that didn't look left or right. Tara's take on facing storms was downright refreshing.

She had her own way of handling things. She had the guts to dare the soaking Nor'easter with nothing more than a thin fleece hood. She talked frankly about his mother's beloved store, and while he didn't necessarily like what he heard, he was glad she'd confronted the situation. Kathy had kept the whole thing to herself as a promise to his mother. Now that he understood the dynamics, he could figure out the best way to go.

He hoped.

# CHAPTER FOUR

As Tara walked toward Old City Monday afternoon, her cell phone rang. She peered at the screen. Her mother. "This has to be a record," she said. "You're the third call I've gotten from Kenneville today."

"Why is that?"

"Mr. Garbowski is wondering if he can sue Mrs. Fowler."

"Why would he do that? She's such a nice old gal."

"She cut down her Norway maple, the only shade for his yard, and she didn't have the decency to consult him first."

"Did you tell him to grow his own tree?"

"I did. It seems he tried, but the shade from her tree killed any seedling he planted. Starved for sunlight, kind of like me right now." She tucked her chin deeper into the collar of her coat as today's wind and rain lashed the city.

"I'm stunned. The only thing I can say is

that everyone is so proud of your accomplishments that they're jumping the gun."

"I reminded him that with hers gone, a new seedling should thrive, and not to be sue-happy."

"I can't believe he interrupted your schooling for a call like that." Her mother sighed. "Who else called?"

"Mrs. Bushing is leaving Mr. Bushing and wondered if I'd be ready to represent her in a divorce by June. I kindly refused."

"They've been married forever. They can't split up."

"Mom, you're missing the point. I never intended to be a divorce attorney. Or to have neighbors suing neighbors over trees."

"Well, what else can you do here, honey? Kenneville's small. It's not like we'd have lawyers who specialize. This way you get a smattering of this and that. It keeps life interesting."

"Or downright crazy," Tara told her. The thought of dealing with chronic complaints and grumpy neighbors hadn't entered her mind when she took up her noble cause three years before. "I'm not out of school yet, and I can't offer legal advice without actually being a lawyer. It's frowned upon."

"Well, folks will take what you say with a grain of salt anyway," Michelle Simonetti

70

assured her, as if that was a *good* thing. "Half won't listen and the other half will disagree. I called to tell you I sent money. I know this year's tight, and I picked up an extra shift at the diner. I sent you a check that's good to cash by Friday."

Tara's heart went soft. "Mom, I'm fine. I got a great job at a bridal salon, and it works out perfectly because the hours are the opposite of my law clinics."

"You're working *and* trying to finish law school?"

"You're working full-time at the bakery *and* waiting tables at night?" Tara replied, knowing her mother would get the point. She did.

"I'm doing this so you and Ethan won't have to do it," Michelle retorted. But then she took a breath, and Tara couldn't miss the pride in her voice. "Good for you, honey. I'm proud of you."

"Back atcha. I've got to go, I'm at work. I'll talk to you soon and don't send any more checks. I'm good here. I promise."

"All right." Her mother couldn't quite hide the relief in her voice, and Tara felt good giving her a reprieve. She tucked her phone away and walked into Elena's. Greg had called a meeting of all the employees, and she'd spent the last six hours wondering what he'd do. Would he close the store? Stay open?

Whatever he did, she prayed he could find peace of mind in the decision. The loss of his mother had blindsided him. To let the business she built slip away had to feel like losing her all over again, and Tara understood how difficult that would be.

The sun broke through the thick clouds about the same time Tara walked through the door, and the combination made Greg feel better about just about everything.

"Tara, sit here." Maisy patted the seat on the bench she was sharing with Myra and Liz. Kathy smiled a broad welcome, and Donna shook Tara's hand while motioning to the sleeping babies tucked in a nearby alcove. "I'm Donna, nice to meet you. My husband's working, but I figured between all of us, we could watch the boys during the meeting."

Greg watched as Tara's mouth formed a perfect circle, and then she did that "I love babies" girl thing, oohing and aahing as if they weren't a fairly common event.

Which they were, of course. The number of strollers and buggies and kid seats on bikes last fall said the majority of double-income-no-kids locals were falling into the "let's have a baby" trap.

But seeing Tara's face and the sweet look of interest as Donna talked about the infant boys made Greg wonder what she'd look like with a baby in her arms.

He switched off the mental path-less-traveled and pulled himself back to the business at hand. His life had been nothing but change for the last six months, and offered just as much in the near future, so entertaining thoughts of U-turns didn't make the short list.

The ladies chattered a moment, then turned toward him, waiting to hear their fates.

He'd walked into the store this afternoon determined to hire a liquidation firm and keep things uncomplicated. Short and simple was best right now. He needed to be at the top of his game at work, and the women here knew that. He'd compensate the staff, they'd apply at the new corporate bridal stores, and while it wouldn't be the same as staffing Elena's, it would be a job. And that's what mattered.

But now? He was face-to-face with the reality of it, with one of Donna's twins stirring in his little car carrier, and Kathy staring up at him as if she knew what he had to say but longed to hear anything else.

He glanced at Tara.

Her face showed no emotion, but it did show support. No matter what he'd decided, her expression said it was okay.

He cleared his throat, and what came out wasn't even close to what he'd intended to say. "We're in trouble."

The women stayed quiet, their attention trained on him.

"Our appointments are down. Our weddings for this year are fewer than ever, and we need to ramp things up in quick order or close the doors."

Their faces fell. Their gazes went tight. He watched as this group of good women prepared to be told they were collectively out of a job.

He shifted his eyes to Tara. "This is Tara Simonetti. She came on board this past weekend in a moment of desperation because we were short-handed."

"Empty-handed, more like it," Kathy said.

He acknowledged that with a tight smile. "True. Well, I thought we'd be training Tara on bridal, but it turns out she trained me instead. And according to her, we're at a crossroads. We either pull together and focus on bringing in more brides, more parties, more overall business over the next few weeks, or we need to liquidate and close the doors."

All eyes turned to Tara, but she didn't make eye contact with the rest of the staff. She kept her gaze on his, and something in her face said he could do this.

"So here's what I think."

The women turned back toward him, waiting. Hoping?

"I want to keep Elena's open."

A sigh of relief rippled through the room.

"But I need your help. I know Donna needs a few more weeks —"

"Kyle said he's ready to take over two evenings and Saturdays starting this week," Donna broke in. "Consider me back for at least sixteen hours a week."

Having Donna back to cover some hours would be a big help. He didn't pretend not to be grateful. "That's huge, Donna. Thank you."

"And I'm fine now," Kathy added.

"And Jean's brother is coming north to help care for her dad, so we can have her back next week too," Maisy added.

"I'll call her," Kathy offered, but caution marked her tone. "Greg, what are your ideas for growing business? There's tough competition out there."

He turned toward Tara. "Your turn."

She didn't come up front, but stayed seated among the women. And then she did something quite amazing in his book. She didn't list her ideas, hogging credit. She turned the tables and asked them theirs, and Greg was amazed by what he heard.

"Trunk shows," Donna offered, the same idea Tara had yesterday. "That way there's no added expense, we have the gowns in store for three days, we have the sales rep from the designer sell the concept of why their gowns are best, and we deal with exclusives the brides can't find in mall stores."

Tara jotted that down as if she hadn't already thought of it.

"We could do better using referral retailers," Kathy admitted. "Reception venues, furniture stores, printers, caterers, florists."

"And we could cross-reference those with specific types of weddings," added Maisy in a tone that said this wasn't the first time she'd made this suggestion.

Greg frowned. "I don't know what that means."

"Themes are the rage right now. There's no such thing as simple anymore." She stood, marched to the front desk, and grabbed a stack of forgettable business cards. "Instead of these, we leave vintage-style cards at vintage and historic venues. For formal hotels and museums, use the more formal design. Artsy-looking cards at the artsy and trendy venues. That way the minute the bride sees the card, she feels the connection to her wedding, her choices, and Elena's Bridal. And it costs pennies."

"That's a brilliant idea." It was, Greg realized, and nothing he would have thought of in a million years, although he looked for instant connections with potential clients all the time. It made sense to do that with his mother's store as well.

"Our location here is huge," Tara offered.

"We're not very mainstream for suburban brides," Donna noted.

"But we're unique, and we can turn that to our advantage," Tara replied. "Bridal parties that come to browse can get coupons to have their lunch or dinner at one of the nearby places. There are enough great spots to gather down here that even the pickiest bride will like that over chain restaurants at the mall. It feeds right into the 'I want my wedding to stand out' mind-set every bridal show and magazine preaches — even to having wedding websites set up for each couple's wedding. I made a list of ways to self-advertise without spending a dime."

"I'm all ears." Kathy smiled, captivated,

and Greg watched as Tara helped build on their ideas.

"We tell the newspapers we're highlighting our Old City location by specializing in old-fashioned weddings. We team up with historic venues —"

"You're in the right city for that," Maisy said.

Donna nodded. "That's for sure."

"We play that angle while making sure the brides looking for a more traditional and formal wedding know we can deliver the entire look from start to finish using the more modern amenities. I've got a couple of possible suggestions we can implement as the boss decides."

"As in?"

She tapped her tablet of paper. "Adding a tuxedo rental area to the store. It doesn't have to be big, just well stocked with stylized fitting jackets. Also, the rental company bears the initial cost, and to garner a new location they're generally good at giving deals on sample tuxes to try on. Their profit lies in the order, so it's a perfect match."

It could be, Greg realized. One-stop shopping. "And?"

"Prom."

He frowned. "Prom?"

Kathy's smile widened, which meant she'd

thought about this in the past.

"The average teen is spending over seven hundred dollars to go to prom. Some go to several in one year. We have this whole section of mothers' attire here." She pointed behind Greg. "And the sales on it are dismal. I suggest turning that into a prom room."

"That brings in a younger crowd," Kathy noted.

"And noisy."

"Possibly bratty."

Tara laughed, not disagreeing with Liz or Maisy. "Teens can be a handful, but think of it as an interesting side business that turns into bridal business in eight years. Or . . ." She waited while they turned their attention back to her. "Wedding gown rental."

Kathy frowned.

Donna winced.

Maisy, Liz, and Myra threw up their hands in unison. "How do we fix gowns for rental?" Liz demanded. "How do we make each bride happy? How can this be done and not make us crazy? I get it that weddings cost great money, but to rent a dress you want to remember the rest of your life? Better they get Uncle Frank to take a video and buy the stupid dress!"

Tara commiserated. "I hear you. So, okay, we nix the rental wedding gown idea. What ideas do you guys think will work? You've been here awhile; you know the clientele better than anyone."

"We need to be on the Internet." Kathy sent Greg a look of apology, as if suggesting this messed with his mother's memory. "With a decent web page, like every other business has."

Tara nodded, jotting quickly. "I've got a friend who does web design. She's got a wedding coming up in September, so maybe we can barter services?" She raised a brow to Greg.

"Truly, right?"

"That's her." Tara poised her pencil. "Kathy, you've been here the longest and you're in charge. Can you talk to Tru, tell her what you envision? You've got the lowdown on all this. Maybe we could do a multipage site and showcase Donna and Maisy's ideas of theme weddings."

"I'd be glad to do it!" Kathy's tone said she'd do anything to help save Elena's Bridal.

"I'll do Facebook," Tara added. "I'll friend all of you. Then we can go through the brides for the past two years and send out friend requests. We can use a picture from

80

the new website as our banner . . ."

"And we can list store hours, specials, and all kinds of things on the business page," added Donna. "I check out my favorite stores that way because there's so little time for actual in-store shopping with the babies."

"Excellent point." Tara noted that and paused. "We need an end game."

"A what?" Kathy turned toward her, brows up.

"A goal, a target, something all this leads to, keeping us all on the same path. But what could it be?"

Donna darted a look of compassion toward Greg. He noted her hesitation and angled his head in invitation. "Spill it, Donna."

She faltered, then said, "A Grand Reopening Gala, incorporating all the things we're changing."

Greg worked to keep his countenance easy. A reopening made the loss of his mother more permanent, but he couldn't afford to work on emotion if he wanted to save her store.

"We could invite the area professionals and make it a complete round-robin effect, possibly developing discounted wedding packages with them." Tara poised her pencil, waiting for his response. "To hold down prices we could do it right here."

"What better place?" asked Kathy.

Greg agreed. What better place to initiate a new lease on his mother's beautiful store than where it all began? "I think it's an excellent idea, and I'll foot the bill for the gala myself so it doesn't come out of store profits."

Kathy's smile of approval said more than words. "I'll work on a list of potential industry partners tonight, and we'll put this plan into action tomorrow." She stood, indicating it was time to close the meeting.

Greg agreed. He'd walked in here with one plan and was leaving with another, but he'd changed worried looks into hopeful expectation, and that hadn't just felt good. It felt right, and that was a welcome change.

Kathy crossed over to Tara. About the same height, she looked the young associate right in the eye and said, "Your being here was no accident."

"It's more like a dream come true," Tara admitted, but Kathy put her hands on Tara's shoulders and shook her head.

"You were meant to find us, Tara. For whatever reason, God put you here, and I want to say welcome aboard. I'm looking forward to working with you."

"Think we can do it?" Tara swept her gaze around the store. "The boss" — she hooked a thumb toward Greg but kept her eyes on Kathy — "gave us a month or so. Whaddya think?"

Kathy dusted her hands together. "I think we'd better get a move on. See you tomorrow. And you." She turned toward Greg, and he'd have had to be blind to miss the gratitude in Kathy's face. "Thank you. Your mother would be very proud of you today."

He waved that off as she moved to the door, but she was right. His mother had believed in second chances. And at this moment, he realized he might have more of Maria Elena in him than he thought.

# CHAPTER FIVE

*Stop watching for Greg to make an unsched-uled appearance. Not gonna happen. You know better than most what it takes to be a successful attorney. It's a time-consuming process. The guy has a life. Ignore the door.*

All week Tara had made a valiant attempt to do just that, but she couldn't help listening for Greg's voice, his laugh. Fortunately, there was plenty to keep her busy. They'd gotten over a thousand likes on their new Facebook page, and the *Daily News* had interviewed Kathy and Greg as part of its Old City campaign.

"Tara, if you're done watching the door, I've got a four thirty appointment coming in that I need you to take."

"I was doing nothing of the kind." She walked around the desk and withdrew the bottle of window cleaner and some paper towels. "Clean entrance windows are vital to our success."

"Mm-hmm." Kathy's expression said she wasn't buying it. "You turn three shades of Vera Wang pink whenever Greg walks in, so don't think you're fooling anybody, darling. Fair skin tells the tale."

"A gift from my mother." Tara frowned, then sighed. "There's a laundry list of reasons not to fall for Gregory Michael Elizondo, starting with the fact that he's my boss. But I forget every single one of them when he walks into the room."

Kathy smiled. "I understand the hesitation, but if no one ever dated the boss, honey, we'd miss out on some of life's great stories. Dating the boss is fairly epidemic."

"Risking a job I need by chancing a bad romance is just dumb." She waved the paper towel wad as she approached the front door. "And we're in opposite corners on just about every important issue known to man. How can that be fixed?"

Kathy pointed up toward heaven. "I've seen a lot of fixes in my time, sweet thing. All I'm saying is that it's never good to draw the line too deeply in the sand, because waves happen. Give life, love, and God a chance."

Tara wanted to do exactly that where Greg was concerned. She gave the front windows a quick wash while Kathy took a phone call.

When she hung up the phone, she waved Tara back to the desk and handed her the four thirty appointment card. "She's coming to look at mothers' gowns."

"I'm going to steam this weekend's veils. Call me when she arrives."

Kathy called her up front about twenty minutes later.

A woman stood quietly at the desk. She turned, and Tara couldn't miss the look of apprehension in her eyes, as if Elena's Bridal was the last place she wanted to be. "Tara, this is Mrs. Dreschler. She needs a mother-of-the-groom gown, and she heard that we put them on sale."

Tara met the woman's look of concern with a smile. "You've come to the right place. May I take your coat?"

The middle-aged woman tugged the coat more snugly around her. "I'll keep it. But thank you."

Tara led her to the area slated to become a prom display room in a few weeks. She turned, ready to ask questions about the wedding, the timing, and preferred styles, but was startled by the anguished look on the woman's face.

"Are you okay?" She stepped forward, unsure what to do. Mrs. Dreschler's cheeks had paled. Her breathing caught as if she was fighting tears, and she seemed terrified, as if the twin racks of dresses might launch an attack at any moment.

"Come here." Tara took her arm and directed her to the nearby comfortable chair. "Sit down, breathe deep, and tell me what's going on. I'm here to help."

The woman stared at her hands a few seconds, then shrugged as if conceding a long and drawn-out battle. "I had cancer a few years back."

"I'm so sorry." Tara took the chair next to her and waited.

"Breast cancer," the woman whispered. "My insurance wouldn't cover reconstruction, and so . . ." She winced, studying the dresses. "Nothing looks right. Nothing fits right. And the bride is a nice young woman, but she thinks I should be able to walk in here and get a suitable gown and it will be okay. And of course it won't."

"Of course it will." Tara added punch to the words with a soft call to Maisy working in the first alterations room. As Maisy strode forward in her typical take-no-prisoners style, Tara reached out a hand. "This is Maisy. Maisy, this is Mrs. Dreschler. We need your expertise to tell us which styles will work with post-surgical mastectomy, and how we can establish a normal and comfortable curve for her son's wedding day."

Mrs. Dreschler stared at her, then Maisy in turn. "You can really do this? I know they sell prosthetic devices, but my skin is too sensitive after the radiation. Most days I don't care," she added. "My husband doesn't care. He's just thankful I'm alive. And my family understands, but for this occasion" — she stressed the last two words — "I want to look and feel normal. Just for one day."

And what did tough, drill-sergeant Maisy do? She reached right down and hauled Mrs. Dreschler out of the chair. "Toss off that coat, dearie. What size are you normally? A ten? Twelve?"

"Twelve, yes." The groom's mother didn't dare say no to Maisy. No one did. She removed the coat and draped it on the chair. Maisy gave her a once-over, then a crisp nod.

"Good shoulders, that helps! And they cut these dresses small, a man's choice, no doubt, utter foolishness. So let's try some twelves and fourteens, because I can trim as needed." She handed Tara pretty gowns in rapid-fire fashion. "This, this, this, and this. And that." She pointed to the rack behind Tara. "And the gold too."

She turned back to Mrs. Dreschler. "Tara's going to take you into my fitting room. I've got some wonderful ways of doing just what you want, but you've got to trust me to know my stuff!"

Maisy's take-charge attitude and self-confidence worked wonders. Mrs. Dreschler picked up her coat, laid it over her arm, and faced Tara. "Lead the way."

Within minutes they'd picked a flowing, blouson gown with tacked, pleated shoulders. The looser fit was perfect for the woman's sensitive skin. With a bit of clever engineering using alteration supplies on hand, Maisy was able to build the look of a normal woman's chest beneath the gown.

"I don't believe it." Mrs. Dreschler caught sight of herself in the triple mirror and sighed. Tears filled her eyes, but they were happy tears this time. "When Mandy said you folks would help me, I thought she was being pushy. She wasn't." She fingered the soft pleats that allowed the top of the gown to fall stylishly, skimming instead of clinging. "This is perfect."

"Well, good!" Maisy beamed. "And, dearie, you look wonderful!"

"I do." Mrs. Dreschler's smile of disbelief widened. "I really do."

Tara chatted with her as she bagged and

tagged the gown, then hung it near Maisy's sewing area for the necessary adjustments. As they approached the front, Mrs. Dreschler gave her a spontaneous hug. "Thank you." She whispered the words, emotion clogging her voice again. "This means the world to me."

The past three years of study and testing and argument flashed through Tara's mind. She'd done what she *thought* was right, but this — helping this woman, working at this delightful shop, surrounded by ribbons and lace — this was what *felt* right.

She left Mrs. Dreschler in Kathy's capable hands to ring up the sale, moved back to bridal, and ran smack into Greg around the corner. He caught her shoulders to keep her from falling, then didn't let go.

She looked up and met his gaze. Appreciation and approval brightened those big brown eyes. He flicked a glance toward the front and gave her shoulders a light squeeze. "That was a nice thing you did."

"Maisy, mostly."

His face said yes and no. "Teamwork is vital in a hands-on business like this. I don't know much about bridal, per se, but I know business, and what you and Maisy just did was wonderful, Tara."

"Thank you." She kept her eyes locked on

his. Greg's grip changed slightly, and the look on his face changed too. He glanced at her mouth as if wondering, and she had to work hard to step back, away from the growing temptation of Greg Elizondo. "Did you come to help shift things around?"

His expression said he recognized her ploy, but his smile said they might revisit things later. The fact that she liked the idea meant she needed to keep her distance.

"I needed measurements for the tuxedo dressing rooms and the hanging racks for displays. Then Kathy and I are interviewing people to staff the tuxedo area. I was wondering . . ."

"Yes?" She moved toward the bridesmaids' racks to replace gowns they'd pulled for earlier customers.

"Can I buy you supper again tonight? After we close up? It's been almost a week, and you must be hungry again."

A cozy late evening with Greg? Her heart said yes instantly. Her head reminded her why this was a really bad idea. "I should go straight home."

She saw his look of disappointment, and a longing washed over her. She'd love to cave and test the waters of romance with Greg, but it was a foolish idea.

The irony of falling for an upwardly

mobile lawyer pushed too many old buttons. Greg represented a side of law that struck first and asked questions later. After losing her father, she couldn't take that lightly.

She shook her head. "The store is booked solid tomorrow, and while Meghan's a walking historical textbook and I'm glad you hired her, she's technologically challenged."

He studied her face as she spoke, and the intensity of his gaze made her long to just say yes, to talk with him. Laugh with him. Commiserate over his losses and enjoy the gentle man living inside the tough-guy suit.

"Understood." Greg turned and walked up front, back to the designated tuxedo area.

Disappointment filled her. She wanted him to convince her, talk her into going out together.

He didn't. He walked away, which only deepened her frustration. He started taking measurements as if inches and feet were the most important things in the world, and she went back to the bridesmaids' gowns, wondering if she'd just blown a chance at something amazing, and knowing she didn't dare find out.

*She wanted to say yes.* Greg could tell by the look in her eyes. And still she said no.

92

Leaving Tara to think about her refusal gave Greg time to do the same, except he was pretty sure he didn't need time. When he wasn't with Tara, he was thinking about Tara.

His phone rang. He glanced at the Manhattan number and answered quickly. "Greg Elizondo."

"Greg, this is Marc Mitchum from the New York office. How are you?"

His heart skipped into faster gear. He set down the tape measure and pretended to be calm, because Friday night calls from New York weren't the norm. "Fine, sir. And you?"

"I'm good, but I've got a few things to talk with you about. I know it's Friday, and Bert told me you'd gone home, so I hope this isn't an intrusion."

Marc had been talking to one of the Philadelphia execs about Greg? Greg's expectations escalated as Marc continued, "We've got an opening here in the downtown Manhattan office, and I know you were interested in being here years ago. Your résumé has come across my desk, so I'm assuming you still have your eye on New York?"

"Yes, sir."

"Good!" Mitchum's voice pitched up. "I

liked what I saw the first time around, but we weren't looking at new grads that year. With our current updates, I'm pleased to revisit your work history."

"Thank you, sir."

"You're welcome. We're meeting to review applications first thing on Monday. I wanted you apprised. We'll notify candidates about interviews at some point following our initial screening."

"Yes, sir."

He hung up the phone and turned. Kathy was watching him from the front desk. "Good news?"

"New York. They're interviewing for new positions. I'm on the list."

She rounded the desk and hugged him, and that made him miss his mother more. "Greg, how exciting! What you've always wanted, a chance to show your stuff in New York."

"Yes . . ."

The moment he said it, Tara appeared in the bridal room with another customer, a bride. She was fluffing the train of a fairly inexpensive gown, and even though her commission rose based on sales figures, nothing in her manner said she wanted the bride to trade up.

Kathy followed the direction of his gaze.

"She's such a wonderful addition to this store."

He nodded, unsure what to say.

"It's rare to meet a person that comfortable with themselves these days," Kathy continued. "Although she absolutely hates the idea of being a lawyer, so that's problematic because graduation isn't far off. No offense," she added as she bumped shoulders with him.

"None taken. She's got a flair for bridal."

"And a heart of gold."

And he didn't, which made him undeserving.

Tara's warmth and common sense set her apart. Was that what intrigued him? Besides the bright and engaging smile, of course, and the great figure, and the skirts that swished when she walked.

His friends would love her, but she'd take one look at his power-hungry coworkers and recognize the lack of everything except money.

Mixed emotions filled him as he walked home later. His chance was finally coming. His years of hard work could come to fruition soon. The dream of landing an office in lower Manhattan was close . . . so close. And it wasn't the money, although he liked to make a good living. It was the prestige of making it to the pinnacle of his field in seven years. His sacrifices were about to pay off, and unlike his father, he hadn't surrendered a family to become successful.

He walked two blocks, then crossed to his side of the street. A neon-colored flyer on the door of the small, storefront Christian mission stood out. Down the road, two elderly men sat huddled around a heat vent, talking, the cold, wet night offering no reprieve.

The situation didn't add up. Greg paused and read the notice, a jumble of pseudo-legalese that said the mission was being closed due to lease infractions. He stepped back and raised his eyes to the sign above the broad, wooden door.

*Old City Mission, est. 1987*
*Nettie Johnson, director*
*All are welcome*

Two churches flanked the ends of the street. Upscale housing, a small park, and high-end stores had migrated to the quaint setting of the new and improved Old City, but the mission had been a Christian mainstay for people as long as he could remember.

He approached the two men. Heads down, they ignored him, as if eye contact put them at risk, and they were most likely right. He

96

squatted so he wouldn't tower over the two older men. "Guys, who closed the mission?"

"Landlord." One old guy spit to the side in disgust. "I expect he don't think we're proper clientele anymore."

"Nettie said she was gonna fight it, but she's just normal folk," added the second man. "Normal folk got no chance against money. She knows it, but she'll do her best. And in the end, it won't be enough."

*Normal folk got no chance against money.*

Tara's story came back to him, how her father's attorney caved to the higher bidder, and he lost his fight for disability benefits. Was this what it came down to in the streets? People in dire circumstances forced onto the pavement because a landlord got a better offer?

He'd look into it further over the weekend. He hooked a thumb left. "My car's in the garage over there. Do you guys need a lift somewhere?"

The men gaped, then the one with the longer beard shrugged. "Too late to get into a shelter tonight." He looked at his companion. "We could use the bridge overhang. If Toby's not there."

"Toby don't like strangers under his part of the bridge," the second man explained.

"Gentlemen." They all turned toward the

97

voice from the nearby brick church. "Come in. Get dry. Spend the night. It's not luxury, but you've got great company." The middle-aged priest smiled toward the statues flanking the door. "And it's warm."

Greg stood. He reached down to help one of the men up and realized the man was missing a limb. The other man followed the direction of his gaze. "Ollie's a war hero, but we don't make a lot of it, do we, Oll?"

"Only when the whiskey's just right," the amputee agreed, and his words offered a quick, cryptic explanation of his plight. "Nettie gave me what for 'bout two years back, and I gave it up, but I'm willin' to start again about now."

"I expect being warm and dry will help." The priest sent Greg a smile of gratitude as the men shuffled in. "But I'll lock up the communion wine. Just in case."

The old men laughed, and the priest waved to Greg and shut the church door. Greg went back down the steps and turned right.

Lights splayed before him, leading to the bank of the Delaware River.

American history had been born here. Nurtured here. Fed here. This land before him had housed presidents and peasants. Independence Park had seen the labors of lawyers and landowners come to pass. A new country born from the gaping wounds of intolerance.

His mother's guidance came back to him, an immigrant woman's counsel spoken to a young boy with great expectations. "Dream you can, and you're halfway there."

Teddy Roosevelt's words, brief and succinct.

Tara Simonetti embodied those words. She saw, she believed, she acted, and all with a rich kindness that made him long to be a better person. And even if he wasn't a better person, maybe he could do something over the weekend to help Nettie Johnson and her peers hang on to their mission.

# CHAPTER SIX

The push of back-to-back bridal party appointments the following Saturday should have kept Tara's mind off Greg.

It didn't.

Her ears strained to catch his voice, and her eyes strayed to the front desk regularly, hoping he'd come in. By late afternoon they'd racked up significant sales and Kathy had booked twelve new appointments for the coming week. "Greg will be pleased," she exclaimed as she finished jotting number thirteen into the book. "And we're plenty full for our afternoon tomorrow. This is a big step in the right direction for Elena's Bridal."

"Is Greg working?" Donna asked as she organized the tiara case. "I thought we'd see him today."

Tara pretended disinterest as she filed the hard copy of each bridal party's sales folder.

"I expect he's hunkered down, doing

lawyer stuff," Kathy noted. "He got a call from New York last week. He's made the short list for a major opening there, and we know that's been his dream from the get-go."

Tara's fantasy ending dissolved.

Greg was a ladder climber. He was driven. And while she liked his strength and aptitude, success at any cost went against everything she believed in. She'd taken up law for the exact opposite reason.

*And you hate it.*

She retracted the thought immediately. *Hate* was too strong a word. She put two sold gowns on the ironing rack and let her hand trail along the lace edge of the nearest one.

She loved this. Who would have thought her heart's desire lay in helping women plan for the least stressful, most perfect wedding day possible?

"You're quiet today, Tara." Kathy exchanged a look with Donna. "What's up?"

"Nothing." She aimed a bright smile their way, but their expressions said they weren't fooled, so she kept the subject on business as usual. "Meghan offered to do the decorating for the reopening. I was thinking of ways I can help her get it done."

"She's got flair, that's for sure," Jean offered as she came up front. "I've got a growing list of reception venues, caterers, rental companies, bakeries, florists, photographers, and linen providers who've accepted the invitations. That's the makings of a great kickoff party."

"We're going to build Meghan's historical display on Monday in that front corner." Tara pointed left. "Unless someone else had their eye on it."

"All yours," Donna replied. "Her sketch is a showstopper. That corner is the perfect place to spotlight it."

"They'll be installing new tuxedo racks while you're building a medieval forest." Kathy smiled. "Elena would love this."

"She would," Donna agreed. "And with every change we make, I miss her more."

"Was she nice?" Tara turned toward Donna and Kathy. "Like Greg?"

"She was far nicer than I could ever hope to be."

Tara turned, surprised. "I didn't know you were here." She touched a hand to her collar, embarrassed because she'd been looking for him all week, and of course he came in the minute she started asking about him.

"Well." He extended his hands. "I am here. I've been working extra this week, but I've got some time now, so I'm going to rough in those tuxedo rooms tonight. That way the drywall guy can finish them on Monday. And yes, my mother was one of the nicest women you'd ever meet. I've always been more like my father."

Kathy rolled her eyes. "Your mother was proud of you. She encouraged your dreams. And from where I'm standing, the way you've helped spur things along here says she raised a pretty nice guy."

"She'd be thrilled that you're getting the chance you've always wanted." Donna slung her arm around Greg. "Mothers want their children to be happy." She moved to put the final gowns away.

Greg turned toward Tara, and she met his gaze straight on. "Some of us are meant to be movers and shakers," she said. "That's a good fit for you, Greg. You're strong and tough. New York won't know what hit them."

Still, she couldn't help wishing things were different. Wishing she could find a way to mentally separate Greg's job from her own values, and from the memory of a simple man who trusted the wrong lawyer.

Tara was right. Greg wanted to be at the top of his game, and he was on the verge of realizing his dream. Why did the thought of success feel suddenly tainted? He'd done nothing wrong.

*Not wrong, per se. But not all that right either.*

He slung his jacket across the back of a chair and rolled out a bag of power tools from the back room. Framing the tuxedo fitting rooms was the kind of muscle work that took his mind off corporate law and New York City. Not to mention an unforgettable woman who had walked in the door a few weeks ago and made him start seeing life and love through very different eyes.

"Are you doing this alone?"

Tara stood between him and the front door. She was ready to go, her coat on, a cute hat pulled down over the mass of golden brown curls.

"The rooms are small, and I'm just roughing in tonight. I thought I'd be in earlier, but —"

"Duty called."

A new kind of duty, but yes, one that felt good by the end of the day. He hoped the city judge would see things his way and smack down the mission landlord's illegal notice of eviction.

She took a step forward. "That didn't answer my question. There's no one to help you hold things in place?"

He shrugged but couldn't deny how her words ignited a spark of hope. "Nope." He gave her a hang-dog expression. "Just me and a really big stack of two-by-fours."

"I'd stay, but I'm not exactly the build-a-room type," Kathy said as she prepared to leave. "Everyone else has gone home. I'll lock up, Greg, but I won't set the alarm."

Tara started to slip off her coat. Kathy ducked her head, but not before Greg saw her smile of approval as she went out the front. "You don't have to do this." He gave the pile of wood a quick glance. "I can erect the walls on the floor, then stand them up. It's not as hard as it might seem, and they're small rooms."

"I've helped my mother with a lot of DIY projects," Tara replied. She grabbed an old sweater from the office and pulled it on to protect the nice clothes she'd worn that day. "And it's not in my nature to walk away when a friend needs a hand."

He stopped laying wood at designated spots on the floor and looked up at her. "What if I want to be more than a friend, Tara? Would you walk away then?"

She had been moving toward him, but then she paused, looking down. "I —"

"Because —" He stood and halved the distance between them. "I managed to stay away all week, when what I wanted to do was drop in here, pretend to help, and see you. Just you. So why don't you look me in the eye and tell me you feel the same way, and then . . ." He smiled and stroked the curve of her cheek with one finger. "Then . . ."

He glanced at her mouth, took a half step closer, and waited, because after staying away for days, the last thing Greg wanted to do was take a step back when he was this close to kissing Tara Simonetti.

Wasn't that what she'd hoped all week too? For Greg to show up and share a smile or a coffee or a lifetime of happiness?

Greg moved closer, until she had to tip her gaze up to meet his eyes, and when she did, the most natural thing in the world was to wonder what it would be like . . .

He didn't leave her wondering long. He wrapped his arms around her slowly, drawing her in, his gaze on hers.

He smiled.

And then he kissed her, cradling her in the strength of his arms while the aromas of fresh-cut lumber and spicy guy-soap filled her senses.

This couldn't be wrong. Not when it felt so absolutely right. And yet, how could two people with polar opposite goals come to common ground?

He paused the kiss and pulled her in for a long, slow hug. "Tara."

He breathed the name as if imprinting his soul, the husky word making her feel precious and beloved.

The desk phone rang. Tara moved to get it, but Greg held her hands. "The machine's on; it's after hours."

The phone quit ringing. But then his cell phone buzzed. He scowled, checked the readout, and stepped away. "Gotta take this."

She watched him stride away, all business, as awareness hit home. Work always came first with the Gregs of this world. It was better to understand that now and not let amazing kisses tempt her into settling for second place or standing witness to his power quest. A man who drew her heart with such fierceness wouldn't just break her heart if things went bad. He'd shatter it.

She hesitated for a fraction of a second, then picked up her jacket, scribbled a note, and slipped out the front door while he took the call.

Her cell phone rang as she trudged toward Germantown Avenue. She grabbed it out, certain it was Greg.

It wasn't.

She let the call go to voice mail and walked home — cold, wet, and disheartened. Greg was wired to put work first, always.

She wasn't built that way, and better to find that out now. But oh, how she wished it were different.

Because she could have spent a lifetime enjoying long, slow kisses like the one they shared tonight.

"I'll be there, Nettie, first thing in the morning."

"Not first thing," the director of the Old City Mission corrected Greg smoothly. "There are church services goin' on first thing Sunday, and the neighborin' churches have invited us to come by and worship with them, even though most of my regulars don't have Sunday-go-to-meetin' clothes at their disposal. We'll meet after services, and I thank you, Gregory. I didn't have a prayer of winnin' this fight 'til you came on board. I speak for all of us when I say we are humbly grateful."

"I'm glad to help." He meant the words sincerely, even though grandstanding for charity broke new legal ground for him.

He finished up his phone call with the Old

City Mission director and hurried back to Tara.

She was gone.

Greg spotted the note, read the short missive, then stared around the small construction area and back at the note again. *Had to go. Sorry.*

The front door opened. He moved that way, glad she had returned, but it was Kathy who bustled through the door. She waved a hand and hurried to the front desk. "My keys! I got all the way home and realized I left my house keys in the top drawer. What was I thinking?"

"I'd have run them over."

She frowned at the pile of wood. "I called but no one answered, and I decided you've got enough on your plate tonight. Where's your buddy?"

"Gone."

"Oh?" Kathy glanced from the work area to Greg and back. "I thought she was going to help you."

"Me too." He sighed. "Guess not."

Kathy looked at him for long, slow seconds, the kind of look that took great measure. She withdrew her keys and came around the desk, then paused in front of him. "She's falling for you, Greg."

He grimaced, because he thought that too,

right before she disappeared. "Strange way of showing it."

"Or maybe she's uncertain where she fits into your busy life."

Greg shrugged that off. "Everyone's busy. In their own way."

"But most of us take time for life in the middle of the busy." The seriousness of Kathy's expression deepened. "You've worked so long and hard that you don't see the difference, probably because you're surrounded by people doing the exact same thing. It feels right because you're in the thick of it. But we normal folk like a day off now and again. And time with those we love."

Remorse spiked his heart. "You're talking about Mom."

She didn't deny the implication. "She loved you more than anything. And she was so proud of you, of your strength, your spirit, your accomplishments. But it's a kick in the head when you have to make an appointment to see your own son."

The regret pierced deeper, because Kathy wasn't far off the mark. "Did she hate me? For being a self-absorbed jerk like my father?"

"Oh, please." Kathy made a face of disbelief. "Your father was a two-timing beltnotcher. He cheated on three wives that I know of. Your ambition to do your best comes straight from your mother, Greg, because you actually care about the outcome. But if you want the fullness of life she had, it's time to take a breath and think hard. Because while God hands out second chances on a regular basis, it's not necessarily a guarantee."

"You mean Tara."

She gave him a quick, motherly hug. "I mean life," she whispered. She backed toward the door. "Don't be so busy climbing up that you forget to enjoy the scenery along the road you're taking."

She winked and waved, leaving him to his thoughts. He built the four short walls methodically, with plenty of time to think, and when he was done, he walked home, past the closed-down mission, past the church with the altruistic priest, past houses and shops that meant little to him because he never took the time to be a neighbor or friend to those around him.

The old stone church at the corner had a lighted sign out front. He'd passed this sign countless times, but tonight the words struck deep.

If I speak in the tongues of men or of

angels, but do not have love, I am only a resounding gong or a clanging cymbal. If I have the gift of prophecy and can fathom all mysteries and all knowledge, and if I have a faith that can move mountains, but do not have love, I am nothing. If I give all I possess to the poor and give over my body to hardship that I may boast, but do not have love, I gain nothing.

I gain nothing.

The simple verse struck him tonight. Was the constant quest for success destined to be his downfall? He'd sailed through life with clear goals until last August when he lost his mother.

He'd never even had a chance to say good-bye. And worse, he couldn't remember if he had kissed her at their last dinner, nearly three weeks before her death. Did she know how much he loved and appreciated her? Did she die knowing the depth of his gratitude?

He stared at the sign, then walked the last block deep in thought. Nettie Johnson said her regular mission dwellers had been invited to share in the neighborhood worship services. As he unlocked the front door of his home, he wondered if they'd mind making room for a money-grubbing lawyer too.

# CHAPTER SEVEN

Kathy had kept Monday morning free of bridal appointments to give Meghan and Tara time to build the old-world display in the most visible front corner while the drywall team finished the tuxedo-area changing rooms. Donna met with the caterer to lock in the appetizer trays for the kickoff party. Two former brides who loved Elena offered to play hostess for the evening, circulating with trays of food so the staff could talk with prospective partners unencumbered.

While most of the staff decided that semiformal dresses from home worked fine, Kathy rented her own medieval-style costume for the gala.

"You look like one of Sleeping Beauty's fairy godmothers." Maisy rolled her eyes at the pink empire-waist gown and cone hat. "You can't be serious."

"I rarely am," Kathy quipped. She fluttered her bell sleeves. "And who would have thought they'd have this in my size? Obviously fairies aren't as tiny as most folks think." She grinned as she paraded through the front of the store. "Folks'll see me coming."

"You can say that again," Liz muttered, but then she grabbed Kathy's shoulders. "Elena would think it's a great idea because it lightens the moment, so thank you for that. But now get in the back and let me mark the skirt so I can tape a hem. Can't have you tripping into some hotel bigwig we're trying to impress."

Greg came in to check the tuxedo corner's progress just before closing. He whistled lightly and high-fived Kathy. "Ready for painting on Wednesday. Perfect."

"And we've double-checked everything," Kathy assured him. "We're good to go."

"I appreciate it." His gaze flicked to Tara as she moved toward the front of the store.

She gave him a "friends only" smile as she logged out of the second computer. "This has been a whirlwind few weeks. I don't think I've ever had this much fun, or been this tired before."

"You've all gone the distance," Greg noted. He motioned to the new displays and the half-empty mothers' area, ready for an influx of prom gowns due to arrive soon. "I think we can do this."

Tara heard the *we* and bit back her first reaction. Greg had been pretty much unavailable these past two weeks, and if that was his version of teamwork, she wanted none of it. She punched out, purposely didn't meet his gaze, and left with Meghan.

"Think he'll race out that door and chase you down, declaring his unbridled affection?"

Tara frowned and Meghan laughed. "Don't pretend you're not over the top. At least it's mutual."

"You're fantasizing. Greg's my boss."

"Which means you get to keep the store when you marry him." Meghan nudged her as they got closer to the bus stop. "Win/win, right?"

"It would be if I wanted to marry the store," Tara replied. "But I've always kinda dreamed I'd come first in my husband's life. Not work first, with me and one-point-seven kids cruising into a well-funded second. That's not the happily-ever-after I've got scripted."

Meghan's bus rumbled closer. She tapped her cell phone. "Text me if you think of anything we've overlooked for Friday."

"Will do."

"And, Tara?"

"Yes?"

Meghan turned as the bus rolled to a stop. "I'd give the guy a chance."

Tara started to sigh, and Meghan held up both hands, palms out. "It's not my business, and we don't know each other well, but I see a gentle heart in that total studmuffin body, and that's a not-so-common occurrence these days."

Tara smiled. She couldn't disagree. But the man she married needed a heart for God and for hearth and home, and right now Greg was batting zero. No matter how she did the math, it came up wrong, and that made the new job she loved a mixed blessing.

# CHAPTER EIGHT

Thursday afternoon the phone rang. "Greg, Marc Mitchum here."

Greg gripped the phone tightly. "Marc, hello. It looks like Manhattan escaped the monster storm that hammered us yesterday."

"Missed us by an inch," the CEO declared. "It caught Long Island, so that meant I stayed in the office overnight, but that's a fairly common occurrence around here. Market conditions have me flying to Tokyo on Saturday, so I'm bringing you here tonight. In the morning we'll go through the required interview process, and then I can make my decision before I spend a week eating food I don't like. My assistant booked a flight for you, Bert's cleared you from the Philly office, and we're good to go."

Good to go? They booked a flight for him to interview in New York on the day of the scheduled gala? This couldn't be happening. "Sir, are you sure you want to rush this? I'm fine with waiting until you get back next week. In fact —"

Mitchum cut him off quickly. "It's New York, Greg. We never wait. Your enthusiasm for your work speaks for you. The major-league clients trust you, and that's the cornerstone of a financial partnership like ours. You'll come here straight from JFK, and the driver will take your bags to the Millenium Hilton. I've got every minute planned. All you have to do is show up as scheduled. Hopefully we'll send you back to Philly tomorrow night with a new job title."

First-class treatment at the worst time ever.

Greg swallowed hard. Wasn't this what he'd worked toward for years? His shot at New York? Why was he hesitating?

"I'll see you later today."

"Good!" Marc hung up without another word, typical for the New York boss. Greg scanned the flight info that Mitchum's assistant had e-mailed, then sighed as the boarding pass printed.

A seven forty-five evening flight back to Philly on Friday.

He'd miss the gala.

Could the women handle it?

Yes.

But shouldn't he be here for it?

*New York's been the goal for years. Don't mess this up. You go, you get tagged as up-and-coming, then you come back here and celebrate after the gala. Sounds like a fast-paced wining and dining extravaganza to me.*

It did, except that being questioned by men who picked your brain while trying to assess your soul suddenly didn't sound all that appealing.

*You've waited a long time for this, putting in years of preparation. And now you get cold feet?*

Greg packed an overnight bag and called a local florist to have flowers brought to the store before the gala, a testament to his confidence in the staff's abilities. He tried calling Tara.

No answer.

He stared at the phone. Should he text her?

No, too impersonal, and what he really wanted was to hear her voice before he boarded his plane. He wanted her to offer an opinion. Beg him to stay.

He sighed, called Kathy to let her know what happened, then caught a cab to the airport. The misgivings he felt as he boarded the plane took him by surprise, but as he settled into his company-provided first-class seat, he saw a pregnant woman with a young child in her arms. She was waiting her turn to navigate the narrow aisle clogged with passengers stowing personal items in the overhead compartments.

Greg stood, reached out, and caught her attention. "Take my seat. Please."

Her expression said the offer was tempting, but she shrank back. "I couldn't, no. But thank you."

He moved into the aisle, reached up and grabbed his carry-on, and smiled. "I insist."

Someone behind Greg cleared his throat.

Greg motioned to the seat and then the little one in her arms. "He'll like this better. Not as noisy."

She slipped into the seat, sat back, and smiled. "Thank you."

"No problem. Where's your seat?"

She grimaced. "Sixty-four B, I'm afraid."

He made his way to the back as the aisle cleared, remembering the soft words he'd heard in church last Sunday. *Whatever you did for one of the least of these brothers and sisters of mine, you did for me.*

The reverend had probably chosen the quote to honor their unexpected mission guests, but the verse spoke directly to Greg. He was paying it forward, and for the first time in years, he not only loved what he was doing, he respected it.

Tara scrolled down her checklist Thursday evening. "Food and beverages are set. Decorations, done. The servers are arriving at six to help arrange the grazing tables. Name tags are made, the theme-specific business cards have arrived, Kathy's got her fairy godmother gown all set . . ."

"Medieval queen," Kathy corrected. "It just *looks* like a cartoon fairy godmother's getup."

A round of laughter greeted her remark.

"And with all of us and Greg, we should have about fifty people here tomorrow night."

"Except that Greg's in New York," Kathy announced.

Tara's heart thumped to a stop. "Now? With the grand opening tomorrow night?"

"When New York says jump . . ." Donna shrugged. Clearly Greg had little say in the matter.

"They had him board a plane about three hours ago," Kathy went on. "Part of the job when you're at Tatelbaum, Schicker, and Knapf."

It took every ounce of reserve to keep her face placid, but Tara gritted her teeth and did it. He'd called her, late afternoon, and instead of answering the phone, she let it go to voice mail. What would he have said if she'd answered? She might never know.

"I'm glad he got the tuxedo area done before his trip," Donna added. "He's footing a sizable bill for tomorrow night's party, and it's nice that he didn't have to hire out too much of the remodeling."

"I was surprised at how well he did," Tara admitted. "I didn't peg Greg as the handyman type."

Kathy sent her a curious look. "He wasn't born in a high-rise office."

"He worked summer construction during undergrad to offset room and board," Jean explained. "The store was doing well, but not well enough to handle an Ivy League education out of pocket."

Tara considered Jean's comment as she gathered the dresses needed for the gala. Former brides would showcase the newest looks, letting the quality of the designer gowns speak for itself.

They closed the store, and as Tara walked to the bus stop, her phone rang. She glanced at the caller ID. *Michelle Simonetti.* "Hey, Mom. What's up?"

"Just checking in," her mother answered. "I wanted you to know that life has settled back into its typical low-drama existence."

They used to laugh together about the lack of news in Kenneville, but the calm, cozy town held its own brand of charm.

"Mostly I wanted to make sure you're okay," her mother added.

Tara breathed softly. "I'm fine."

"Well, I'm not so sure about that," her mother replied in a voice she employed when making a point. "I know my daughter, and I know you've got a lot on your plate right now, but when I talk to you about working at the bridal store, I hear excitement in your voice. That makes me happy."

"And your point is?"

"I don't hear that same girl when we talk about law, so my question is this: Why don't you stay and work at the bridal store if that's what makes you happy? Because if you're happy, I'm happy."

Quick tears smarted in Tara's eyes. She dashed them away, avoiding eye contact with the other people waiting for the bus. "Three years of law school and mega loans, for starters."

"But if you had a choice," Michelle pressed, and Tara was too tired and too bummed about Greg to argue. "If you were to choose, which would it be? To stay in Philly and help run the store? Or come

124

north and represent crotchety neighbors and grumpy wives whose husbands forgot their fortieth anniversary?"

Tara knew which she'd pick, but she also knew there was no real choice. She'd made her decision three years before when she accepted the terms of entrance into Beasley School of Law. Now she had to pay the price, even if her heart was firmly tucked into Elena's Bridal. "Moot point, Mom."

Her mother laughed, then sighed. "It's not. You're stubborn, and you think you owe the world a good, honest lawyer. But the truth is you need to be true to yourself, honey. Leave the past in the past and forge ahead. Grab your own dreams, new dreams, and run with them."

Tara longed to do just that. If she were to chart her dreams, they'd start with Greg Elizondo and end with living in Old City, raising some cute kids and running Elena's Bridal with Kathy and the gang. But that wasn't on the list of possibilities, so she kept her true wishes quiet. "I know what you're saying, Mom, but it's not that easy."

"Easy has nothing to do with it," Michelle declared. "Life's too short to saddle yourself with a job you don't like based on a decision you made when you were eleven. Did you know that over 15 percent of law school grads never practice law?"

"Is the tough job market supposed to make me feel better?"

Her mother laughed. "It's supposed to make you see you're not alone. Lots of people change career paths as they mature. Your bend in the road is just a little pricier than others."

Tara started to reply, but her mother interrupted. "Don't say anything now. It's better to take some time, take it to God, and see what happens. You've got months before graduation, but if this isn't what you thought it would be, if someplace or someone has drawn your focus in a new direction, then go for it, Tara. No one wants you unhappy. Just think about it, okay?"

"I will," Tara promised. The bus pulled up, and she drew a breath and added, "And, Mom? Thank you."

Her mother's voice softened. "You're welcome, honey. Love you."

"Love you too." She climbed onto the bus feeling lighter. Could she walk away from three years of rigorous education? Was that the height of stupidity or the common sense of growing maturity?

She wasn't sure, but the thought that she might have a viable choice lightened her steps.

# CHAPTER NINE

The lower Manhattan financial district surrounded Greg like an overgrown architectural maze. Tall, imposing buildings bracketed narrow streets. Coffee shops dotted the landscape like trees in a park. Wind-tunneled air bathed his face, the night chilling as dark descended.

The antiquated structure of Trinity Church rose before him on his walk, a blend of history and majesty. The historic graveyard lay tucked between the buildings, surrounded by a wrought-iron fence.

Weathered tombstones dotted the small plot, the dark night making the old dates indiscernible. At one point, this had been a neighborhood of people, places, and dreams, folks who worked together, worshipped together, and waited for their loved ones' ships to come into the harbor below.

There was no neighborhood feel now.

Gorgeous, yes, in its own way. But when

he envisioned life, a life so close he could almost reach out and grab it, it wasn't here, in Manhattan's cool, calm collection of high-rises.

It was in Old City, a niche where history was celebrated, not relegated. It was with Tara by his side, working, playing, shaping his mother's store into a new millennium showcase. A place where their kids — two, he hoped, but maybe she could be talked into three — could romp and play among the other young families, rich in the past, alive in the present.

As he approached the hotel, bells from the church began to ring. He tried the church door. It opened under his hand. He stepped inside and slipped into a back pew.

He'd walked into the middle of a candlelit evening prayer service. Attendance was minimal but heartfelt. A couple of homeless people had claimed pews on the far side and were curled up, sound asleep, away from the cold city night.

*When I was hungry you fed me. Naked, you clothed me.*

The image of the two sleepers stirred his heart. God had already given him so much. What need did he have for more?

None, he decided. He had more than enough already.

The Serenity Prayer came back to him, his mother's counsel: "God grant me the serenity to accept the things I cannot change, the courage to change the things I can, and the wisdom to know the difference."

When the service drew to a quiet close, he slipped across the back of the church, left a contribution in the church's offering box, and did the same for the two sleepers down on their luck.

*When I was hungry you fed me . . .*

An opportunity for change dangled before him, if only he had the courage to reach out and take it.

With God's help and Tara's love, he did.

The following morning he met with Marc Mitchum, withdrew his name from consideration, and headed back to Philly. He'd make it just in time for the gala, and hopefully in time to see Tara before the event started.

But if not?

Well, they'd have the rest of their lives to work things out. He'd make sure of it.

Tara and Jean scanned the list late Friday afternoon to ensure they hadn't missed anything.

Displays? Done.

Models? Ready!

Food? Being catered by a nearby culinary academy, reasonably priced and proud to show their stuff.

Greg's flowers and floral displays from friends of the Elizondos decked the sales areas. The soft scent of spring blossoms filled the air.

A dream come true. A night that would have been perfect if Greg were there, but he wasn't, and most likely he would be following his own dreams in New York before long.

Tara's conscience jumped in with a mental scolding. *What if Ruth had abandoned Naomi? What if she'd followed her mother-in-law's direction and returned to Moab? Where would her happy ending be now? Be patient. Trust. And by the way, that dress looks marvelous!*

"Tara, does this look right?" Meghan interrupted her thoughts. She was retucking the Maid Marian–style gown display for the tenth time that afternoon.

"Touch it again and I'll lock you in an alterations room, Meghan. I know where they keep the keys, so don't test me."

Meghan burst out laughing and stepped away, hands up. "I'm going to get changed. Can you handle this customer?" She nodded toward the front.

"Absolutely." Tara draped the organza bunting over her shoulder and moved forward. "Hi, I'm Tara. Can I help you?"

The woman glanced around. A wide smile split her broad, bronzed face. "This is just plain beautiful inside here, Miss Tara. I can see why Elena's has been a cornerstone in Old City for so long! I am Nettie Johnson from a few blocks over, and I am here on a mission."

"For a dress?"

She laughed and shook her head quickly. "For Mr. Greg. Is he here?"

Tara shook her head regretfully. "He's in Manhattan until later tonight. Can I help you?"

"Oh, no need!" The woman's smile deepened. She reached out and grasped Tara's hands in hers. "We are flyin' high at this moment, and I just wanted to come by and give Gregory a big hug and a public thank-you for what he's done. We not only get to keep our mission right here in Old City, but the landlord has agreed to fix an abundance of things he has been puttin' off for years! And all because Greg did battle for us. He is a special man, and our staff and clients are deeply indebted to him. He will be in our daily prayers, for certain."

"Greg helped your mission?" Tara tried to

do the math and failed. "When?"

"These past two weeks, once he saw we'd been closed down. Oh, he is tireless, that one! They've got a big write-up in the paper today, but I didn't want him just to read about savin' us. I wanted to tell him myself. I'll come by again once he's back home."

Awareness flooded Tara.

Greg hadn't been working night and day to impress New York. He'd been working to save a homeless shelter and food kitchen. Shame bit deep. She had jumped to conclusions and never given Greg a minute to explain himself, or his work. "Yes, please. Do that. I'm sure he'd love to hear this from you. You know, Ms. Johnson —"

"Oh, now, I'm just Nettie to everyone. It's simpler that way."

"Nettie, we're having a party tonight to celebrate the reopening of Elena's Bridal," Tara told her. "Why don't you stay and eat with us? Meet some other people with shops here in Old City?"

"I'm not dressed for partyin'." Her round, brown eyes glanced down. "Though I am right partial to this dress."

Tara scanned Nettie's polka-dot dress and broad-brimmed hat, then smiled. "I think you look perfect for partying, and we'd love to have you."

Kathy glided by wearing her ridiculous and endearing medieval gown with the matching high, cone-shaped hat. "Do stay. I'm Kathy, and I just heard on the news what Greg did. I have to say I'm absolutely delighted, proud, and not one bit surprised." She let her gaze rest on Tara, but she spoke to Nettie. "Things started changing around here the first weekend of January, and they've just gotten better every week. Come with me, Nettie. We can hang your coat back here."

Kathy guided Nettie to the coatrack they'd tucked at the back of the media room, an area staged to showcase the bridal store's ideas. Soon this would be a prom room, but for tonight, Truly had put together rolling media presentations on Donna's big-screen TV to show aspiring business partners the potential of linking to the newly renovated and renamed Elena's Weddings and Bridal, Inc.

Tara watched Kathy take Nettie under her wing while she tried to digest this new information about Greg, but the arrival of the first guests took precedence. Smiling bridal servers emerged to take coats and offer refreshments to the local business partners.

Compliments flowed. Conversation

buzzed. And about thirty minutes in, Tara turned and spotted Greg, talking with a tall man in an expensive gray suit.

Her heart fluttered, then sank.

He'd made it. He'd come back in time for the gala. And there he was, talking to another suit without even saying hello to her.

*As I recall, you've given him the cold shoulder lately. Kind of rude, cupcake.*

Quick happiness turned into quicker self-recrimination. She turned when the wedding planner from a line of distinctive hotels asked about the newness of their program and projected success ratios.

"While the specifics of this wedding program are new . . ."

Tara's heart went into overdrive as Greg answered the question from directly behind her. And when he put a firm hand on her waist?

Total heart-spin.

"Elena's Bridal is steeped in a history of tradition and service. That was my mother's goal from the beginning, and now?" He took a step forward, smiled down at Tara, and reached out to shake the hotel executive's hand. "It's ours." He gave Tara and the scattered staff a look of approval. "I'm Greg Elizondo, the owner of Elena's Weddings and Bridal."

"Good to meet you." Several other industry professionals stepped up to meet Greg.

Tara tried to slip away.

His hand on her waist said he wasn't letting go.

She kept her smile in place and tried to wriggle free once more.

Nope.

Finally Greg held up a hand for Kathy's attention. She raised an eyebrow. "Kathy, can we pause the music for just a moment?"

"Of course." She moved to the front desk and hit a switch.

An expectant quiet descended over the crowded bridal room.

Greg grabbed Tara's hand and moved to one of the short, wide bridal stools in front of a triple mirror, designed to show the bride all aspects of her gown. "Ladies and gentlemen, forgive the interruption. I've just returned from New York. I arrived late, and I'm hoping to meet with every one of you this evening. But it seems I have some pressing business at hand, so if you'd indulge me a moment." He went down on one knee and gazed up at Tara.

Heat flooded her cheeks.

Emotions roiled within her. And seeing Greg like this, ready to declare his love in front of all these people when he should have been courting their business and not her heart . . .

It made Tara realize she would love him no matter where he lived.

"Tara, this isn't exactly how I envisioned this, but given the last two months, it's most likely what we should get used to."

The truth of that made her smile.

"Will you marry me, Tara Simonetti? Will you run my mother's store with Kathy and the gang and live with me and grow old with me? And if God sends us a few cute kids, I'd be the happiest man on earth."

Marry him.

Run Elena's.

Babies.

The heat in her cheeks grew, but the warmth in her heart overflowed. "Yes, yes, and yes! But what about New York?" she whispered as he stood and withdrew a stunning marquise diamond from a velvet box.

"We'll visit there," he promised, smiling. "But this is home. And if I have my way, it always will be." He slipped the diamond onto her finger, gave her one last lingering kiss, then smiled. "And with all of these nice people counting on our new corporate enterprise" — he turned and gave the gathered professionals watching a wave of acknowledgment — "can I talk you into a quick wedding? Because while wedding planning is our business, I'm hoping we won't have a whole lot of time to plan our own."

Tara laughed, hugged him, and nodded. "We'll talk later." She smiled up at him, then down at her ring. "Right now we've got work to do."

# CHAPTER TEN

Tara would have married Greg on the steps of City Hall if necessary, but her mother and Kathy joined forces. "A quick wedding is fine," Kathy scolded, "but Elena's doesn't do weddings without thought, so you two hang on to your hats, go about your days, and in a few weeks, we'll have a wonderful wedding in Kenneville."

Would it snow?

Was there an ice storm looming?

"It doesn't matter," Kathy promised. "We're using an inside venue and weather will do what weather will do. Go back to writing your final paper and leave me alone, Tara."

She finished her final paper, and Greg drew up wedding-package contract agreements with multiple professionals on board. They booked six packages the first week, and eight the week after.

The ladies' combined efforts sold seventeen vintage-style independent gowns and booked thirteen full wedding parties.

Instead of closing the doors to Elena's, they'd increased their staff, reached into the community, and incorporated a new business model.

But nothing loomed as bright and beautiful as her upcoming wedding day.

Crisp, bright light filtered through stained glass windows. Flowers adorned the sanctuary, and soft piano music welcomed the guests into the historic, small church tucked on Franklin Street in Kenneville.

Tara's mother stepped into the bride's room. Quick tears filled her eyes. Her brother, Ethan, followed, saw the rise of emotion, and frowned. "You promised not to do that."

"I might have been wrong." She sniffled, grabbed a tissue, and hugged Tara. "You look so beautiful, honey."

"You look all right." Ethan grinned her way, then grabbed his own hug. "For a sister, you're not too bad."

"I do my best." She laughed up at him, then touched his face. "We've done okay, little brother."

His expression reflected the meaning behind her words. Despite the harshness of losing their dad, the financial struggles and emotional hurdles, they'd both come out fine. Just fine.

"There's a groom out there looking mighty handsome." Her mother smiled as she double-checked Tara's veil, her train, and the tucks of her ivory satin gown. "And the whole community has come out to celebrate with you."

"Not an empty pew in the place," Ethan noted, smiling. "Pretty impressive, sis."

"Mrs. Bushing organized the sweets table and made the prettiest wedding cake," her mother added as she picked up Tara's small bouquet. "And Mr. Bushing made pots of pulled pork barbecue for the buffet."

"Without fighting?" Tara asked, laughing.

"Well, they used separate kitchens, but they're fine now, buzzin' like a couple of happy bees. I think . . ." She took a step back, swept her gaze over Tara, and smiled. "We're ready."


Pachelbel's Canon in D.

Greg turned. His buddy Tim gave him a nudge, then nodded in appreciation as Tara stepped into view on her brother's arm.

*Stunning.*

She looked beautiful in a ballroom-style dress he wouldn't have foreseen in a million years. Sweet, funny, practical, frugal Tara had chosen a fairy-tale gown.

And it fit.

She should have looked left and right, acknowledging the sweet neighbors and friends who'd come to celebrate on this bright, early spring day.

She didn't. Looking forward, she smiled at him, only him, and his heart did the Grinch-trick, expanding exponentially.

She passed the pew filled with Elena's employees. With quiet deliberation she nudged Ethan to pause for just a moment and grasped Kathy's hand.

Tears streamed down Kathy's cheeks. For him? For his mother? For the moment?

Probably all three, and when Tara bent and kissed Kathy's cheek, Greg felt like his mother was there, with them, completing the circle.

She smiled at the rest of the crew, turned, and caught his gaze.

Her smile grew.

She and Ethan took those last few steps, and when Ethan reached out to shake his hand, Greg sensed the kinship of family, forever linked.

His mother was gone. Her father was gone. But in the beauty of the moment and the sanctity of the ceremony, he felt the full circle of family surrounding him.

And when the final blessing was given, Greg Elizondo turned, lifted Tara's veil, and kissed his bride, taking his sweet time with the happily-ever-after he hadn't expected.

Church bells pealed to announce their exit. Flower petals dusted the sidewalk, and as the bells rang above them, Greg stopped Tara on the steps for one more kiss, a pledge of life, love, and honor, no matter what came their way.

With God's help, living in the quaint surroundings of Old City, Pennsylvania, it was a promise they both could keep.

# EPILOGUE

"She'll be too cold. It's not even fifty degrees yet," Greg fussed. He reached for another blanket and handed it to Tara. "Just in case."

"No one's going to notice her pretty little Easter dress if we have her bundled in seventeen blankets. She's got the cute pink coat Kathy made her and a hat from my mother. She's fine, honey."

"You think?"

Tara resisted the urge to laugh at him, because one look at his face said he was sincerely concerned. "Yes. But if you want to carry her over to church for the Easter service, she can snuggle in with her daddy."

That thought brightened his eyes and relaxed his jaw. "Come on, Laynie. Daddy will cuddle you all the way to the church."

He bent and lifted the six-month-old little girl. She smiled up at him, patted his cheek, then nuzzled into his neck.

"She's got your number." Tara laughed as she tugged her coat on. "Daddy's little girl."

"Daddy's two best girls," he corrected her with a lingering kiss. "Who'd have thought two years ago that my life would be like this now?"

"Knee-deep in diapers and representing women's shelters and soup kitchens instead of entertaining international clients on Wall Street?" Tara teased. "We are so blessed, Greg. Who'd have thought that saving the Old City Mission would lead to being the contract attorney for an international Christian outreach?"

"Amazing and good." He settled Laynie along his hip as he pulled open the door. The baby grabbed his ear, babbling something adorable. "Elena Michelle Elizondo, Daddy can't close the door if you're doing that."

"Let me." Tara pulled the door shut, then stepped into the cool, midspring morning as neighbors along the way came out of their homes. "Laynie, look. It's your first Easter parade."

"It is." Greg kissed the baby's soft brow. "What do you think, Laynie? Everybody's all dressed up and going to church together."

Folks waved from across the street. Mission clients called greetings to neighbors as they positioned donated flowers along the mission's steps.

Another young couple came out of a highrise at the corner pushing a little boy in a stroller. As the church bells tolled, people filled the streets, walking toward the old brick house of prayer.

Another church rang in, and then another, a chorus of resurrection and joy, a new day. As Greg's hand clasped Tara's, she raised her gaze to his.

They'd both lost loved ones over the years, but God had given them a brand-new beginning. New jobs, a cozy home, a baby girl, and a strong neighborhood community. Old buildings, vintage stores, rustic stoops, and new love.

An older woman passed them and smiled. "He is risen!"

Greg answered the way his mother had no doubt taught him long years ago: "He is risen, indeed!"

And Tara walked beside him up the broad steps of the historic church, knowing she could never ask for anything more.

# ACKNOWLEDGMENTS

This fun novella wouldn't exist without the grace of the Hall family, owners of a renowned independent bridal store in Rochester, New York. "Bridal Hall" was a longstanding and wonderful part of the Western New York bridal industry for decades. As employers, they were marvelous, kind, and caring. As friends, they're more so! They offered jobs to two of my children in "Tuxedo Hall" as Beth and Luke worked their way through college, and on slow winter nights Ed Hall would say, "Bring your books and study if it's quiet. Make good use of your time!" Also, big thanks to Matt and Zach Blodgett, my two boys who attended the University of Pennsylvania. Their years in Philly gave me a chance to know and love the city, from the streets of Old City to the hills of Valley Forge, a wonderful place to visit and live! And a huge shout-out to the missions and soup kitchens reaching out to the needy in our communities. Bless you for your living example of Christ's words among us!

# DISCUSSION QUESTIONS

1. Deciding what to do with your life at age 18 . . . or 21 . . . can be a daunting task. The law school statistics bear that out. Fifteen percent of graduates never practice law. Do you know people who bore the brunt of education and then changed their lives or careers abruptly? Is that crazy or wonderful?

2. Greg Elizondo thinks he's like his father. Of course he is, in some ways, but as an adult his future lies strictly in his own hands. How often do we blame our pasts or our parents for choices we made on our own?

3. Tara's eager-to-please personality is almost her undoing. She wants to help others, but the reality of what her small town lawyer career would be like doesn't exactly jive with her mental image! Have you ever had a true wake-up call from the Holy Spirit? One of those "what were you

thinking?" moments? How did it change or affect your life?

4. No one said the right person would come along at the most opportune time. Oops. Greg is faced with two dreams . . . the woman God planted before him and his long-awaited goal of a seat in the big house of corporate law in Lower Manhattan. His trip there seemed ill-timed, but it was actually perfect timing. Has that happened to you, where the worst timing ever turns out to be ideal? Oh . . . that God!☺

5. Greg has lived in Old City and walked the streets for decades. He grew up here and pursued his education and dreams in Philadelphia, but he never paid much attention to the Old City Mission or the nearby churches until the mission closed down. How did God's timing play a pivotal role in Greg's life, his choices, and his perspective?

6. Greg, Tara, and the bridal crew at Elena's Bridal had to reinvent a new normal to keep the store running. With the advent of internet shopping and free delivery, have you seen changes in your local shops now that they have worldwide competition? My research trips highlight the difficulty of keeping a shop running in a tight and competitive economy. How important is it

to a community to keep those local shops open?

# ABOUT THE AUTHOR

Award-winning author **Ruth Logan Herne** is the author of over a dozen novels for Love Inspired and Summerside Press. The mother of seven children, she loves kids and pets. She is married to a very patient man who is seemingly unthreatened by the casts of characters living in her head. Visit her website at ruthloganherne.com, e-mail her at ruthy@ruthloganherne.com, and visit her on Goodreads or at www.seekerville .blogspot.com

■ ■ ■ ■

# IN TUNE WITH LOVE

## AMY MATAYO

■ ■ ■ ■

*This book is dedicated to my Nana —
Aileen Millsap Longfellow —
because I think she's pretty happy I
turned out to be a writer.*

# PROLOGUE

"You really are obsessive, you know that?"

April stifled a sigh. She was so tired of people saying that same thing to her — from Brenda the waitress to Daniel the night manager and now Jack the bartender — and that was only tonight. She'd heard this line at least a hundred times since she moved from Chattanooga into her sister's Nashville apartment last month and started working here.

Besides, who cared if she liked to write? Was it really *that* strange a hobby?

True, not everyone wrote lyrics on gum wrappers and bar napkins like she was currently doing. And then maybe there was the occasional roll of toilet paper she pilfered from the men's room because the women's room was always out when she needed it most, and what was up with that? And maybe it was a bit weird when she ripped the tags off new bar aprons and used them to jot down notes, but when a girl was out of toilet paper and napkins and gum wrappers, what was she supposed to do?

But obsessive? That was ridiculous.

"I am not obsessive. Just thorough."

"Last Friday you wrote eight words in Sharpie on my arm."

April rolled her eyes. Jack could be so petty with details. "They were the perfect rhyme, and I didn't want to forget them."

"Then next time write on your own arm."

"I was wearing a white sweater with really tight sleeves."

"I was wearing a white shirt too! I had just gotten in from performing in a wedding!"

"Who gets married in the morning, anyway?" April sighed. "Besides, you're a guy and it washed off, so what's the big deal?"

"The big deal is I had a date later that night before I had a chance to even attempt to wash it off — which took a mix of rubbing alcohol and baking soda to remove, by the way — and no girl likes a guy she just met that shows up with the words *I'll pay you a dime for a good time* written on his arm."

"Some girls do." She winked, fully aware it was a lame attempt at flirting. Jack was . . . *Jack.* Dark hair, well-built, and . . . and . . .

okay, sexy. *Sexy* is the word she would use to describe him. But he would never be interested in her. "Besides, she went out with you again, didn't she?"

"After a lot of explaining from me that the words were written by my psycho coworker and weren't the worst pickup line ever in history."

Psycho coworker. More proof that she didn't stand a — *wait.* Did he just insult her writing?

"It wasn't a pickup line!" As if her songs could be compared to a pickup line. Those sorts of lines were cheesy. Classless. In contrast, her art was high quality, intellectual. Even if no one had signed her yet. April frowned and put her pen down. "I guess my break's over. What table do you want me to take this to?" she asked.

Jack set a tray in front of her. "Take this round of drinks to table seven, and then you're up. Make it a good one. You never know who might be watching." He smiled at her.

In only a few weeks, Jack had become a friend. All he would ever be.

April frowned, grabbed the tray, and headed to the table, not the least bit concerned when she saw Jack pick up the napkin and read what she had written on it.

161

After she dispensed drinks to the waiting customers, she grabbed the microphone and headed toward the stage. This song would be a good one. Her best one yet.

She felt her confidence level swell, until she glanced over at Jack from his spot behind the bar. He held up the napkin . . . then proceeded to make gagging gestures with his finger and tongue. She actually heard herself laugh mid-note.

"You're late," Jack said, producing a sign-in sheet and a pen while Daniel pulled up a barstool.

"No, I'm not. I'm not supposed to start work for . . ." Daniel checked his watch, then shrugged. "I guess I'm late."

And that was the great thing about Daniel. He never had a problem admitting when he was wrong. In Jack's opinion, the world would be a better place if more people were like him.

"No matter," Jack said. "We're not that busy tonight. The most pressing thing I need you to do is refill the toilet paper in the men's bathroom. Looks like we're out again."

"April?"

Jack drummed his fingers on the counter. "That girl has a problem. Every time I see her she has pieces of it stuffed in her pocket, tucked under her arm, probably even inside her bra." Both men took a second to reflect on that. Finally, Jack took a breath. "Did you know she even wrote with a Sharpie on my —"

"Yes, you told me a couple of times. Or twelve, but I think I lost count sometime before closing last Tuesday night."

"Point taken. But seriously, that girl . . ." April was a little on the obsessive-compulsive side; still, she was cute. And in his twenty-six-year-old opinion, cute trumped crazy any day of the week. "Where is she, anyway?" Jack looked around but didn't see her anywhere.

"Her shift is over. I saw her in the parking lot on my way in. She said she started laughing during her last performance and couldn't stop. Had to walk off the stage. Can you believe that?"

Jack couldn't help the grin that worked its way across his face. "That might have been my fault."

Daniel raised an eyebrow. "What did you do?"

"Made fun of something she wrote right before going onstage. And I might have acted like I was vomiting while she was up there trying to sing."

Both men laughed. It was mean, but it was funny.

"Okay," Jack said. "Go fix the bathroom problem, and then come take over for me. I'm up in five minutes." Jack shoved a mug under the Coke dispenser and pulled the lever, mentally reciting upcoming lyrics in his head. He handed the filled glass to a customer.

"That reminds me," Daniel said, snapping him out of his thoughts. "Bill Jenkins called after you left last night. He's coming in tomorrow night, so be ready with something."

Jack's head snapped up at that. *Bill Jenkins?* Bill Jenkins, who had personally signed every third singer in Nashville this past decade *and* gotten them all record deals? Okay, except the ones who shot to fame because of that stupid television singing show. That Bill Jenkins? His face must have registered his thoughts.

"Yes, that Bill Jenkins," Daniel said, standing from his seat. "So have something ready."

Jack swallowed, because that was the problem. He had nothing ready. Nothing at all. Dread shot down his spine and landed inside his legs. Feeling the weight of a thousand rejections resting on his shoulders, he grabbed a cloth and began wiping down counters, intent on finishing the mundane part of his job before the entire purpose for his existence began. He worked here for one reason and one reason only: because this place was where many of Nashville's heavy hitters had worked before fame came knocking. Jack figured it was only a matter of time before the same thing happened to him. At least he hoped time would be that kind. Then again, he knew of many who'd spent entire lives waiting tables and passing out beer only to find twenty years had passed without a single nod of encouragement by anyone who mattered.

Jack often prayed he wouldn't be relegated to the same fate.

But now that Bill Jenkins was showing up, he feared he just might be.

Two hours and three songs later, Jack tossed his apron on a hook by the back entrance and walked into the stale night air. Even outside, the area smelled of cheap alcohol and day-old urine. A sad state of affairs considering this was one of the nicest bars in town, situated in an upscale neighborhood and catering to Nashville's finest. Then again, a bar's a bar. Some just didn't know when to stop. Jack stepped around a particularly disturbing patch of wetness and opened the door to his Honda Accord.

That's when he spotted the paper plastered against his windshield.

He frowned, then leaned forward and grabbed it. He turned the bar napkin over in his hand, studying the way the black words written on it bled through to the other side. He scanned them and scanned them again, his pulse picking up speed as realization dawned.

Lyrics. They were lyrics. Only four lines, but some of the best four lines he'd ever had the privilege of reading. For a split second he thought of April; wondered if they could be hers. But the words were clever. Engaging. Definitely the start of something that could be a hit. He'd read plenty of April's lyrics. These definitely weren't hers.

Jack looked over his shoulder and stuffed the napkin in his pocket. *Have something ready,* Daniel had said. And like an answer to prayer, these words practically fell from heaven and landed on his car. Jack wasn't the kind to reject small favors, so as soon as he got home, he would get started.

He'd come up with something if it took all night.

# CHAPTER ONE

*Three years later*

"I just don't see why it matters," April said, trying to remain diplomatic. Trying not to unleash a torrent of words all over her sister's head. "The dresses are yellow, Kristin. Yellow. It's not like pink clashes with it, so who cares?"

Her sister's almond-shaped eyes narrowed to resemble hot, burned pumpkin seeds. April had never seen eyes shrink and change that fast. Clearly one of them cared.

"Who *cares*? Doesn't *matter*?" Her sister's arms flew upward, automatically tossing the volume of her voice higher with it. "I asked the wedding coordinator to keep the color pink out of this wedding, and I meant *out of it*. It's so cliché. It's so overdone. It's so generic."

April didn't think now was the time to point out that all those words meant exactly the same thing. She bit her lip and commanded the grammar nerd inside her to shut up.

"When we were little, pink was your favorite color, so maybe it's a sign."

Kristin glared at her. "A sign of what — that I'm no longer four years old? Thanks a lot for pointing out that I'm getting old."

One — Kristin was twenty-five. Exactly three years older than April.

Two — this conversation was stupid.

But Kristin didn't think so. "I'm so angry with her right now I could scream!"

Which was exactly what she was doing. April glanced behind her to see people all over the Target parking lot staring at them. She gave a little wave and a pathetic smile and turned back to her sister.

"Well then, the good news is the co-ordinator quit so you'll be able to avoid any more screaming for today. There's always an upside."

"You're not helping, April." Kristin's head came down to rest on the car door. April heard a sniffle, then another. Yelling and crying — this day just kept getting better and better. "How could she quit on me four days before the wedding? It's *four days* before the *wedding*!"

April stepped forward and patted her sister's back. What else could she do? She was trying to give comfort, trying to be supportive, trying not to think of the fact that it was nearly three o'clock in the afternoon and she had lyrics to write and coffee to drink and a pedicure appointment in an hour, and of all the things on her list of things to do she could not miss that. Her feet were embarrassing, her toenails chipped and jagged, and she would not walk down the aisle as the maid of honor with gross feet. She would, however, rethink the color she'd already mentally chosen. Pink was not the way to go in this situation.

"Because she's rude and thoughtless and completely unprofessional, that's why," April said. She didn't add that her sister was also rude and overbearing and ridiculously demanding and if she, herself, had been the wedding coordinator she would have quit months ago. There was nothing wrong with the color pink. Or with omitting the receiving line — no one liked those anyway. Or with doing away with the traditional cake and replacing it with cupcakes. But her sister had dismissed every creative idea the lady came up with. Not surprising since Kristin was currently studying for the state bar exam, and lawyers were some of the most unimaginative people April had ever met, if her father and his friends were any indication.

So, truthfully, April was a little proud the coordinator quit. Still, she had to help somehow, if only to make her sister feel better.

"If there's anything you need me to do, just let me know." She checked the time on her phone. Forty-nine minutes and counting.

She almost didn't notice when her sister's head snapped up. "Really? Because you could do it."

April squirmed against the tightness in her chest. It squeezed her like a snake intent on swallowing her for dinner. "I could do what?" Denial. Denial was her friend.

"You could be the coordinator. It's just for four days."

Just four days. That was like saying the Battle of the Alamo was just four days. Like saying God created the heavens and earth in just four days. April wouldn't survive. She couldn't work as fast as God, and even if she could, she would end up killing her sister. And as much as she needed some alone time to write, solitary confinement in a prison cell wasn't currently on her bucket list of things to do.

"Um . . ." she studied her fingernails. "I

don't know. I'm a little busy right now and
—"

Kristin huffed. "Busy doing what?"

"Busy working. Writing songs. Trying to land a record deal. It all takes time, and I just don't see how —"

"You've been doing that for over three years now." Kristin made a disgusted sound. "It's about time you accepted the fact that it will probably never happen. I need your help. You can go back to writing your little jingles on Monday after the wedding."

Jingles. And this is how her family saw her, every last one of them. As if it was her fault she hadn't yet been discovered. Her fault that the right place and right time hadn't yet surfaced for her. Her fault that a guy she worked with had ripped off one of her lyrics three years back and made a huge success of himself while she still passed out drinks and peanuts at the same stupid dive bar.

April took a deep breath and forced herself not to hate Jack Vaughn. As always, it took work, especially considering she'd heard a rumor he was in town for a few days. The idea alone sent a ripple of anger up her spine, one she quickly commanded to go away. To think she once had a ridiculous crush on him. April nearly gagged just thinking about it. Besides, Kristin needed her. They were *sisters* — and friends. And despite their differences in opinion, they really did love each other.

"Okay, I'll do it."

The relieved look on Kristin's face made relenting worth it. "Thank you. You won't regret it, I promise."

"What do I need to do?" April asked.

For the first time all day, her sister smiled. "Really, not that much."

# Chapter Two

If ever she had cursed her belief in humanity and the truth behind a spoken word, it was now. *Not that much,* her sister had said.

Not that much, her butt.

April blew a strand of hair out of her face and tied another ribbon around a bag of birdseed, holding the yellow silk ball and stick in place so it would stop leaning to the side for the love of all things holy while she tried once again to keep all of it together. She wasn't sure who came up with the idea, but she knew one thing: whoever decided birdseed bags needed to resemble cake pops should be required to put these together themselves. But it was up to April. Everything was up to April.

For fifteen solid hours now, wedding crap was all she'd had time for.

"Are you almost done with those?" Kristin popped her head around the corner, a giant look of concern crinkling the space between her eyebrows as she took in the stack of unfilled cloth and bucket of birdseed. "Because I need help with the place cards and you have better handwriting than me."

And this was the excuse for all the work she'd been doing unassisted since she accidentally fell into the job of wedding coordinator yesterday afternoon. April was apparently better at everything. Better at making birdseed bags. Better at polishing bridesmaids' shoes. Better at stacking monogrammed matchbooks inside clear glass hurricanes. Better at everything.

And now better at writing names on place cards so that everyone in attendance could sit at chairs preassigned by Kristin. April didn't care where anyone sat. April didn't care if anyone sat at all. At this point, April didn't care if her sister flew away to Jamaica or Aruba — wherever crazy, high-maintenance brides went to elope with their poor, unsuspecting husbands-to-be.

But as had become customary, she smiled. Sucked it up. And answered. "I'll be done in just a minute and then I can help you."

"Okay, thanks." Kristin waved her fingers and walked away, only to pop her head in a second later. "Oh. One more thing."

Something about the way she said those three words made April's blood run cold.

Maybe it was the slight lilt in her voice at the end brought on by the artificial effort to sound casual. Maybe it was the way each word was carefully enunciated, as though Kristin needed extra time to really make sure her sister knew what came next was important. Or maybe it was the simple fact that every piece of bad news Kristin had ever delivered in life began with those same words. When April was seven: one more thing, your goldfish died. When she was ten: one more thing, Santa Claus isn't real. When she was sixteen: one more thing, I accidentally made out with your boyfriend. And when she was nineteen: one more thing, Jack Vaughn's song "Confidence" hit number one on the country charts.

April was sick of One More Things, and it was about time her sister knew it. She tied a bow around another bag and tossed it in a box. "What did you do now?"

Kristin's eyes went wide, the picture of false innocence. "What makes you think I did something?"

"I know you did something. Spit it out, Kristin."

She shifted in the doorway. "The wedding singer quit this afternoon."

April blinked, waiting for the rest of the story. She would like to say the news surprised her, but in reality she was shocked the whole hired staff hadn't quit by now. Kristin was a diva. Verged on a tyrant. Would probably go down in the books as the worst bride ever in the history of brides, and she'd seen the movie *Bride Wars* so this was saying a lot.

"I'd like to say I'm surprised, but then that would be a lie and lying is a sin and — oh my gosh, do you want me to *sing*? Because I'll do a lot for you, Kristin, but I'm not singing in your wedding." April flattened another piece of material and spooned a small pile of birdseed in the middle of it.

"No, I'm not asking you to — wait, why wouldn't you sing in my wedding?" Kristin crossed her arms and glared down at her. "It's not like you don't sing in public all the time. And don't tell me you've developed a sudden case of stage fright because I won't believe you. You sing for a living, April. And you're telling me you wouldn't sing in my wedding if I needed you to?"

Her sister, ever the drama queen. April sighed. "I don't have stage fright, but I do have a very real fear of crying in public. So if you don't mind, I'd really rather not look like a sobbing idiot in front of three hundred people while I sing twelve stanzas of 'Wind Beneath My Wings.' "

"Aw, you think you'll cry at my wedding? That's so sweet."

"Of course I'll cry. You're my sister and I love you. Plus, I cry at Hallmark commercials."

Kristin made a face. "You're so emotional. But 'Wind Beneath My Wings'?" Kristin made an unflattering noise. "As if *I* would choose that overdone song. But I don't need you to sing. I hired someone."

"Then why are we having this conver—*wait*. You hired someone already?" There was no way — no way — Kristin could have hired someone that fast. Aside from April, she knew no one in the music scene, and a replacement that fast would have to be done on a favor. But who owed her a favor?

"Um . . . it was more like a chance encounter than anything else." April watched while her sister reached up for a strand of hair and began twirling. Twirling, twirling, twirling. And more than the One More Things and fake smiles and all the other regular habits Kristin used to mask guilt, hair twirling was the biggest sign of wrongdoing. Always had been. She raised an eyebrow at her sister and repeated the question. "Kristin, who agreed to sing last minute? Because I can't imagine that anyone around here would —"

Then she knew. Like a cat knows when someone is dying and a child senses stranger danger, she knew.

And just like that, prison found its way to the top of her bucket list, because this was totally and completely and entirely grounds for murdering her sister.

"Has anyone seen my brain? I can't seem to locate it," Jack said, raking his hands through his hair before burying his face in his palms. "What the heck possessed me to agree to sing in that wedding? I don't even like that chick, but it was almost like my mouth opened up on its own and said yes before I could stop it. I'm a musician — I have a great career — so how in heaven's name am I suddenly playing the part of Adam Sandler in that lame nineties movie?"

*"The Wedding Singer?"* His manager, Brian, peered at him over his laptop screen. They sat at Jack's mother's kitchen table drinking coffee. Jack always made a point of stopping in to see his mom when he rolled into town. With a rare weekend off and the new tour kicking off next weekend, neither he nor his manager were in a hurry to do much of anything else. "I think that movie came out in the early two-thousands."

"Whatever. I'm still starring in it. Will

probably be forced to wear some blue tuxedo with a puffy ruffle shirt and sing some cheesy ballad." His head came up, eyes wide with horror. "If she makes me sing 'Wind Beneath My Wings' —"

"She wouldn't dare," Brian said. "Besides, I saw that chick in her tight blue skirt. I'm not surprised you said yes. Not surprised at all."

"Please," Jack said, "You don't know this girl. She could have been standing there in a fringe bikini and I still would have found her repulsive. I only said yes for one reason." Guilt. Guilt and a fair amount of self-loathing. Pair those two attributes with a healthy dose of shame and a guy could be talked into just about anything. But he didn't say that. In fact, he said nothing. It took Brian a minute, but eventually he caught on.

"And the reason is . . . ?"

"I owe her sister something." That was as close to the truth as he dared to admit. He couldn't tell his manager his entire career was launched on a stolen song. It didn't matter that he didn't know it was stolen until exactly four weeks after it was released and playing on an hourly basis on the radio. It didn't matter that over a month of television appearances had gone by before April began to flood his phone with text messages demanding an apology, a retraction, money. It didn't matter that Jack spent the next two months panicking before he finally sucked it up and called her back, or that she had subsequently ignored all his calls — at that point likely too angry and hurt to bother acknowledging him. It didn't matter that she'd written only four lines and Jack had built an entire song around them — he'd spent three years rationalizing that pathetic idea — but his conscience wouldn't let him deny the hard truth that stealing a little was the same thing as stealing a lot. People went to jail for both.

Sometimes Jack suspected jail was where he belonged. Despite the poor conditions or the fact that he might be eye candy for the sexually frustrated, he wondered if landing his butt in solitary for a few days would make his guilt magically disappear.

It was a long shot, he knew, but he still couldn't help consider the possibility.

"You owe who something?" His mother walked in, the picture of health and stability and normalcy — something he appreciated more and more as life got crazier. She wore her usual uniform of mom jeans and pullover sweater. No matter how many times Jack encouraged her to go shopping and treat herself to something more than JCPenney or Sears, she wouldn't do it. There were definite benefits of having money, but other than this house that Jack purchased for her last year and a cleaning lady who came once a week in spite of his mother's objections, she didn't bother enjoying any of them.

"No one, Mom. I was just filling Brian in on the history of this town." Not exactly a lie; just a few details left out to protect the less-than-innocent. Namely, him.

"Oh, tell him about the Belle Meade Plantation," she said, fishing a black mug out of an upper cabinet and setting it beneath a shiny chrome Keurig, a purchase Jack had made the last time he visited. "It's one of the most beautiful landmarks in Nashville. You should take him to see it while you're here."

And this is what his mother did. Made plans for Jack to tour the city every time he came into town, despite knowing he had only two days set aside before a grueling concert schedule took over every second of the next seven months of his life. Sightseeing was the last thing he wanted to do. But ever the dutiful son, he agreed.

"Sure thing, Mom. I'll try to fit it in."

He wouldn't, but she didn't need to know that. His mother was the best woman he'd ever met — provided for him and raised him alone, when the only thing they could afford was a trailer park on the outskirts of town and Ramen noodles most nights for dinner. The last thing he would do was hurt her, not when she was excited about the idea of Jack playing Nashville tour guide. But the only thing about sightseeing in Nashville . . . sometimes you ran into people you'd rather not see.

Jack stared at the table, his thoughts a swirling tornado wrapping itself around the same familiar subject.

April Quinn.

He knew he owed April everything, and for the last three years his conscience had begged for release. And now it would have it in the form of a big, fat face-to-face with her. He had no idea what he would say, no idea how he would feel seeing her after all these years. But he knew one thing: if he had to sing ninety-seven verses of "Wind Beneath My Wings" on repeat, he'd do it the entire wedding to keep her from slapping him.

# CHAPTER THREE

The next morning Jack picked up two grocery bags and set them on his hips, then turned to walk to the car, trying to change his attitude but failing miserably. He hated grocery shopping. Hated it almost as much as mowing the lawn and unclogging a hair-filled drain. But his apartment contained nothing edible except for a bag of stale Doritos he didn't recall buying and one unopened can of beer tucked away in the back of his refrigerator. Brian was taking yet another nap, so Jack figured now was as good a time as any to get the errand over with. Which meant he'd spent the last half hour of life cursing his existence.

But every internal foul word that had flitted across his brain in the grocery store was nothing compared to now.

He stepped off the curb and stopped short. Twenty feet away from him stood April Quinn depositing bags inside the trunk of her car. She reached for the last bag inside her shopping cart and turned back around, giving him a nice view of her backside. So he looked. Of course he looked. Until it occurred to him that any second now, she would notice him standing there and quite possibly yell at him across the parking lot.

Jack decided to make himself invisible. After looking over his shoulder to make sure April was still preoccupied, he walked in the opposite direction toward his own car. Everything went well until he made the bonehead move of setting both bags on the back of his Lexus to retrieve car keys from his pocket. Just as he fished them out, one bag toppled onto the other bag and both started shooting contents onto the ground. While he lunged to grab them, his hand hit the panic key. His car alarm blared across the parking lot like a bullhorn announcing a battlefield retreat while Jack just stood there among the carnage.

He clicked the *Off* button and surveyed the disaster.

A carton of eggs lay upside down with four — maybe five — yolks oozing out from the top. An untied bag of apples rolled underneath cars and in the driving lane, fruit heading in too many directions to rescue. Jack watched as a minivan obliterated one. Cereal toppled end over end, but it was cereal, so nothing much happened there, thank God. But the chocolate milk fared worst of all. One side busted and gushed brown liquid in a puddle around his feet. He had to jump out of the way to keep any from getting on his new two-hundred-dollar leather combat boots. A silly expenditure, but he swore it was love at first sight even though he didn't believe in that crap. Seeing no hope for his situation, he gave the heavens a great big eye roll and bent to retrieve an apple. The eggs could stay there and scramble in the hot afternoon sun for all he cared.

"Need help with that?"

Jack's spine stiffened even though he was kneeling down. Who knew spines could do that? But apparently spines could because his did, right then and right there, making it painful and awkward to stretch for more apples. So he gave up trying and straightened, dread and nervousness filling up every crevice of his insides because he would know that voice anywhere. Only this time, it rang with a definite chill. That same sound haunted him at night when he lay awake with nothing on his mind except time and emptiness. It taunted him from its place in the crowd as he stood onstage and pretended to be a songwriter. It jabbed at him in his dreams that played out like real-time memories on repeat. He'd listened to her early messages so often he could recite them on command.

Jack, where did you find that napkin? It wasn't yours to take.

Jack, where did you get those lyrics? And don't even think about telling me it's just a coincidence.

Number one, huh? I hope you're proud of yourself, Jack.

How do you live with being so dishonest, Jack?

She'd said so many other things in those first few months, but these were the questions he remembered the most. Because these were the ones he wished to undo. The ones he wished to deny. The ones he asked himself daily.

Yes, he was proud of his career. But no, he wasn't proud of the way he got here. For every second of every day, his regrets were many. Still, regret did nothing to prepare him for what he was sure to face when he locked eyes with April for the first time in three years. Wanting to get it over with, he inhaled all the air around them and slowly turned around.

Nothing prepared him for her smile. Or for the fact that three years had done scrawny, short, wispy April Quinn a whole lot of favors.

April kept the smile pasted on her face, unwilling to give him the satisfaction of seeing any other emotion. Maybe he felt guilty. Maybe he felt remorseful. Maybe he felt bad that his career took off instead of hers, which would have been justified.

But she wouldn't let him see her feeling anything except happy. Happy, happy, happy. Despite the past two days spent doing every freaking thing possible for the Sister Bride from Hell, Jack Vaughn was going to see her happy. So she smiled. The sweetest, kindest, Southernmost, fakest smile she could muster. And she kept it there while his mouth opened and closed, the famous singer-songwriter at a sudden loss for his own words.

Imagine that.

"Um, I think I can manage it myself. But thanks."

An apple dropped from his hands and rolled across his foot before it disappeared under a black Volvo. April nearly laughed at the awkward picture it made, but then she saw Jack wince and saw him shift and saw an embarrassed flush as it made its way up his neck, and then she felt . . . sorry for him? Frustrated, she straightened her shoulders and demanded indignation to return. Like an obedient puppy she'd been carrying around for three solid years, it did. With a little added anger to make things interesting.

She held that smile in place and said, "It looks like you're handling things really well, so okay then." She didn't even try to mask the sarcasm in her voice. It was bound to come out eventually anyway. "It's great to see you, Jack. Can't wait to hear you perform at the wedding." She turned to go, bitterness perched like a devil, wings flapping wildly as it shouted obscenities from its spot on her left shoulder. If she weren't such a nice girl she would probably encourage it to keep going. Instead she slapped it away, then stomped on it for good measure to make sure it was good and dead.

Sometimes it was such a pain to be naturally nice.

"April, wait."

Sometimes it also sucked to be such a slow walker. She turned back around and worked up that smile again, but even she could feel the way it faltered.

"What? Do you need something else?"

She expected him to stutter; what she got instead was a wry grin. "Why'd you stomp your foot like that when you walked away?"

And just like that the tables were turned. "I didn't stomp my foot."

His grin only deepened. "Oh, but you did. Kind of an odd display of anger in the middle of all that smiling you did, in my opinion."

So he'd seen through her façade. Now she was ticked off. "No one cares about your opinion, Jack."

He shrugged, arrogance practically dripping from that wavy head of gorgeous hair. Wait. She didn't just think that. His hair was disgusting. Even worse than that tan, chiseled face. April gave herself an internal beat down for noticing.

"Actually, quite a few people care about my opinion nowadays, if you want the truth."

And finally, there was her opening. "As if you would know anything about the truth. Good one, Jack. You're so hilarious."

She should have felt better at the way he blanched. Swallowed. And looked instantly sorry.

But she didn't. Instead, she watched him

nod and offer the first admission of wrong-doing she'd ever heard him say. "You're right, and I deserved that." He looked over her shoulder for a long minute, locked in a faraway stare. Finally, he looked her in the eye. "I'll see you at the wedding, April. Thanks for your offer to help."

And with a sad smile, he climbed inside his car, leaving a pile of mutilated groceries on the pavement behind him. April stared after him until his car disappeared, slowly beginning to realize they now shared the same raw emotion.

Just like that flash of a smile Jack had just given her, sadness wrapped its arms around her and squeezed tight.

# CHAPTER FOUR

"You said what?" It was the third time in two minutes Kristin had asked that same question with that same horrified lilt on the last word, and April was more than sick of it.

"I told him he was just so hilarious. That he wouldn't know the truth if it bit him on the butt." Maybe she hadn't exactly worded it that way, but that's what she meant. If he was a smart guy, he would figure it out.

Her sister ran the pad of her index finger across her eyebrow to wipe away a phantom drop of nonexistent sweat — there's no reason to sweat when you're not doing anything but giving orders to your personal slave of a sister — and glared at April. "Why would you say something like that? I need him to be in top form for the wedding, not worried that you're going to have some meltdown in front of everyone while he's up there trying to sing. For once in your life, think of someone besides yourself, April."

A harsh laugh escaped before she could stop it. "Oh that's rich coming from you. *Think of someone besides myself?* Kind of like you were doing when you asked him to sing in the wedding in the first place? Who were you thinking of then, Kristin? Who were you thinking of then?" April hated the way her voice had risen to such a high pitch, but there was no stopping it. Hysterical and whiny were sometimes her thing.

Like self-righteousness and arrogance were sometimes Kristin's thing. "I was thinking of you. It's way past time to put this whole grudge thing you're holding against Jack behind you. It isn't healthy. It isn't smart. And unforgiveness isn't good for the soul. Plus it causes wrinkles."

"It does *not* cause wrinkles, and I'm twenty-two. Hardly at a place in life where I need to worry about them."

"Sure, you say that now. But someday you'll thank me when you're in your forties and still look like you're twenty-eight."

April rubbed the space between her eyebrows, trying and failing to figure out how a conversation about Jack Vaughn's jerkiness had headed south on a path that practically waved a pink banner endorsing Botox injections.

"Can we get back to the subject at hand, please?" she asked her sister.

"Sure. You need to forgive Jack."

"This has nothing to do with forgiveness. This has to do with ethics and morals and taking things that don't belong to you."

Kristin sucked in a breath. "April, it was a song. You don't even know if he took it on purpose, and besides, it's not like he robbed a bank or something."

And this was the response her family often gave, much like the *jingles* statement her sister had made yesterday. It was only a song. A song that just happened to be *the* song that skyrocketed Jack's singing career. And sure, maybe she was jealous. Maybe she was angry. Maybe she was even a tad bit vengeful. But deep down, all she really wanted was an apology. Nothing elaborate; nothing grandiose. But it's hard to move on and really make peace when an offense has never been addressed in the first place.

But it was pointless to talk about it with her sister. She didn't understand. In fact, no one really did.

"You're right, at least he didn't rob a bank." Sometimes it was easier to smooth the waters than to walk through a rising current of lectures. Today, April decided to aim for calm.

Kristin lowered her mascara wand and smiled at her through the bathroom mirror. "I'm glad you're finally coming around." She'd been practicing her wedding makeup for well over an hour — applying and removing and switching up color pallets only to apply and remove all over again. They were currently on round four, and in April's opinion every single application looked the same. "And I'd like to hear your thoughts on that eventually, but first tell me what you think of this look."

"I think it's perfect," April said on a sigh, swallowing any hopes for an understanding conversation.

"You've said the same thing about all of them," Kristin pointed out. "I need your opinion, April. I'm not just doing this for the fun of it. I have less than seventy-two hours to find the right colors. How am I supposed to do that without your help?"

"Maybe Mom can help you when she comes tomorrow."

Kristen just looked at her. "Dear Lord, is that tomorrow?"

"Yep." April picked up a tube of lipstick and pulled off the cap. Gold. Gold looked good on her. "I'm sure she'll be ready to

194

give you all sorts of opinions, especially when she sees the church."

Both girls grimaced. "She's going to hate it. Every bit of it. She wants a high-society wedding on my very tiny budget. Even what they've chipped in isn't going to give Mom the showpiece she's dreamed of."

April rubbed her lips together. "Whatever. She's still mad at me for working at a bar and trying to make it as a songwriter instead of marrying a doctor. We're both huge disappointments."

At that, they laughed. "They'll deal with it eventually," April continued. "Besides, if you want my opinion, they should be proud to have two daughters who make their own way instead of becoming clones of their parents. At least we're not spoiled rotten. Or, at least one of us isn't."

Kristin jabbed her in the side. "Very funny. But speaking of opinions . . ."

Now that she was in a slightly better mood, April tried to focus once again. "Okay, what color is this? Purple? Violet? Mauve? I don't remember what you told me."

"It's a pale wine." Kristin fluffed her hair and shook it a little, then turned her face from left to right, examining and critiquing her image from every angle. "I think I've narrowed it down to this one or the nude theme. Which one did you like better?"

If she'd had a coin in her hand, April would have flipped it over and called out the lucky answer. As it was, she had nothing in her possession right then but an old hairbrush and her sister's well-used tube of L'Oréal lipstick. Neither one was all that flippable. She came up with an answer anyway.

"I say go with the nude. It's safe, it's classic, and it goes with everything. Plus I don't have time to see anything else. I have to get to work."

Jack started sweating when he hit the parking lot. He hadn't been here since he walked out three years ago — his last night on a job that had opened more doors than he ever thought possible. Since then, life had been a whirlwind of opportunity and introductions and press junkets and travel on his rapid rise to stardom. He wouldn't trade a minute of it. Wouldn't change it for the world.

Except now he felt like he was walking into a time warp of delayed disaster — the whirlwind of fun quickly morphing into a hurricane of impending doom.

April still worked here. He'd found out

that awesome piece of news earlier when he called in to check on the performance he was set to give an hour from now. And presently, he was begging his Maker that tonight might be her night off. And begging wasn't an exaggeration. The words *please, I'll do anything you say* had gone through his mind at least a million times in the last hour, coupled with the phrase *I'll even start going to church.*

Not that he shouldn't have been doing that already, but still.

It took less than two seconds to realize all that begging was for nothing. The door had barely shut behind him when he saw a familiar apron skimming the thighs of a not-so-familiar set of legs that would have sent any red-blooded American male's pulse racing. He remembered those legs from three years ago, *and* from the five minutes he'd spent alone with them in a parking lot yesterday. April had changed in a lot of ways, all of them favorable. All of them positive. All of them pretty darn good.

His eyes traveled upward until they connected with hers. He swallowed and took an involuntary step backward; the scathing glare she nailed him with wasn't so favorable. He guessed some things hadn't changed after all, despite a hot set of legs.

Jack squared his shoulders and walked forward, thinking he was Jack Vaughn. Jack Vaughn didn't cower. Jack Vaughn didn't worry about what other people thought. Jack Vaughn certainly wasn't intimidated by a waitress in a bar, especially not one who just dropped a tray of beer all over an unsuspecting dude's lap. When the man looked up and sent April a murderous look, Jack forgot his hesitation and moved forward to help.

"I'm so sorry," April was saying. The horror in her voice tore at him a little. "I don't know what happened, the tray just tipped before I could stop it." She set the now empty tray on a nearby table and yanked a few napkins out of a metal holder, using them to pat the guy down. Jack didn't think she realized how inappropriate she was being, but he didn't stop her.

"Lady, quit pawing at me." The customer ripped the napkins from her hand and used them on himself, swiping at his shirt and pants and leaving a trail of paper napkin dust all over himself. "Look at me! I'm a mess!" He flung his hands in the air and stood, pushing his chair back in the process and creating the beginnings of a small scene. "This is going to cost you." He pointed a thick finger in April's face, a gesture that made Jack's blood simmer. "I want to see your manager right now."

April nodded. "Okay, I'll —"

Jack couldn't take watching anymore. "Hey, man, I'm pretty sure that was an accident. Why don't you let the girl get back to work, and I'll buy another round for your table?" Jack fished a hundred dollar bill out of his wallet and handed it to the guy. "And maybe this will replace the pants."

Just as he hoped would happen, the guy blinked at him, his jaw dropped just enough for Jack to know he'd been recognized. This was the best and worst part of fame — the worst when people wouldn't leave you alone, the best when it could be used to help out a friend.

Although in this situation, he used the term *friend* in the loosest way possible.

"Are you Jack . . . ?"

"Sure am. And I need to get ready to sing." He offered his hand, hoping it would seal an end to the situation. "So are we good here?"

The guy shook his hand and nodded, all traces of anger diminished to the point that Jack doubted he would even remember tomorrow. "We're good. But I will take you up on that round." And with that, the guy smiled.

Jack laughed and assured him he would place the order, then turned to face April. If he was being really honest, he was rather proud of himself. It wasn't just anyone who could diffuse a situation like that. It took someone special to swoop in so quickly and rescue a woman. It wasn't just any day that —

"I didn't need your help, Jack, and I darn well don't appreciate it." If anyone had been standing behind him, they would see his self-congratulatory thought bubble leak, deflate, and float to the ground. "Next time you want to throw your weight around, do it at the expense of someone other than me. Got it?"

And with that, April snatched up her tray and marched away, leaving Jack Vaughn — *the* Jack Vaughn with the really cool career — wondering what the heck just happened.

# CHAPTER FIVE

His eyes had been on her all night, but she had made it a point not to look at him. Not when she served customers, being careful to hold the tray steady to avoid more accidents. Not when he walked by at the exact moment she dropped a pen while taking an order, nor when he picked it up and handed it back to her. Not when inspiration struck and she jotted new lyrics on a receipt a customer had left behind. And not when he took the stage just after nine o'clock to begin his scheduled performance.

Definitely not then.

Of course, by that point it was easy to avoid eye contact. The place was so crowded that April could barely see three feet in front of her, never mind the stage. Jack Vaughn was popular, it seemed. More popular than even she had guessed. So popular she suspected they broke the fire code one hundred people ago.

That made her even madder. Didn't the guy care that they could all die in a fire if . . . if . . . something she couldn't think of went wrong? Didn't he care that people were sweating, that all this body heat had upped the temperature in here at least ten degrees? Didn't he care that it now smelled bad in here all because he had chosen tonight of all nights — the last night before her weeklong wedding vacation — to need an ego boost offered by nearly four hundred screaming fans, several of whom clearly forgot to wear deodorant?

And another thing, why was he so maddeningly good looking? Even *that* annoying fact was a thorn in her still-not-quite-small-enough side.

Seriously, she had been on a stupid low-carb diet for over a month now and only four pounds had come off. Which left her only three more days to take off the remaining ten. Math wasn't her strong suit, but the numbers weren't adding right. Something told her she might fall short by nine pounds or so, which made the cookie she'd eaten behind the counter an hour ago seem slightly more justified.

Unlike this whole performance Jack was currently in the middle of giving. Nothing about this entire situation felt justifiable.

The whole thing was so incredibly unfair. So ridiculously —

"April, did you hear him?" Brenda, the only waitress who had worked here as long as April, jolted her out of her thoughts with a quick grab of her arm. "He just asked for you."

April blinked. "Who asked for me?"

"Jack Vaughn! Do you not notice the whole place is staring at you? Answer him, April!"

She felt her mouth open, felt her breath growing thinner and thinner as she searched the room for something . . . anything . . . that made sense. She still hadn't found it when Jack's voice finally registered in her ears.

"I'm not sure she heard me the first time, so I'd like to invite her onstage again to sing with me if she would. April, are you interested? You pick the song."

In the three years she'd worked here, in all the times she had written lyrics on napkins and jotted notes on discarded name tags and even marked up her own palm when nothing else was available, this exact moment had always been in the back of her mind like a recycled dream from childhood. A talent scout, a well-known manager, and — most common of all — a famous musician would appear from nowhere and ask her to sing. Hear her voice and fall in love with it. Listen to her lyrics and give her a platform to share them with the world. Sign her on the spot and teach her to ride the wave of stardom. This dream happened so often she could recite every nuance, plot point, and disappointing ending.

"April, what do you say? I've heard you sing, and it's about time the rest of the world got to hear you too."

And now she spotted him, almost like the crowd had parted in that brief moment just to give her a glimpse of the hopeful expression written on his guilt-ridden face. And he really did look hopeful. He really did look like he wanted her up there beside him. He really did look sincere.

It was just like her dream, in the flesh and incredibly true.

But there was one problem.

Not once — not in the hundred or so times this dream had played through her mind in the past three years since she had found the courage to take on this job and the hope that came with it — did she ever imagine herself turning around, dropping everything in her hands, and running away.

Sometimes during a concert, Jack would

pause the performance for a minute — a dramatic break that was made to appear spontaneous but in fact had been overly rehearsed — then scan the crowd looking for a woman to join him onstage. Screaming would ensue, followed by the shouting of names and the occasional attempt by a fan or two to mount the stage uninvited, until Jack finally picked the girl. She was always pretty. Always on the voluptuous side. Always standing next to a boyfriend because Jack liked to see them get mad. And — he would never admit it out loud — always blond.

But never, not once, had anyone refused to join him. Even more preposterous — never had one resorted to running away from him. To say he was mad was an understatement. To say he wanted to finish this stupid song he was stuck singing and punch something was dead-on accurate. But he had to keep performing, plus wrap up two more songs before he could jump down and leave this place. All because April Quinn had just rejected him in front of several hundred screaming fans.

He knew she was mad, but he still thought she would see the invitation as a compliment. The opportunity of a lifetime, even. An unbelievable chance to show the world what she was made of. And maybe he was also a little hopeful that his one simple act of kindness would get April to stand next to him in that tight little dress.

He was a man. Of course he'd noticed. He'd been staring all night.

Not that it mattered, because clearly her bitterness ran deeper than he thought. Well, her anger wasn't healthy, and it was time she realized it. And if he had to be the one to tell her . . . then fine. He would. As soon as this last song was over.

"We've got one more for you tonight," he said into the microphone. The noise grew and swelled above the already ear-splitting roar he'd been listening to for the better part of an hour. "I hope you've had fun, and I hope to see all of you back here sometime soon." They were customary platitudes and nothing more; Jack was never coming back here. "But until then, you've got one more chance to get a little crazy!"

And with that, his fingers grazed through the opening riff of "Crazy Little Thing" — his most recent release. They'd been waiting for it all night, and within seconds, the crowd jumped and roared. But all Jack could see was that feminine figure retreating into the back of the bar.

Only one more verse and two more choruses to go, and then he would retrace her footsteps.

It was time he and April Quinn reached an understanding.

# CHAPTER SIX

"I said go away, Jack. And I meant go away."
He banged his head once, twice, three times against the doorframe. It was the fourth time he'd done this, and — who knew? — it really could give a guy a headache. But he wasn't leaving until she opened the door. He just needed to figure out a way to get her to do it. So far begging, bribing with dinner, and offering to cowrite his next hit song with her hadn't worked. He'd reached the end of his creativity, and he was out of ideas. Unless a bolt of lightning struck or God himself reached down and zapped him with a sudden burst of inspiration, he would be standing in this hallway all night. And of all the places he could imagine pulling an all-nighter with a pretty girl, a narrow, dimly lit corridor lined with industrial-sized bottles of ketchup, mustard, and mayonnaise wasn't it. He hated mayo; even the sight of it made him nauseous. Jack

rolled his eyes toward the ceiling just to have something else to look at.

"I'm not leaving, April. Not until you talk to me."

"Then you're going to be standing out there until the rapture hits, because I'm not talking to you before then."

*The rapture?* Whatever. The sound of her muffled voice had long since driven him crazy, and not in a good way. He could tell she'd been crying, could hear the wetness in her voice despite the fact that it was laced with the kind of anger that meant she wanted to kill him. The combination managed to soften his attitude toward her, while at the same time it gave him a stronger urge to see her.

"April, there's a crowd out there. Do you really want to cause a scene in a place like this?"

She made an exasperated noise. Even through the closed door, he could hear the murderous undertones. "Says the man who just created the biggest scene this place has seen all year. Nice try, Jack. Why don't you go sing some more? Maybe this time do a striptease or two to really drive your female fans wild? Oh! It could be your last chance to *get a little crazy.*" She laughed at her stupid joke.

And it was stupid for sure. He couldn't help it if that song had shot to number one overnight. The fans picked the hits, not him.

"I've never done a striptease in my life, and I'm sure not going to start now." He scrubbed a hand over his face. "April, open the door."

"No."

"Open the door."

"Again, no."

"I don't understand why you're being so difficult."

"I don't understand why you're still standing out there."

Jack pressed a fist to his forehead. Women. You couldn't deal with them, yet you couldn't kill them either. At least not unless you planned it really well and didn't get caught. And so far he hadn't been able to figure out how.

"April, we need to talk. Other than the last ten minutes I've been standing in this hallway, I've dealt with your silent treatment for three long years now, and frankly I'm getting pretty tired of it."

He knew that would work. The door flew open with a bang, and before he could say *uncle,* a wild pair of eyes attached to the same body as a pair of fists emerged — one pair glaring a hole through him as the other pair shoved his chest and knocked him backward. He hit the wall, and a jar of mustard grazed his shoulder on its way toward the floor. Thankfully it didn't bust open; it did, however, land on his foot. Hard. He stopped himself from letting out a yelp. He would *not* look like the immature female in this weird situation.

"What the heck was that for?" he yelled.

"Are you kidding me with the three years of silent treatment?" In a complete unsurprise, she managed to yell even louder. She also used three fingers to jab him on the shoulder. Repeatedly. "I left you a million messages, and you ignored all of them. And before that, I seem to remember you snatching up my lyrics, writing yourself a whole little song around them, and never saying another word about it. If you were having to endure a silent treatment from me, you're the only one who knew it because you disappeared like the coward you are!" She jabbed him again.

He'd had more than enough. Nobody called him a coward and got away with it.

"First of all, I didn't know they were your lyrics until it was too late to do anything about it. The song was already on the radio, April. Second of all, I called you back, but you ignored my messages. And if you were so angry that you couldn't even talk to me, why didn't you sue? Or at least go to the press?" He backed up a step and ran a hand through his hair. "Some people interpret a lack of initiative as a lack of interest. And you did neither, so —"

"I hired a lawyer! I called the newspaper! I did a lot of things back then that I wish I'd followed through with." Her wild eyes focused a bit, but she still looked slightly rabid — like the foaming-at-the-mouth thing was a real possibility.

"You really called a reporter? Then why didn't the news break? My career would have fizzled before it even had a chance to start."

April sighed, long and slow. "I said I called the newspaper, not that I talked to a reporter." She shook her head, clearly embarrassed by something in her memory. "I accidently got transferred to the classified section, where I remained on hold listening to really bad Muzak for fifteen minutes. Eventually I got sick of it and hung up."

Jack barely won a battle with a smile struggling to break free. Barely. This wasn't the time for lightheartedness, and he still had something to tell her. Something he didn't want to say, but he had to get this girl on his good side somehow.

"April, I'm sorry. Really, I am." There, he'd apologized. She had no choice but to get over it now. "I really don't know what else to say."

It was silent so long that he looked up. Her gaze met his with a sad, wary smile. "Thanks, Jack. But honestly, sometimes sorry isn't enough."

She didn't mean to say those last words, except she did. Because even though *sorry isn't enough* was in direct contrast to the forgiveness she had been raised to believe in, this time it was just the way she felt. She believed Jack was sorry. Sort of. From her earliest memory, she'd had an unusual talent for reading people — and she could read Jack. The man had remorse invisibly tattooed inside the worry lines on his well-scrunched forehead. He also wore cockiness like a pair of expensive new shoes, and that wasn't going away anytime soon.

She just didn't know if she could bring herself to forgive him.

"Did you really not know the lyrics belonged to me?" She didn't know why, but suddenly she thought his answer might contain the key to this whole forgiveness thing.

Might.

Jack pinched the space between his eyebrows. "I didn't. Not until I heard your first message. And then . . . I don't know, I just —"

"Didn't know how to stop it?"

Jack studied his feet as though searching for a way to disagree. But she knew he couldn't, just like she knew there wasn't a way to answer it that would satisfy either of them. April didn't know if there ever would be. The only thing she knew right then was that her shift had just ended. She tore off her apron and rolled it into a ball, then looked up at Jack with what felt like a weak smile.

"This is it for me. I think I'm going to head home and pretend this day never happened."

He finally looked up at her. "Come on, it couldn't have been that bad. You got to see me again, after all."

She made a face before she could stop it. It just figured that she would be the only woman in America less than thrilled at the chance to talk to Jack Vaughn, especially considering her dream of making it big in Nashville. *Oh, the irony.*

She sighed. "From what I've heard, you talked to my sister the other day. Otherwise known as Bridezilla. Otherwise known as the bane of my existence. Otherwise known as the woman who makes more demands than Paris Hilton at a sample sale. Otherwise known as —"

Jack gave a soft laugh, and something about the sound wreaked a weird sort of havoc on her heart. "You lost me at Paris Hilton, but I did talk to your sister. She seemed a little stressed."

April didn't know if she detected sarcasm or not, but she went with it anyway. "Yes, I'm sure she's stressed. Because what bride wouldn't be going crazy when she's busy ordering her sister to call the caterer, take care of decorations, rewrite wedding vows, pick out a negligé for the wedding night, make plans for —"

"Wait — she expects you to write the vows?"

April didn't consider this the most outlandish item on the to-do list she'd just recited, especially considering the fact that wedding night shopping had forced her into three Victoria's Secrets, one Fredrick's of Hollywood, and another store that she would never speak of again, ever. Not even under the threat of the torture chamber or being forced to give up ice cream for a month. Both pretty much equaled the same thing.

She nodded. "Among other things. I think I've rewritten those vows a hundred times, and each time she nixes them based on a couple of words. Sometimes only one. I've recited them in my head so much that I'm a little afraid I'm accidentally already married to her fiancé."

This time Jack threw his head back and laughed. He had a nice jawline. Chiseled. Slightly unshaven. She liked unshaven.

April hated herself for noticing.

"I don't think it works that way, but I could be wrong."

"Let's hope you aren't. Sam's a great guy and all, but he's a little shorter than I like. Not to mention he's been dating my sister for three years. I believe in a lot of things, but sharing boyfriends isn't one of them."

Jack raised an eyebrow and glanced down at himself. "You like your men tall, do you?"

April wanted to punch herself right in the middle of her big mouth. Of course she would say that out loud. And of course Jack was over six feet tall. "Not super tall, definitely not as tall as you." She raked her gaze over his features to communicate her displeasure. There. That should do it.

Maybe.

"April, I'm thinking . . ." With a hesitant smile, he dragged in a slow breath and all

216

she could think was *please quit thinking, please quit thinking.* But as her usual luck would have it, Jack's mind was in full working order. "You're off work, I'm finished performing. Do you want to get coffee or something? I'd like to find out more about how you got talked into wedding-night shopping. Interested?"

April gave a little laugh. No, she wasn't interested. No, she couldn't care less what he wanted to find out about her. No, she didn't want to talk to him. She didn't even like coffee.

Which was why she couldn't believe it when her brain seemed to forget their earlier altercation and her mouth opened completely without any help from her and said, "Sure. Coffee sounds great."

# CHAPTER SEVEN

"That isn't true. Just because a person is famous doesn't mean he's shallow. Not all of us like full-body massages and seaweed wraps."

"You're telling me that if a girl showed up at your house on Monday morning with a table, essential oils, and a jar of mud, you wouldn't lie down then and there and let her get to work?" April took a sip of her chai green tea latte — something she had never ordered before but made herself choose under some weird sort of coffee shop duress — and set it on the table between them.

"Well, of course I would if it was free and she had nothing better to do. I just wouldn't let her show up every morning for the same reason." Jack folded his hands in front of him and looked around the room before settling his gaze back on April. "I would, however, draw the line at the mud. Seems like such a strange thing to spread over a person's body, and I'm not buying the stupid health benefits."

April raised an eyebrow. "So you've heard of them?"

"Of course I've heard of them. I just wouldn't pay for it, not when this entire state is made of red clay. That works just as well. And it, my friend, is free."

Once again, April's stupid heart gave a stupid flip in her chest. This was Jack Vaughn. So why was it getting harder and harder to remember all the reasons she was mad at him? It was time to give her brain a little refresher course. Time to step up the put-downs.

"At least we've established that you're cheap."

"Sweetheart, I grew up in a single-wide trailer. You have no idea."

Again with the flip, and this time it added a little thud. The term *sweetheart* certainly wasn't helping matters. She picked up her mug just to have something to do with her hands. "I forgot about that. Does your mom still live there?"

Jack picked up his napkin and tore a piece from the end. He smiled, a small amount of wonderment filling his expression.

"No, I bought my mom a house in Franklin last year. She objected until we unpacked the last box, but I'm glad she lives in a better place now. I owed it to her after all she sacrificed to raise me."

So much for stepping up her game. The thought of him taking care of his mother lost her a few dozen anger points. "How does she like it?"

He set the napkin down and looked at her. "She likes it fine, but she won't willingly spend a dime of my money unless I force her to. Like last month, I offered to take her to get a pedicure and buy her some new clothes. She told me she owned a perfectly good pair of nail clippers and what was wrong with her new Vanderbilt sweatshirt?" He shifted in his seat and pulled the white mug to his lips, but April saw the way he grinned. The mug wasn't big enough to hide it.

April laughed. It surprised her, but it felt good. "I suppose you should count your blessings."

"Why?" His eyebrow came up.

"You could have a line of family members only interested in your money. Your mom *could* be the type who asks for a monthly stipend to fund trips to Rodeo Drive and the plastic surgeon."

Jack set his cup down. "Those family

members exist. Believe me, they exist."

"Uh-oh. Long-lost uncles?"

"And aunts and cousins and best friends from high school I supposedly hung out with whose names I don't even remember."

April shrugged. "Sucks to be you."

The sentence held steady in the space between them, both of them aware of the words left unspoken. April would love to be him, would in fact *be* him if he'd been more of an honest person a few years back. Thankfully, she smiled.

"New subject," she said.

Jack barely suppressed a sigh of relief. "Back to the seaweed wraps," he said. "Are you telling me you would regularly subject yourself to that awfulness just because some idiot says it's good for you?"

April smiled up at him over the rim of her cup. "Not only would I subject myself to it, I would gladly pay the fee no matter how much it costs. Every single day. Because that's the difference between you and me, Jack." She leaned forward and looked him in the eye, well aware it was a flirtatious move but suddenly not in the mood to care. She was having fun. She was having fun with a man. She was twenty-two years old, available, and maybe it was the late hour or the fact that she was tired or the idea that going home alone to an empty apartment right now sounded more depressing than going to her sister's wedding dateless — which was her current plan. But for now, April was having fun with a man.

She wished the man wasn't Jack Vaughn, but that seemed to be just the way her life worked.

He blinked at her. "What's the difference?"

She blinked back. "The difference of what?"

He gave her a curious look. "You didn't finish your sentence. You said, *that's the difference between us, Jack.* But you never said what those differences are. And unless you want me to start guessing —"

"No, don't guess," she blurted. But for the life of her, she couldn't remember what they had been talking about. Quickly, she retraced her steps — the idea that she was young, that she didn't want to head home to an empty apartment, that Jack Vaughn was attractive. Wait, she had *not* been thinking that, so where did the thought come from? She forced her brain back into compliance. They had been talking about seaweed wraps and massage appointments and —

"I'm not cheap. That's what I intended to

say." She wanted to give a little victorious fist pump to commemorate her sudden surge in memory, but refrained. Thank God for good judgment.

"I might argue that point," Jack said. "I haven't gone on a date in years that cost me only eight bucks. You just might be the cheapest woman who ever lived."

April gave him a long look and motioned for the waiter. That little dig was going to cost him. In the form of a slice of cheesecake. Maybe two. No one called her cheap and got away with it.

She was feisty; he liked it. She was incredibly hot; he liked that too. She was also quick to put him in his place, something he hadn't seen for a couple of years now. He liked that most of all; probably a little more than he should. But something about April Quinn had him feeling instantly connected, and that was something he didn't need. Not at this point in his career. Maybe not ever.

But every time he considered taking her home, he came up with two new reasons not to.

She was funny.

He wanted more coffee.

Traffic was bound to be busy at midnight.

She had just ordered cheesecake. A move

he saw right through but somehow liked anyway. Note to self: never call April Quinn cheap. Although if that's what it took to spend more time with her . . .

And above everything else, he wanted to see more of April Quinn.

This was the worst reason of all. He needed to get out of here before the desire to spend time with her took over. Before he found himself asking for another date and another and another.

Under the table, something kicked at his shin. He looked up into April's amused face.

"What was that for?"

"You disappeared. It's one thing to call me cheap. It's another to check out on our date altogether."

His mouth tilted, his signature wicked grin that almost always worked on women. "Is that what we're on? A date?"

She shrugged, stifled a yawn. "Just repeating what you said earlier. Personally, I would call it more like a peace offering given by you, yet still up for debate on my end. I haven't decided whether to accept or not. Maybe I'll have some pie while I think it over."

Apparently the signature grin thing didn't work on April.

Jack raised an eyebrow. "Cheesecake and

pie? Are you trying to put on weight while you do all this thinking?"

She gave him a look. "Careful Jack, you should never call a woman fat. You never know when she might retaliate. You could be up onstage singing or —"

"Why didn't you sing with me tonight?" He hadn't meant to ask the question, but the opportunity had practically landed in his lap.

"Because I knew why you asked, and I wasn't about to make it that easy for you. If you want to smooth things over with me, you'll need to get a lot more creative than that."

*More creative than pulling her up onstage for a duet?* He was Jack freaking Vaughn. It didn't get more creative than that. He swallowed all the retorts that floated through his brain and tried to think up a response — one that didn't make him sound like an arrogant jerk. It wasn't easy.

"You got any suggestions? Something in particular you want me to do?" She probably wanted him to sign over all his royalties. Give her a writer's credit. Make a public statement declaring his guilt. Make a ridiculous apology on camera. He might have done that a couple of years ago, but not now. No way. Not happening.

Again, she shrugged. She almost looked . . . annoyed. "Well, I can tell you right now I don't want anything obvious. It's not like I want back pay or anything. That would be ridiculous." She laughed a brief, impatient laugh, one that had him baffled.

*She didn't?*

Jack drained the rest of his mocha latte and set the cup in front of him. "Then what do you want?"

April looked at him a long moment before giving him a barely perceptible smile. "I don't know, Jack. But I'm sure you'll think of something."

# CHAPTER EIGHT

"If you would use your brain, you might be able to come up with a better idea. One that hasn't been used by every bride since 1964."

For the third time today, April refrained from chucking something heavy at her sister's head. Her sister, who April considered to be her best friend on occasion. Her confidante. Her go-to-gal when everyone else left her all alone. Now April wanted to do the leaving, but of course she was stuck nine feet in the air, propped on a ladder, hanging white and cream paper lanterns from the reception hall's black ceilings. She knew the effect would be beautiful, but frankly, she wouldn't mind gathering all this paper crap in a pile and lighting it on fire.

"What is wrong with Christmas lights?" She hooked the lantern onto a nail and descended a few steps to take in the effect. "White lights are beautiful and will only enhance the planet and stars effect you seem to be going for."

Kristin sighed again. The sound had been so frequent all morning, April was beginning to suspect carbon dioxide was the only element left to breathe in this room. "Christmas lights are so overdone. They scream *I'm not original.* Frankly, they also scream *cheap.* I thought you were better than that, April."

It was all she could do to keep her mouth shut. April was so tired of that word being used to describe her. "They aren't cheap, especially if you get the LED white kind."

"I didn't mean —" Kristin made an impatient noise. "Just . . . I like the lanterns, but not the lights. Think of something else. Something no one has done before. Something people will be talking about for years and years to come."

"You could hang live snakes from the rafters. That would get people talking."

"That isn't funny, April."

She hadn't been kidding. At this point, she would do anything to move past decorating for this stupid wedding, even letting a snake bite her over and over and over. Because maybe it would be poisonous and maybe she would be admitted to the hospital and maybe she would have to stay there for days and days and days while someone else served her food and fixed her hair and gave her massages — all the things she'd watched Kristin enjoy all week.

She didn't exactly know if they offered free massages in hospitals, but that wasn't the point.

April was sick of being in charge; *that* was the point.

"Okay, then tell me your bright ideas. Because I'm having trouble coming up with anything else, and furthermore —" April froze, felt that weird sensation when your stomach drops into your toes and then bounces straight back up into your esophagus, and swallowed. "Oh dear God, they're here."

Below her, Kristin reached for her throat and cleared it — as if that one small act could dissipate the tension that had just swooped in and added a grayish pall to their day of wedding decorating. Their parents. Their parents were here. Which meant they were likely exhausted from their two-hour drive from Chattanooga, because who wouldn't be? Silent disapproval wrapped around them both like an extra-large sweater as the door closed behind them.

"I see you started without me," Gloria Quinn said. Her statement carried the same edge it would carry if she'd said *I see the Democrats are in control again* or *I see you ignored my advice and wore the color red anyway* or *I see you've put on a few pounds* — all of which April had heard at least once in the last year alone. "And paper lanterns, Kristin? I would have gone with electric ones, the iron kind you can buy at Crate and Barrel or one of those other cheap catalog stores everyone raves about even though I have no idea why."

*Crate and Barrel was cheap?* April bit back a retort. Next to her, Kristin whispered a low criticism.

"Electric lanterns. Thanks a lot, April. Why didn't you think of that?"

April ignored the dig and addressed her mother. "Because electric lanterns would have required a rewiring in the entire lighting system — outlets would need to be added and switches installed and I really didn't think you would want to pay for it. Besides, paper lanterns are eco-friendly and much easier to store after the ceremony is over."

As expected, Gloria's face relaxed. Her mother, the only ultraconservative April knew who was also zealous about environmental causes. Admirable, sure. Except she was usually more passionate about them than she was her own daughters.

"Then I guess I can live with them." She

clicked her tongue. "But I draw the line at Christmas lights." At Kristin's breathy laugh, her mother's eyes narrowed. "Kristin, tell me you didn't decide on something that tacky."

Kristin paled. "No, it was —"

"It doesn't matter. I'm here now, and everything you've done up to this point will look so much better when I'm finished with it." Her mother took in the reception hall with a disapproving frown, then set her sights directly on her sister. "Kristin, who on earth is your wedding coordinator? Because I insist you fire her this minute."

Kristin gasped. April glared.

She'd been here all of five minutes, and her mother had somehow managed to insult both of them.

"It's about time you showed up," Kristin said when he walked through the front door of the reception hall. "We've been here two hours already."

And now Jack was on the receiving end of Kristin's wrath. What a perfect start to the day.

The second he stepped out of his car, Jack wanted to climb back inside like the coward April claimed he was last night. Now he wished he'd followed that instinct. He'd never been more afraid in his life — not when he signed his first contract or recorded his first album or stepped onstage for the very first time. Of all the things that frightened him in life, he could think of four that topped the list.

April.

April's sister.

April's mom.

April's dad.

All four stared at him now, and all likely knew what he had done. He'd never met April's parents, but he knew that her father was a lawyer in Knoxville or Chattanooga or some other Tennessee town that wasn't Nashville. He knew they had money — not a lot, but enough to be annoyed that their daughters weren't more dependent on them. Jack admired that about both girls. It took guts to start with nothing and make something of yourself.

"I'm sorry?" The words sounded more like a question than an admission of wrongdoing. Because he wasn't sorry. He was late. The world would keep spinning with or without his painstaking rehearsal of whatever cheesy ballads Kristin had chosen for him to sing at this dang wedding. Still, a promise was a promise — even a foolish one made under the pressure of intense guilt. "I didn't know we were on a time crunch." He set his guitar case down by the door.

"Well, we are."

"Kristin, stop being so controlling," April said. "At least Jack actually showed up. Give him a little credit for that."

April's words surprised him. Before he thought better of it, he slid her a wink, one that she accepted with a slight blush. That reaction made him happier than he'd been in a while. But not as happy as her next words made him.

"Mom, Dad, this is Jack. He's the wedding singer, newly hired."

Jack didn't expect the introduction. A cold shoulder, maybe. To be ignored, quite possibly. But definitely not an introduction that didn't sound remotely hostile. This place wasn't technically a church, but he wondered if maybe a miracle was taking place anyway.

April's parents had watched this entire exchange, but now her father stepped forward and extended his hand. "Nice to meet you, Jack. You from around here?"

Jack offered a firm handshake just like his mother had taught him years ago. "I am, though I'm not here as much as I used to be."

"Jack and I used to work together," April offered.

And this. This surprised him more than anything, because —

"You're Jack Vaughn?" April's mother gasped. Her father frowned, and now it was only a matter of seconds before —

"Jack Vaughn? *The* Jack Vaughn?"

So many people asked that question, awe and admiration painted all over their features. Neither could be found on the faces of April's parents. Annoyance. Irritation. Distrust, for sure. And *there* was the hostility missing from earlier.

They knew. Oh crap, did they know.

"Yes, I'm him." Jack swallowed the mass of nerves suddenly clogging his throat and searched for something to say. Thankfully, he didn't have to scramble for long.

"That's him, and he's here to sing on a favor to Kristin. So go sing, Jack. It'll be interesting to hear what lovely songs she has picked out for you." Sarcasm. April used it well.

With a half smile, Jack picked up his guitar case and microphone stand and gestured for his bandmates — his pared-down bandmates because only his keyboardist and drummer agreed to join him, the other two losers claiming they were still owed vacation time and shouldn't have to give the days up just because Jack was an idiot — to pick up equipment and follow him.

Jack wasn't too far away to hear Gloria Quinn's whispered words. "Kristin, you can't be serious. After what he did? I would like to think you care about your sister's feelings a little more than that."

"I do. It's just that —"

"Now, who picked out this awful fabric for the rice bags? And what are they supposed to be? They look like very poorly designed lollipops, and the construction . . . just shabby. A complete disappointment. Amateur." She clicked her tongue and tossed one in a nearby wastebasket. Jack didn't miss the way April's face bloomed red; she was angry, that much was obvious. But there was something else. April almost looked weary. Maybe . . . defeated? She reached up to rub her eyebrows, and that's when he had an idea.

April had told him to figure out a way to make it up to her, and Jack had the feeling he'd just discovered a way to do it.

# CHAPTER NINE

Jack sighed and set his guitar on the stand. Rehearsal hadn't gone well. Not because they were out of practice or the band wasn't in tune, but because Jack had developed a sudden inability to sing in front of people. An odd bout of stage fright. He hadn't suffered from it in recent memory, not even at the bar two nights ago. Then again, it seemed to only involve those people whose well-known personal dislike of him ran deep.

And April's parents hadn't stopped glaring at him all afternoon.

Jack shut off the microphone and jumped off the makeshift stage, rubbing his hands together because really, he had no idea what to do. Torn between wanting to see April and wanting to flee this pit of tension and hostility — funny, considering a happy, supposedly joyful wedding would take place in this room tomorrow night — he stood back and waited for a decision to fall from the sky and smack him in the face. But like always, he waited for no reason because nothing happened. April continued filling miniature shot glasses with birdseed and yellow drink umbrellas because her mother had deemed all her previous work worthless and tossed those sucker-looking things into the trash. A small collection of gold balls lay heaped in a mound inside the trash can — like a pot of gold at the end of the rainbow, if the pot of gold lay on top of a collection of discarded coffee cups and yesterday's Chinese takeout.

The trash smelled awful. Someone needed to take it out.

Jack's eyes drifted away from April as he took in Kristin placing and replacing name cards around white linen-topped tables. Her mother reassembled gigantic arrangements of cream-colored lilies and white roses, proclaiming that the local flower shop was inept and completely without taste and for the love of God could they not tell the difference between a freshly cut flower and one that had clearly been refrigerated for more than a day? The level of outrage on this particular point left Jack perplexed, but then again he wasn't a chick and maybe this is what women worried about.

For maybe the millionth time in his life,

he silently thanked God for making him a man.

He also silently begged his Maker for a little grace. In about four seconds, he would need it.

"So did everything sound okay to you? Because if you had something different in mind we could always change things up a bit." Kristin hovered over a pile of multiple types of ribbon mounded on one of the round tables. She chewed her lip, heavy on the concentration, as she glanced up for the briefest second.

"It sounded great." Her enthusiasm equaled a disappointed meteorologist's pronouncement on the perfectly normal weather during non-hurricane season. *It's pretty. Not a cloud in the sky. Nothing to report here. Not even a single death.* "The only thing I didn't hear you play was 'Open Arms.' It's on your set list, right? That's the song we were listening to when Sam first asked me to be exclusive. You have to sing it."

*"Open Arms"? By Journey?* The "Open Arms" that was about thirty years old and had probably been played more at weddings than even "Wind Beneath My Wings" — which he drew the line at and would continue to draw the line at until the end of

238

time? Or until the end of this particular wedding since this was the last and final time anyone would refer to him as a wedding singer ever again.

But . . . "Open Arms"? Surely she was kidding.

"Um, no. I didn't see that one on the list I was given. Maybe somehow it got left off."

"Well, make sure you add it. Sam would be so disappointed."

From a few yards back, April laughed. She tried to cover it with a sudden hacking cough — one that Kristin bought but Jack could spot as fake even if he hadn't been standing ten feet away from her. Right then, Jack decided to close the distance. Maybe it was a small kinship he'd felt with her since their little date last night. Maybe it was because she felt like the only familiar person in the room. Maybe it was just that at this particular moment in time they shared a private exasperation with Kristin. Whatever the reason, he felt like being around her. Even if her parents flung imaginary daggers at his chest as he approached.

He picked up a birdseed cup. "Now, are people supposed to drink those or hand them out to the birds? Which, if you want my opinion, seems to skirt the line of encouraging alcoholism among God's winged creatures."

"Thank you for sharing."

"And then another thing —"

"Put that down, Jack. The last thing I need is for you to spill it. Then I'd have to clean it up and start over." April looked up at him, a look of pure exhaustion on her face. Still, he didn't miss the edge of a smile. "Except for your lovely rendition of 'Open Arms' that I simply can't wait to hear tomorrow night, you're finished with rehearsals. So why are you still hanging around? A sudden need to fill birdseed cups?" Before he knew what had happened, she grabbed a stack of twenty-five or so and shoved them in his hands. "I'll take that as a yes, so here you go. Finish these in the next fifteen minutes and I'll buy you some ice cream." As soon as the words left her lips, her eyes widened as though she couldn't believe her impulsively bad idea.

"I haven't been bribed with ice cream since I was seven, but I guess I'll agree to anything if it means you're taking me out on another date."

She pushed back a strand of hair that had fallen in her face. The move was cute, the slightly disheveled look suddenly doing all sorts of good things for her. Something inside his chest gave a little twist, something he tried to ignore as best he could. It didn't work all that well, not even when she took the opportunity to throw out another insult.

"You asked *me* last night, and going out for coffee doesn't count as a date. Neither does ice cream. And besides, we're only going if you finish on time." She glanced at everything he still held in his hands. "And right now, it's not looking real good for you."

He looked down, then back up at her. If he calculated right, he had nearly thirteen minutes left before time ran out. And he was Jack Vaughn.

Jack Vaughn never backed down from a challenge, especially not one thrown down by the most interesting girl he'd been around in years.

Nine minutes. Nine minutes, and he'd finished filling every last cup. Meanwhile, she had managed to complete less than half his total and still had to return to the reception hall to finish them before the rehearsal started in three hours. Not to mention she still wore the gym shorts and the tank she'd pulled on in a rush first thing this morning, her hair was still knotted at the back of her head, and she wasn't wearing a stitch of makeup. She was a mess walking next to

Jack in his perfectly manicured wedding rehearsal outfit.

"You have ice cream on your chin."

And this lovely observation only confirmed it. April frowned and rubbed the ice cream away.

"Did I get it all?" she asked.

He tilted his head and studied her. "The vanilla, yes. But you still have a chocolate chip stuck to your cheek." Before she knew what was happening, Jack reached out and brushed it away, the warmth of his fingertip staying behind long after contact had been broken. April willed her heart to settle and stared straight ahead, reminding herself to take one step and then another, one step and then another. It was the only way to make sure she wouldn't trip and fall over her own feet, which currently felt like unset Jell-O shaking in a bowl of mixed-up nerves.

"I shouldn't be allowed to go out in public," she said. Beside her, Jack laughed.

"Every time I wear a white shirt — every single time, I'm not kidding — I drop something on it. Coffee. Chocolate cake. Once even a Sharpie when I was trying to write my own name. So I know what you mean. The affliction affects me too. Has since I was a kid."

April couldn't help the grin that stole over

her face. "You know, you'll be wearing a white shirt tomorrow night at the wedding. I'll hate to see what you look like at the end of the night."

Jack opened the car door for her and she climbed inside. For just a moment, he rested one arm on the passenger door and peered down at her. "Something tells me you wouldn't hate it at all. Something tells me you're secretly hoping I'll be covered in filth before I even climb up onstage."

"Busted. Although in my defense, seeing you a complete mess might be a good way to get Kristin to loosen up a little. Maybe I'll do the same with my dress. Smear a little chocolate on it. Add a few rips to the hem. Who knows? We could start a hot new trend." April smiled at her lap. "And then, of course, seeing you that way might ultimately help make me feel better."

Jack stepped back. "Come on, April. You told me to get creative. To think of something to make everything up to you. Surely you think I can do better than that. And speaking of what we're wearing, what color is your dress?"

It was the way he said it. It was the way he said it coupled with the excited gleam in his eye. That's what began April's unraveling, one tiny thread at a time. Jack had something planned. Jack had taken her words to heart and had actually begun to work on them. And as he stepped back and closed the car door, then took his time walking around to the driver's side, the feeling stayed with her.

Jack Vaughn had a plan. Which could only mean one thing. Jack cared about her. At least a little.

"It's yellow. My dress is yellow."

April couldn't keep the smile off her face the whole way home.

# CHAPTER TEN

Jack slipped his arms through his tuxedo jacket and studied himself in the mirror. He hadn't worn one of these straightjackets since prom, foregoing them even at awards ceremonies and other friends' weddings in favor of tailored jackets, expensive tees, and black Converse. He was a musician; he could get away with anything and call it artistic expression.

Today wasn't one of those days, especially with Kristin Quinn as the bride.

Jack buttoned himself in and frowned, a little uncomfortable with how closely he resembled a groom at that moment. But then just as soon as that feeling came . . . it left. Maybe one of these days he would be. Maybe someday soon he would meet a girl, fall in love, and find himself walking down the aisle to meet her. He fully expected that day not to occur for the next decade or so, at least that's how he had things planned.

It's what he felt most comfortable with in his mind.

Which is why the sudden image of April in a wedding dress his imagination conjured up had him feeling particularly uncomfortable.

He shook off the mental picture and reached for a pair of gold cufflinks, taking a moment to attach one and then the other. Satisfied that his look was complete, he headed for the door. He barely got the thing open when he spotted April across the church hallway, looking down at her feet as though trying to find something. She looked stunning. He hated that superficial word, but it was the only way he could think to describe her. Her hair was pulled up, her slender neck a smooth line of tanned skin from hairline to collarbone. He traced it down to her bare upper back, taking in the way her waist narrowed and disappeared underneath the clingy silk fabric. His eyes traveled lower . . . lower . . . until he caught himself and swallowed. She was stunning. Absolutely gorgeous.

He was frozen in his own doorway, unable to move, until he realized she had turned around and was looking right at him.

"If you're finished ogling me, do you think you could come help with this?"

Busted. The word she used last night, suddenly appropriate right now. He felt his stupid face turn red, a sensation he hadn't experienced since high school. So many incidents from those years crashed over him like a hurricane of bad memories. He wouldn't go back there for anything, not even if it meant Katie McKeen — most popular girl who never once gave him the time of day — sat on his lap at lunch, shared her order of ketchup and fries, and kissed him on the mouth while the entire cafeteria watched in awe.

A dumb schoolboy fantasy that stayed with him through sophomore and junior year. And maybe a little bit of senior year, too, but that wasn't important.

"I wasn't ogling you." The lie bled red all over him, and inwardly he cursed. "What do you need help with?"

"I dropped Sam's wedding band and now I can't find it anywhere. Help me and I'll dance with you at the wedding." It was a sarcastic comment, meant to sound amusing. The disappointment Jack felt surprised him.

"I'm singing. I won't be able to dance with you."

He didn't miss her frown. Or the way she covered it with a tug on her hair and a small smile. They were both bothered.

"I was kidding. But I saw the way you filled those birdseed cups yesterday. You were practically racing to finish them on time. I've never seen anyone work so fast, and for nothing but a single scoop of chocolate."

"It was a double scoop, and there's nothing wrong with chocolate."

"Only boring people get plain chocolate."

"Must be the reason you went with the super-exciting chocolate chip."

In response, she smacked him on the arm. Using her very smooth, shapely arm. And funny thing, he liked being hit. By her. As far as he was concerned, she could do it again and again.

"Would you just help me for a second? If I don't find this ring, my sister will freak out, and I'm just really not in the mood for that today."

"Your sister needs to chill." Jack shot a quick glance at his feet. Something flashed right next to the sole of his shoe. "Is this it?" He leaned over and picked it up, then handed it over.

Instead of the relieved smile he expected to see, she rolled her eyes. "Of course you would find it without even trying. I've been out here looking for ten minutes."

"What did you expect? I'm Jack Vaughn. I can do anything I want."

For the first time ever, he regretted that line as soon as it escaped his mouth. If April's expression was any indication, the words were definitely a mistake.

"It would seem that way," she said with a shrug. And without another word, she slipped the band over her thumb and disappeared behind the door to the room that housed the rest of the wedding party. Jack could hear a half dozen excited conversations going on inside the room.

He swallowed. He had so much to make up to her. He only hoped today would put him on the road to getting there.

"What do you mean you lost it?" Kristin's shrill voice carried across the room. "I bought it as a gift and gave it to you only yesterday. How could you lose it?"

"Kristin, those things were so tiny, I'm not surprised she lost hers," April said, rushing to the bridesmaid's defense. "Why in the world you thought it was a good idea to buy everyone a single pearl to commemorate the day completely escapes me."

Kristin let out a long, labored sigh, so loud it was likely heard at the altar. "Because everyone knows pearls signify fertility if you wear them in your shoes during a wedding ceremony, and I want to have lots of children." April just looked at her. If Sam were a smart man, he would already be out the front door and looking for a cab to take him a million miles away from here.

"That doesn't mean everyone else does." April said slowly, already planning to lose hers accidently on purpose.

"Suddenly I'm glad I can't find mine," Brenda, the bridesmaid who had just been given the lecture, muttered under her breath.

"I don't understand why everyone can't just do their jobs and cooperate a little more," Kristin — remaining firmly in meltdown mode — said into her hands. April just smiled at Brenda, the two of them sharing what might possibly be the only lighthearted moment of the entire day, week, or black hole of a month.

"Kristin, what are you yelling about?" Their mother, ever the picture of calm, cool, and collectedness in her blue silk suit and Jimmy Choo heels, walked into the room and closed the door — her thin lips pressed into a disapproving line.

And as Kristin started to cry about the benefits of fertility pearls and Brenda and the other bridesmaids looked anywhere but at Kristin, April swallowed her frustration and quietly left the room. She needed air. Of all the places she wanted to be in this moment, cowering on the receiving end of one of her sister's tantrums wasn't one of them. There was really only one place she wanted to be.

Back in the hallway with Jack.

April pressed a hand to her stomach, thinking surely she had come down with a strange bug or something. Because . . . the hallway with Jack? Anywhere *at all* with Jack? The idea was ridiculous at best, horrific at worst. She'd been furious with Jack Vaughn for three years now. It wasn't like she could just give that up in less than a week's time and suddenly develop some sort of odd kinship with the man. And kinship wasn't even the right word. Affection was closer to it — no. She decided then and there to stick with kinship. It was safer. Accurate. The most correct way to describe how she felt.

She was totally lying to herself.

Still, the wedding was getting ready to start, she had a pearl to dispose of, her feet already hurt, and she hadn't seen Jack in ten minutes or so.

It had been the longest ten minutes of her life.

251

# CHAPTER ELEVEN

This had been the longest hour of Jack's life.

Weddings just weren't his thing.

Not the one-by-one parade down the aisle. Not the endless words about love and faithfulness by the pastor-for-hire — or in this case Kristin's pastor because she actually went to church here. Not the candle lighting or the vows or the mind-numbing words of encouragement spoken throughout by assorted unknown family members. Since when did family members speak? No, none of this was particularly his thing.

He glanced up at the stage, his gaze landing once again on April's slender form. Okay, maybe this wedding offered one thing.

April. April had definitely become his thing.

Truthfully, he shouldn't even be here. He needed to be at the reception hall getting his band ready to perform. Instead he sent

252

them on ahead, unable to bring himself to leave while April was still here. Besides, he was invited. And who was he to turn down a kindly offered invitation by the bride?

A man who was learning to have a thing for weddings, that's who.

Throughout the ceremony, Jack hadn't stopped staring at her. At the way she stood proudly at her sister's side, taking charge of the veil, the bouquet, the ring, the every-thing. At her figure in that formfitting dress. At her eyes — the way they shone with unshed tears. As mad as she'd been only an hour ago when she marched up to him right before the ceremony started, he didn't expect the emotional side of her to come out. Then again, every chick he'd ever met cried at weddings. Obviously she was no exception. But something about her tears tugged at him.

Maybe because it was easy to imagine her crying those same tears after she discovered he had stolen her lyrics. Partial lyrics or not, it was time he finally stopped lying to himself. They were hers. Rightfully hers. And on the back of her creativity, he'd made millions.

All week he'd worked to convince himself that pocketing her napkin years ago wasn't a serious offense, rationalizing that someone needed to have the courage to make good words like hers available to the public. April hadn't had the guts; still didn't have them or she wouldn't be working in the same bar wearing the same apron and singing the same nightclub ballads.

That's what he'd told himself.

Now the only words floating through his mind were *liar . . . selfish . . . cheater.* All of them on repeat. Well, he was tired of the labels. Weary of the mental taunt. There really was only one way to rectify that grievance, only one way to make the accusations stop launching toward him like hand grenades aimed straight for his head.

He just hoped he could actually bring himself to go through with it.

April was annoyed with her sister. Fed up and sick of her demands and weary of being Kristin's personal punching bag for the last week. No one should be treated the way she'd been treated the past several days, and she'd had enough. More than enough, and she was ticked off.

So why in the world was she crying?

Because her sister was getting married, and she would miss everything about their one-on-one relationship. Quiet conversations late at night from the living room sofa in the apartment they'd shared for the past three years. Fights over which one of them used the last of the conditioner and placed it back on the shower shelf for the other to discover it empty. Grocery store trips and split bills at the checkout — always in half and always annoying because Kristin's tastes ran decidedly more expensive than hers. Living with her sister was a pain in the butt. She was bossy and messy and lazy and selfish to the core.

But Kristin was her sister. April would miss her so much it hurt just thinking about it. She swiped at a tear threatening to run down her cheek and smear her perfectly applied makeup. But then another one followed it and she gave up. It didn't matter if anyone saw her cry. She loved her sister; it wasn't anything to be ashamed of. Their love ran deep.

"April, pay attention," Kristin whispered. "Why are you choosing my wedding to daydream?"

Their hatred . . . it also ran deep.

"I wasn't daydreaming," April shot back. "What do you want?"

"It's time for the rings. If you're not too busy, could you hold my bouquet?"

April forgot her tears as her gaze turned hot. "Stop complaining and hand it over.

Geez, you'd think this moment was all about you." She grinned at her unintended words, and just like that her anger dissolved.

As did Kristin's. It didn't take long until both of them were giggling. Onstage. In front of everyone. At a wedding. A wedding that had cost a lot of money and time and effort to impress the socially upward. At the exact same moment, they remembered their mother and the heated glare she was likely sending from her spot on the front row. April tried to catch a glimpse of her, but as luck would have it, her eyes connected with Jack's and stayed there before she had the chance.

And then, of course, April forgot all about her mother. Because Jack was staring right at her, the sweetest look of concern lining his features. She could get used to that look. She could swim in it and hang out inside it for a while and probably never want to leave. And more than anything else at that very moment, it was what she wanted.

April blinked. Why, of all the men she could one day meet, was she thinking these things about Jack Vaughn? And why, when she was standing at her sister's side, holding her bouquet, listening to their heartwarming handwritten vows that she had personally written and rewritten a half dozen

256

times, did she suddenly wish she were a bride in her own wedding?

That was a problem. One so big, April barely recognized herself.

And as she listened to her sister exchange vows and rings and a kiss with the man who had just become part of their family, April didn't see an end to this problem.

Worse, as she chanced a look at Jack out of the corner of her eye, she no longer thought she wanted one.

# CHAPTER TWELVE

The moment April stepped into the reception hall with the rest of the wedding party, she knew. She halted her steps, sucked in a breath, listened to Kristin scream, and she knew. The entire room had Jack's fingerprints all over it, because who else had this kind of money? Her parents were well-off, but they had been given strict instructions by Kristin not to go overboard. Kristin wanted a normal Nashville wedding.

But this. This was anything but normal.

One look at Kristin's face, though . . . Clearly her sister was just fine with it.

The room had been transformed into something so grandiose, April had never seen anything like it. Reminiscent of five-page spreads in *InStyle* magazine, April almost expected celebrities to be sprinkled along the perimeter — holding crystal goblets filled with Dom Pérignon, decked out in tailored Armani tuxes, draped with sparkling twelve-carat diamonds.

In a word, this place was unbelievable.

Gone were the birdseed cups with the little yellow umbrellas they had worked to assemble just yesterday afternoon. Instead crystal champagne flutes were filled with creamy white rose petals and stacked in a pyramid pattern that began on the floor and stretched nearly to the ceiling. Gone were the small, neatly arranged bouquets draped with yellow ribbons and gingerly placed in the center of the tables. In their place, mounds of moss and ivy and every white flower imaginable hung in a mass along the ceiling, attached to light-strewn wooden trellises. Gone were the simple white linen tablecloths that had been rented at a nearby party store and positioned over plain wooden tables. Billowy silk fabric replaced the plain linen — mounded high and draped to the floor. Each table gleamed with over-sized lighted candles and spotless silver place settings.

The only thing April recognized were the paper lanterns, but they had been moved to the four corners of the room, hanging in an asymmetrical pattern and back-lit in a way that made them appear to float on air. The room felt like a dream. April fully expected Cinderella to descend a magic staircase followed by fairies waving sparkling wands. But even as April took it all in, even as she scanned the room with her mouth hanging open because for some reason she couldn't seem to close it, even then everything combined wasn't the most shocking feature.

The photographer with the massive camera and the *People* magazine credentials hanging around his neck was the most shocking . . . and outlandish . . . feature.

*People* magazine?

What in the name of everything holy was *People* magazine doing here? More importantly, who were they here to interview?

Kristin latched onto her arm, squeezing like April's bicep was a stress ball meant for kneading and twisting and reshaping into something more pliable. April fully expected fingerprint indentions to remain long after she let go, which wouldn't be anytime soon.

"Did you know about this?" she asked. If April thought for even the slightest second her sister would be upset about the change in décor, her breathy, high-pitched squeal put that fear to rest.

"I had no idea. Still have no idea what is happening . . ." She let the sentence hang as Jack walked up to her, a shy smile curling one corner of his mouth.

"I hope you like it," he said, looking truly

concerned that both women would be angry. Gloria Quinn chose that exact moment to enter the room. Her shocked gasp could be distinguished even over the hum of two hundred guests. April had never heard such an unflattering sound come out of her mother's mouth; the woman had forever preferred decorum and reservation over the reveal of honest emotion.

"What on earth has happened here?" But like both her daughters, the words were laced with dreamy incredulity rather than offense. "It's like an entirely different world than the one we left last night." If April had been in the frame of mind to giggle, she would have chosen this moment to do so based on her mother's spellbound words. But she felt a little dazed herself. Dazed and completely baffled.

"I have no idea," April answered, seeing that Kristin was still too out of it — spending her time craning her neck to see the flowers, the arbor, the lights that she seemed to be counting one by one — to speak. "But I think Jack may have had something to do with it."

Three heads snapped in Jack's direction, all laced with varying degrees of uncertainty. Yet they each wanted the same thing: an answer.

"You did this?" Everyone heard the underlying tone of accusation in Gloria's question. It was slight, but it was there.

Reluctantly, Jack nodded, a kindergartner approaching his teacher's desk to explain a missing assignment. "I did. I heard you talking about what you would do if you had more time, so I took it upon myself to take care of it. I have connections and a few people who owe me favors, and . . . I hope you don't mind?"

April's breath caught as she stared at her sister. Did they mind? Because she didn't think they minded. She didn't even think they minded if he offered to put the whole family up for the week at an upscale resort in Fiji. In fact, maybe she should make that important fact known just in case —

"Of course we don't mind." Kristin, clad in twenty pounds of silk and lace and tulle and pearls, flung herself into Jack's arms. He looked as surprised as April felt.

It was the first time she could remember anyone in her family displaying anything besides anger toward Jack Vaughn. It was a weird sensation. The death of a pact. The end of an unspoken mission to unite in their hostility where he was concerned. And as she watched her sister locked in a hug-fest with the guy who used to be her bitterest rival, every negative emotion she'd ever held against him dissolved. Finally, after all these years, April was no longer angry.

What she felt for Jack didn't resemble anger at all.

# CHAPTER THIRTEEN

"And then my coordinator quit last-minute and I had to fill the role myself. Doing all this work was exhausting, especially with only four days to make it happen. If anyone deserves a vacation, it's me."

And this was the sort of crap April had been listening to for the last two minutes as her sister answered questions for her upcoming mention in *People* magazine. The article would highlight Jack's return home before his upcoming tour began — the magazine had asked for a feature on him for months, which he had consistently turned down until now — but of course Kristin's wedding had been part of the deal. It was a favor. A way to make peace. An olive branch extended by a guy trying to make good on a past gone wrong. Kristin had grabbed on to that branch and shredded a few leaves in the process. Her excitement was an electrical current charging through everyone in the room.

Except April. *Doing all the work was exhausting?*

"Um, I seem to remember you having a little help," she said, unable to take it anymore.

In response, Kristin waved her off. "This is my sister, April. She stepped in a couple of times when I needed some extra help. But for the most part, I was on my own. And let me tell you, when that happens right before a wedding as high profile as mine, the stress level is sky high . . ."

April turned away before the desire to punch her sister took over. This wasn't the time or place. Next week — right after Kristin returned from her honeymoon — that was the perfect time and place. April made a mental note to mark it on her calendar.

"Interview is going well, I hear." Jack walked toward her, on a short break from singing. The band was providing background music for the moment; his time off wouldn't last much longer. "I could hear her talking from the stage. Sounds like you should have stepped in to help more, slacker."

The gleam in his eye kept her from scheduling a personal beat down for him too.

Punching two people in one day sounded just so exhausting, anyway.

"Yeah, poor Kristin. Having to do all the work in between massages and pedicure appointments must have been a killer. I'm not sure how she managed to handle it all."

When his face broke into a grin, she felt her irritation give way to something else. Something that was growing increasingly hard to ignore. She swallowed and gave it the old college try. Even though she knew it wouldn't work. Because she hated college in the two years she'd attempted to go. Found it a complete waste of time.

Besides, musicians didn't need college anyway.

"That's Kristin, at least the one I remember. A hardworking control freak."

"You got that last part right." She stared at him a long moment. "You sound good up there. Yet I'm still waiting to hear 'Open Arms.' It's the one I'm really looking forward to."

"I'm sure you are. Nothing more fun than seeing a musician make a fool of himself onstage," he said. "Although it won't be the worst thing I've ever done."

April laughed. "I want to hear that story sometime." She caught herself, aware the words sounded like an invitation. An offer

to make herself available for a future . . .
date? She swallowed, trying to measure her
level of excitement. Was she excited? Would
she welcome another chance to see him
again after tonight?

If the way her pulse raced was any indication, she would. She definitely would.

She blinked up at Jack just as a slow grin
began to tilt his mouth. "I'm still here
tomorrow night if you want me to tell it to
you."

She bit her lip on a smile. "Sure. Can't
think of anything I need to do, plus I'm off
work."

He nodded. "Great. I'll buy you some fries
and we'll hang out."

That earned him a scowl. "Coffee, ice
cream, and fries? You spend less money on
dates than my fourteen-year-old boyfriend
in eighth grade."

He frowned. "You were allowed to date in
eighth grade?"

"That's not the point."

He shrugged. "Fine. I'll take you to Husk."
When he couldn't quite hide a smile, she
knew she'd been played. Husk was of the
nicest restaurants in Nashville. At least this
was what she'd heard. Not many lounge
singers with an income like hers could afford to go there, especially considering she

refused to borrow money from her parents.

"Much better. And bring whichever credit card has the highest limit, because I'm ordering the most expensive thing on the menu, plus dessert."

Finally, Jack laughed. "I expected as much."

April glanced over his shoulder. "Don't look now, but Kristin is glaring at you. And motioning for me to get you back onstage."

He sighed. "Great, just great. I'm not sure how I found myself back in the role of the wedding singer, but whatever. 'Open Arms' is coming right up." He turned to walk away.

April laughed. "I guess I should find some lucky guy to slow dance with me. Then it can become our song too . . ."

Jack looked over his shoulder at her. "Hold up on that dance. I have something special planned for this song."

April just looked at him. *Something special?*

She watched as he took the stage and reached for his guitar, then approached the microphone once again. But instead of beginning the opening riff of the famous Journey song, this time Jack began to talk. And as he launched into a monologue of love and commitment and faithfulness, April's legs and arms and head grew numb.

Nothing could have prepared her for his words.

"Jack, what are you doing?" April whispered under her breath. But even though her voice was barely audible, the panic . . . the strain . . . the terror was unmistakable. He was out of his mind. He was insane. He was completely . . . completely . . .

She couldn't believe what he had just done.

"April, what do you say. Will you come up here with me?"

Her hand fluttered to her throat. She felt her head slowly move side to side. "I don't think I can —"

"April, please." Jack's voice was pinched with hope. A hope she didn't have the heart to kill twice in one week. Especially since he'd just announced to the entire place that —

"April, you cowrote 'Confidence'?" the kid standing next to her said. "The song we used for our senior prom theme last year?" At her reluctant nod, he kept going. "That is so cool! Why didn't you ever say anything?"

"I just . . . didn't." She was still in a state of shock and indecision and stuck in a haze of not knowing what to do. *Go onstage?*

*What in the world for?* And then her feet began to move. Before she knew it, she was climbing four steps, then turning to face a crowd of two hundred expectant people, all of whom began to cheer. Her sister smiled from the front, tears streaming down her face.

Before she was able to think, before she took a single breath, before she could even consider doing what Jack asked of her, she had to know. She covered the microphone with her hand and leaned closer, scanning his face with her eyes.

"Why did you do it, Jack? What in the world possessed you to tell everyone now?"

For the smallest second — so small she almost missed it — she saw his confidence drain. Vulnerability took its place.

"Because you deserve it. You're a great songwriter, April, and I've known it for years. It's about time the rest of the world knows it too." His eyes took in her features as he reached out and brushed a strand of hair out of her face. "I'm sorry, and I wish I could undo it, but I can't. Can you forgive me for that stupid, stupid mistake?"

Unable to speak past the lump in her throat, she simply nodded.

Jack's relieved smile filled his face, and he looked down for a moment. "What do you

270

say? Will you help me?"

She frowned, just so confused. "I guess, but what am I helping you with?" she asked.

Three seconds later, she wanted to take back that question. Would she ever, ever learn to keep her mouth shut?

# CHAPTER FOURTEEN

"I thought about killing you. Did you know that?"

"I saw the way you were looking at me. I think you more than thought about it. When you approached the stage, it was all I could do not to duck and run for cover."

"Coward."

"Where you're concerned, I'll gladly claim the label."

April smiled, then spooned another bite of her crème brûlée into her mouth, closing her eyes for a second to really savor it. If someone held a gun to her head and forced her to make a decision, she would say it was the best thing she'd ever tasted. But then she opened her eyes and saw her brownie fudge sundae practically giving her a guilt-ridden stare down and paused that thought. Because it was awfully good too. Maybe even better than the caramel cake with buttercream glaze she'd polished off a few minutes ago.

The rumors were true. This really was the best restaurant in Nashville.

"I have never seen another human consume more food than you."

She eyed him over the rim of her steaming mocha latte — also a winner in tonight's quest to make Jack Vaughn pay one last time. Literally. She shot him a grin.

"Dude, give me an hour and we can start this meal all over again. No one beats me in a food challenge, ever."

He made a bewildered face and shook his head. "Yet you're the size of a toothpick."

She shook her head, though she was secretly flattered. "More like a pair of chopsticks stuck together and shoved inside a white paper package."

He smiled at her weird logic and motioned for the waiter. "Whatever. Can we please get the check?" he asked.

"Too afraid to stick around and see if I can do it again?"

He pulled out his credit card and handed it off. "I don't doubt your abilities. But my bank account is telling me not to push my luck."

Jack stood and walked around to her side of the table. But instead of helping her up like she expected, he leaned close to her ear. "But April, I would buy you five more dinners just like this one if it meant I could spend more time with you."

She swallowed, thankful the restaurant's dim lighting kept him from seeing the pink, red, purple of her suddenly flushed cheeks. Her mind played a card game of make-a-match inside her head, but she couldn't come up with two similar thoughts, let alone any that were the least bit coherent.

"Okay." That was all she had; the only word her stupid brain could think of to say.

As if sensing her awkwardness, Jack simply breathed a quiet laugh and led her into the night air.

"So I forgot to tell you — you're a great singer."

"That may be true, but I'll never forgive you for the way you found out."

"First of all, I heard you years ago. Second of all, forgiveness is a virtue, and I'm pretty sure it's a commandment."

"I'm equally sure you're wrong on both counts. Forgiveness is a choice, one I'm refusing to make at this particular moment." She shrugged. "Maybe tomorrow. Maybe the next day. Maybe . . . one week from not at all."

She felt his foot kick her backside. "Come

on, April. Give a guy a break. There's never been a better rendition of 'Open Arms' performed by a woman before."

"Correction — there's *never* been a rendition of that song performed by a woman before except at high school talent shows in the eighties. And we both know nothing good came out of that decade."

"I was born in that decade."

April shrugged. "Exactly."

He laughed. "I deserved that."

For the next several moments, they walked in silence, bypassing his car and leaving the parking lot entirely, neither of them in a hurry to go home. April crossed her arms to ward off a shiver of sudden nervousness, then looked up at the stars and offered up a little prayer for calmness. It was weird being alone with him . . . intimate in a way she had never felt before, not with any guy she'd dated. Up until now, all her relationships had been casual. Controlled. April keeping them at arm's length even as they tried to pull her as close to their bodies as they possibly could — a constant tug-of-war.

In a word, this experience was new.

With Jack, she felt different. Like she could tell him her deepest secrets and not be afraid he would share them. Like she could put on a comfortable pair of sweatpants and her oldest T-shirt and he would still find her beautiful. Like she wanted to know everything about him and wanted to be known herself. Like —

"What is that?" He swiped something out of her pocket. She tried to snatch it out of his hands but didn't move fast enough. When he held it up to further inspect the item, she lunged.

"Give me that!"

He laughed and raised it out of her reach. "Someone doesn't want me to read this." He looked up at the white cotton square. "And would you look here. It's a bar napkin with words on it." He could barely speak around the stupid way he laughed. "This looks a lot like song lyrics to me." Her mouth dropped open when he started reading them out loud. " 'When I was young I dreamed of writing your name on my heart —' "

"Jack! Give that to me!" She jumped to grab it, but failed.

"Not until I finish reading it." Jack held it over his head and kept going. " 'But then I woke up alone and discovered my heart would barely start . . .' "

Finally, she snatched it from his grasp. "Jack, that's private. Something I wrote last night after the wedding. It isn't even that good." She fisted it, tucking it out-of-sight inside her palm.

His smile softened as his gaze grew more serious. Then he reached for her hand, bringing it slowly between them. She had no choice but to loosen her grip — everything inside her had melted. It only made sense that an iron grip would give way as well.

Slowly, Jack pulled the paper from her hand. "It seems to me," he said, a soft smile curving his lips, "that one night several years ago, I came across a napkin a lot like this one. And written on it were some of the best lines I've ever read."

April blinked up at him, a wave of emotion rolling through her at the long-awaited compliment. All she'd ever really wanted was affirmation, and he was the only man who could give it to her.

"I went about everything all wrong back then, but now . . . Now I'd like to read them. And if they're good, I'd like to record them. And I would like you to come to the studio and help me out on my next album. I'd like to see a lot more of you, April. If you're okay with it?"

She sucked in a breath, felt the first prick of tears begin to sting right behind her eyes. "I'm definitely okay with it. I'm okay with all of it, because I want to keep seeing you too." She cleared her throat when her voice caught, and tried again. "And it would be the best thing that ever happened to me if —"

"Although there's a good chance they could be awful, and then our deal would be off."

April's mouth fell and she gave him a little shove. "I don't write bad lyrics. Ever. In fact, I'm good at everything I do."

It took her a minute — a few seconds past the lazy grin that stole over his lips and the wicked gleam that lit behind his eyes — to realize what she had said. But then when he reached for her waist and pulled her toward him, searching her eyes for permission just before leaning in to kiss her, she no longer cared.

His lips roamed over hers, tasting and teasing and gently coaxing her to let him in. Her mouth parted willingly. Mint and chocolate — she identified both and added a few more flavors the longer they kissed. They kissed through a car horn sounding and a cell phone buzzing and a misstep on April's part that had her tripping backward before Jack used both hands to steady her. Through it all, they never broke apart. And the longer they stayed there and the longer they explored each other and the longer she went without grabbing more than a strained breath, April realized a couple of things. One, she *was* good at everything she did. And two . . .

He was even better.

# ACKNOWLEDGMENTS

Thank you to my publisher — Harper Collins/Zondervan — for inviting me into your group. As an indie author who often finds herself flailing alone, it's nice to have found a place to belong. I appreciate your entire team of sweet, encouraging people.

I would like to thank my readers for coming back again. It's always a humbling and thrilling experience when someone buys my books, especially when you take the time to give a nice review or sweet face-to-face comment. I appreciate every single one of you, and I'm forever grateful.

A huge thank you to my fantastic agent, Jessica Kirkland. Without your guidance I would still be staring at a screen, wondering what the heck to do with all the finished manuscripts stored inside my computer. Thankfully you always know what comes next. You're savvy when I am clueless, sharp when I am dull, excited when I am lifeless, a marketing genius when I am not (which is always since I hate marketing). I'm eternally blessed by you.

Thank you to my awesome editor — Jamie Chavez — for your willingness to read this book and for taking my very rough manuscript and turning it into something (hopefully) worth publishing. I learned so much about writing from you, and I appreciate your wisdom.

To Nicole Deese — my "writer wife" — for every encouraging word you've ever spoken. If words came to life and I tried to stack them in a room, all your kind ones wouldn't fit inside. You cheer me up when I'm down and eagerly volunteer to slap me when I'm filled with self-doubt. Only a real friend would do something so sweet. God made a great person when He made you, and I am privileged to know you.

To Alec Stockton, for sharing my love of creating things from nothing but imagination and a computer. It's nice to know someone who identifies with my weirdness. Or coolness, as I prefer to call it.

To my sisters, Tracy and Emily, for being my best friends and for not giving up on me when I'm under a deadline or going through last-minute freak outs. I love you both. Thank you for loving me.

To my parents — Hal and Jan Millsap — for raising three pretty awesome girls. At least I think we're awesome. Other people might think differently, but whatever.

To my extended family — both the Millsap side and the Matayo side. I couldn't ask for a better group of people to belong to.

To my kids — Jackson, Lilly, Landon, and Rowan — for being the loves of my life. You four sacrifice more than anyone so that I can achieve my dreams, and I'm grateful for each one of you. I'll love you always.

To my husband, Doug, for loving me, sticking with me, and encouraging me through the craziness.

And to Jesus Christ, for saving my life. I'm messy and ridiculous and constantly screwing up, but your grace makes all the difference.

# DISCUSSION QUESTIONS

1. Jack builds a hit song out of a few lines of lyrics that don't belong to him. Have you ever passed off someone else's work as your own? If so, did you get away with it, or did it backfire?
2. April has worked the same job for years, hoping to make it big in a town full of musicians just like herself. Have you ever had a dream so big that you were willing to do anything to make it happen? How long did it take?
3. Jack agrees to perform in Kristin's wedding out of guilt. Is there anything you've ever agreed to do because of a need to "make it up" to another person?
4. April writes lyrics on anything she can find — napkins, toilet paper, other people's arms. Do you have any habits like April that might considered "quirky"?
5. When Jack questions April, he learns that she doesn't want money or "anything

obvious" to make up for stealing her lyrics. Instead she wants him to "think of something creative." Do you think Jack's solution was a good one, or do you think April was crazy not to demand payment and recognition?

6. April's sister is a bit of a diva when it comes to planning a wedding. Is there anything in your life that has temporarily changed you or turned you into an irrational person — be it from stress or another outside factor? Can you give an example?

7. In the end, April forgives Jack and they wind up dating each other. Do you think you could forgive someone that much who stole something so personal from you?

# ABOUT THE AUTHOR

**Amy Matayo** has a degree in journalism from John Brown University. She worked for seven years as senior writer and editor at DaySpring Cards until the birth of her first child. Amy was a freelance writer for David C. Cook before pursuing writing full-time, and she focuses on edgy, contemporary books for women of all ages. She is the author of *The Wedding Game, Love Gone Wild,* and the upcoming *Sway.* She lives with her husband and four children in Arkansas.

Visit her website at www.amymatayo.com.
Facebook: amymatayoauthor
Twitter: @amymatay

■ ■ ■ ■

# NEVER A
# BRIDESMAID

JANICE THOMPSON

■ ■ ■ ■

*To my four daughters, Randi, Courtney Rae, Megan and Courtney Elizabeth. (Yes, I really have two daughters named Courtney!) Four weddings in four years?! How did we survive! What a blissful time, and what a blessing, to see you all happily wed.*

# CHAPTER ONE

The morning my older sister, Crystal, announced her engagement, our whole family celebrated. Well, all but my dad, who mumbled something about checking his bank balance as he headed toward his computer to get online.

Mama did a funny little dance on her way to make Crystal's favorite pancakes, all while singing a rousing chorus from her favorite praise song. My grandmother burst into tears at the news. She gave Crystal a thousand kisses on each cheek — approximately — and launched into a passionate speech about the joys of married life. I chuckled at her enthusiasm as she boot-scooted her way out of the living room to call all her friends.

And me? I gave Crystal the biggest hug ever — and then stood there, waiting for the words every sister anticipates: the invitation to serve as maid of honor. I'd earned the role, after all. Twenty-two years of living under the same roof with my everything-has-to-be-perfect older sister had more than qualified me for the job. And the whole family knew orchestrating events was my special gift. Hadn't I planned all the birthday parties since I was ten?

Now, if I could only get Crystal to stop staring at that over-the-top, princess-cut diamond on her ring finger, we'd get this show on the road.

It took a few minutes for her obsession with the engagement ring to subside, but she finally got control of herself. She grabbed my hands and squealed, then released a happy sigh. "Oh, Mari, isn't it wonderful? I'm going to be Mrs. Phillip Havenhurst. Finally!" She brushed one of her platinum blond locks aside and giggled. "His parents have a membership at the River Oaks Country Club. According to *Texas Bridal,* it's Houston's top venue for weddings. I mean, who gets that? Certainly not girls like us. It's such an honor. I feel like a princess."

I felt a little more like Cinderella at the ball. Hanging out with Houston's upper echelon would be nerve-racking at best. I'd never really been much for the country club set, even though most of the people in our upper-middle-class community strived for such luxuries. Me? I'd rather get married on the beach, any day. Or at our church. Certainly not at a hoity-toity place like River Oaks Country Club, and definitely not surrounded by people who preferred caviar to nacho cheese dip.

I was more than a little concerned by her news about the venue. "Does Dad know you're getting married at the country club? No wonder he's checking his bank balance. He's probably in a panic."

"Maybe it won't be as bad as we think." Concern flashed in my sister's blue eyes. "Phillip's father has connections. I'm sure he'll help work out something. I hope."

"Maybe, but it's still going to shake Dad up. I mean, the food costs alone will be crazy. Are you sure you don't want to get married at the church? Did you see how they did up the reception hall for Nikki Raymond's wedding? It looked amazing, almost like a high-end wedding facility. It can be done. If we have time, I mean. Have you set a date?"

"Yes. Mid-May. That gives us just four months. But don't worry, Mari. We're definitely getting married at the church. The reception just won't be there. Phillip's parents probably wouldn't like that. Remember, I told you what kind of lifestyle they're used to?" For whatever reason, the sparkle in Crystal's eyes faded as she spoke those words. Just as quickly, it reignited. "Anyway, it'll be great."

"Of course it will." I did my best to sound reassuring and tried not to focus on the wide financial gap between our two families.

"Besides, I'm only getting married once. I want it to be amazing."

"It's going to be amazing, Crystal. And you, of all people, deserve the perfect wedding. You're the most giving person I know. I can't wait."

"Me either." She took a couple of steps in my direction and gave me a warm hug.

"So, um, have you given any thought to bridesmaids?"

"Of course! I've been dreaming about my wedding for years." She released me from the hug and then listed several friends, cousins, and other relatives as possibilities, covering eight or nine people in the process. With each name, my heart felt a little heavier.

*Hello? Did we forget someone?*

"But I've limited it to five. One sister —"

*Yes!*

"— one cousin, and three best friends. One from high school, one from college, and one from church." She turned and faced me. "I think that number is just right. Don't you?"

"Yes, but one of them" — I paused and gave my sister a pointed look — "will technically be a maid of honor." I cleared my throat and prayed she'd take the hint. "Right? So it's really four bridesmaids and a maid of honor." I squared my shoulders and waited for Crystal to confirm what I already knew in my heart.

"Right." She nodded. "The maid of honor handles a lot — the bridal shower, a bachelorette party, and quite a few things on the actual wedding day. So choosing the right person is key."

"Of course. And I —"

"I know Sienna will do a great job."

"Oh, thank you, I —"

*Wait. Did she say Sienna?*

Crystal reached into her purse and came up with a piece of paper with a bunch of notes scribbled on it. "I know Sienna might seem like an odd choice, but I've known her since we met at camp as little girls, and she's been my best friend ever since. Besides, I owe her. She's the one who introduced me to Phillip, remember?"

"Well yes, but —"

"I know, I know." Crystal gripped the note

in her hand. "I can guess what you're thinking."

"You can?"

"Yes. She wouldn't have been your first pick."

"I . . . well . . . no."

"She wasn't really mine, either." Crystal sighed and then took a seat on the sofa. "If you want the truth, Phillip's mother suggested it. Sienna's mom is one of her best friends."

"You don't have to bow to Mrs. Havenhurst's wishes, Crystal. She's not even the mother of the bride, and it's your wedding."

"I know." My sister didn't look convinced. She glanced at the note and then looked my way. "But I don't like to stir the waters. I never know what to do when Phillip's mother starts giving me her . . . opinions. Sometimes it's easier not to debate her, you know? She doesn't have a daughter, so she's been kind of planning her son's wedding for ages, I guess."

"Well, yes, but again, it's your wedding, not hers." I took a seat next to her. "You should be able to have anyone you like stand next to you."

"It's okay, Mari. Really. Sienna is a little, well, self-centered and spoiled, but she's a good friend, and she'll do fine. I hope." A

298

little sigh followed. "But I know what you're thinking. You would've picked Gillian, right?"

"Gillian?" *Um, no.*

"It's true that I'm closer to her these days. We work together at the hospital, after all. I see her every day. I toyed with the idea of asking her. And I even thought about Cassie. She's my favorite cousin, and we got really close on that last mission trip. And Brianna, of course, was my college roomie, and we certainly bonded over all those all-nighters, studying for exams. I just have so many wonderful people to choose from."

*What am I, chopped liver?*

Crystal leaned back against the sofa and reached for a throw pillow, which she hugged to her chest. "But Phillip's mom convinced me Sienna's the right choice, and I agree. I mean, she was there for me through the breakup with Phillip, and I've shared my deepest, darkest secrets with her."

*Well, hello. You've shared them with me too. Remember? Who talked you down from the ledge just three months ago when Phillip put the brakes on your relationship?*

Crystal's eyes pooled with tears. "Oh, Mari!" She tossed the pillow aside, grabbed my hands again, and gave them a squeeze. "I'm so excited."

"Me too." And I meant it. In my heart of hearts, I meant it. Even if it took brushing aside any crumbs of bitterness from my heart. My one and only sister was getting married. I needed to be there for her.

"I do need to ask one special favor of you, Mari." She gave me a pleading look. I recognized the pouty lip, of course. I'd seen it a zillion times before.

"What's that?"

"Well, you haven't met Phillip's cousin, Tyler."

"Ooh, he has a cousin?" Potential love interest, perhaps?

"Yes." Crystal's nose wrinkled, and I could read the concern in her eyes. "See, here's the deal. Tyler is only fourteen."

"Fourteen?" I swallowed hard.

"He's going to be a groomsman, of course. I mean, they're cousins, after all, both of them only children. I know, technically, the two aren't close in age. And Tyler is, well, socially awkward."

"Socially awkward?"

"He's always telling goofy jokes at the wrong time, interrupting people when they're talking, dressing oddly just to get attention. Stuff like that. You know the type, right? I think some boys just go through this when they're sloshing their way through puberty."

"I'm confused. What does this have to do with me?"

"Oh, I'm sorry." Crystal giggled. "I got distracted. You know how the bridesmaids and groomsmen are paired up. Well, Tyler will need a partner for the ceremony."

"You're pairing me up with the socially awkward fourteen-year-old?" At this news, I leaned back against the sofa cushions and pinched my eyes shut. What was she thinking? After a few slow breaths, I opened my eyes and looked at my sister. The happiness in her eyes almost made me think I could handle all this.

Almost.

"I knew you would understand, Mari! Oh, and don't worry . . . he's just your height. Of course, that would make him a lot shorter than the other boys his age, but, if you don't count the acne, he looks a lot older." Crystal's nose wrinkled once again. "As picky as Mrs. Havenhurst is, I'm surprised she hasn't insisted her sister-in-law take him to a dermatologist. I mean, it's not really my business, but in a roundabout way, it kind of is. You know?"

No, I didn't know. And I didn't care to, thank you very much. She'd lost me at the words *fourteen-year-old.*

"I knew I could count on you, Mari. You're the sweetest person I've ever known. Of course, with you and Tyler both being five foot two, you guys will be at the end of the line, but I knew you wouldn't mind that part. You know, his coloring is even a lot like yours — sandy blond hair, blue eyes."

"Wait. End of the line?"

"Well, sure, Mari. I mean, you're" — she paused and her nose wrinkled for the third time — "petite."

"You mean short."

"Well, five foot two is a great height . . . for you. But the other girls happen to be taller. So I'm putting everyone in order according to height. That's another reason Mrs. Havenhurst suggested Sienna — she's five nine, the tallest in the bunch. Cassie's five seven, so she'll be the first bridesmaid. We'll work our way down from there."

"Gee, thanks."

"I didn't mean it that way." She gave me a puzzled look. "Are your feelings hurt, Mari? Please tell me they're not."

I couldn't really answer without lying, so I hesitated before finally coming back with, "Just having kind of an off day."

"Well, get back on again, okay?" Crystal clasped her hands together at her chest and released a girlish sigh. "I'm counting on you to stay focused. We have a wedding to plan!"

So my sister did want my help. Maybe I should just stand back and let Sienna perform her job as maid of honor, and wait for Crystal to tell me what she needed me to do. I certainly didn't want to overstep like a certain future mother-in-law already had.

And from the look of sheer joy in Crystal's eyes, I'd better snap out of my bad mood and focus on the bride to be. This was all about her, after all. With a forced smiled, I made up my mind to do just that.

# CHAPTER TWO

Less than a week after their announcement, Crystal and Phillip invited all the bridesmaids and groomsmen to our house for a Saturday afternoon BBQ. As much as I hated to admit it, my jealousy toward Sienna tainted the event for me.

I'd known the buxom blond since childhood. Of course, she wasn't buxom as a kid. Then again, she wasn't shapely as a teen, either. The drastic change in Sienna's physique had only come about recently after a so-called week of vacation in the Caribbean. A week at the plastic surgeon's office was more like it. Still, I tried not to focus on her Double D's, though tonight's ensemble — a bright-pink and lime-green fitted dress with low-cut bodice — made that difficult.

"Suck it up, Buttercup." Dad's voice sounded to my right.

I startled to attention and turned to find

304

my father standing next to me, his blue eyes twinkling with mischief.

"I'm sorry. What?"

"I said, 'Suck it up, Buttercup.' " He nudged me with his elbow, then leaned down and whispered, "I know what you're thinking."

"You do?"

"Yep. You can't stand that girl. You've hated her ever since she stole your sister's boyfriend in sixth grade. I never cared much for that Joey O'Shea, anyway."

"Me either, but *hate* is a strong word. I just can't stand that she always draws so much attention to herself."

"Let's get real." My father chuckled. "We both know why the guys can't look away."

"I know, I know." *And those Double D's aren't even real.*

Still, it bugged me. Even Tyler — the socially awkward fourteen-year-old — had been rendered speechless by the effervescent and curvaceous Sienna. Then again, the gawky stare might be Tyler's norm.

"That's not the only reason you're upset, is it?" Dad gave me a sympathetic look. "I see what your sister's done to you. You and that gangly kid with pimples have been coupled up for this shindig, right?"

"We're *not* a couple. Ew."

"Right, right." He slung his arm over my shoulder and pulled me into a bear hug. "Well, you get my point. And you have two choices: either you can spend the next four months moaning and groaning about it, or you can suck it up and do the right thing."

"That's the point. I *always* do the right thing, and look where it's gotten me — standing at the end of the line."

"At least you're in the line. Did I ever tell you the story about my older sister eloping and leaving the whole family out of her big day? Broke my mother's heart. Mine too." Dad's carefree expression shifted as his lips curled downward in a frown. "Anyway, I'm just happy Crystal is a family girl. She's involved all of us in her wedding plans, and I'm grateful. It's gonna be a wonderful day" — he pursed his lips — "even if the reception is at the River Oaks Country Club at sixty-five dollars a head."

I started to respond, but something — rather, someone — caught my eye. Walking through the front door was the most gorgeous specimen of a man I'd ever clamped my eyes on. Something about the solidly built, dark-haired fellow looked familiar, but I didn't know why. The other bridesmaids gathered around him, all giggles and smiles, greeting him like an old friend.

Weird. I had met Phillip's other two friends before, but was I the only one who had never met this one? Sienna practically lunged herself into his arms with a boisterous giggle.

"I don't believe it." Dad almost tripped over his own feet as he took a couple of steps away from me. "T-that's Derrick Richardson."

"Derrick Richardson?" The name sounded familiar. And the confident stride and broad, white-toothed smile looked familiar too. Wow, this guy would be a shoo-in for toothpaste commercials.

Commercials.

TV.

That's where I'd seen him before. I felt sure of it. He starred in a television commercial for Accentuate Bank, my employer.

"He's an actor?" I whispered to my dad.

He snorted. "An actor? Only if you call his work on the ball field acting. He's the best right fielder the Astros have ever had, kid. You need to get out more. Go see a game or two. Why your mother raised you to love theater instead of sports, I will never understand."

"Ah, he's a ballplayer, then. Whatever." I shrugged, feeling a little less impressed than before. I'd never been much for sports, especially baseball. Who had the patience to sit through all those innings just to watch grown men jog around those little placemat things?

"But he does a TV commercial for Accentuate Bank too?" I asked.

"Now that you mention it, I think he does."

"I knew it."

Tyler appeared to spring to life in Derrick's presence. The gawky teen wedged his way through the crowd of girls and, with a goofy grin on his face, came to a stop directly in front of the guy, then stammered, "D-dude. You're D-Derrick R-Richardson."

"I am." The handsome ballplayer extended his hand in Tyler's direction. "And you are . . . ?"

"T-Tyler Havenhurst. I think." Tyler grabbed Derrick's hand and shook it with great zeal. "My cousin talks about you all the time. He thinks you're great."

"Well, I'm honored to be your cousin's best man, Tyler. Phillip's been a good friend to me since high school, though we haven't seen each other very much the last few years."

"I've been dying to meet you. I think you're great too."

Tyler continued to shake Derrick's hand.

"You *totally* saved that last game. We were down for the count, and you came through for us. We owe you, man."

Derrick gently drew his hand away and shrugged. "Happened to be a good night, I guess. I've had a few rough ones too. Trust me."

Cassie sidled up next to me and giggled. "Ooh, if Derrick Richardson has any flaws, I don't see them."

I couldn't really argue that point. Still, I didn't understand why everyone seemed to be fawning over this guy. Except for the gorgeous physique, he appeared to be perfectly normal.

My father headed off to greet our new guest, then disappeared outside to tend to the meat on the grill. The yummy scent of barbecue permeated the house as the back door opened. Yum. I could hardly wait. Let the others make a big deal about the baseball player. I'd stay off in the shadows. That's what the fifth-in-line bridesmaid usually did, right?

Phillip introduced Derrick to the rest of the group, and before long everyone was gathered around the food table, nibbling on appetizers. Derrick and I both reached for the nacho dip at the same time and our hands bumped.

"Oh. Sorry." I pulled my hand away.

"No problem." As he withdrew his own hand, his beautiful brown eyes locked with mine. "I would never fight with a girl over nacho dip. You go first." He gave a funny little bow and flashed a boyish smile. Yep. Great white teeth. Definitely a shoo-in for a toothpaste commercial. Or maybe those teeth-whitening strips.

My heart did a funny little fluttering thing, and I released a slow breath. No way would I make a goober of myself over this guy like the other girls had done. Better stick to business.

"Thank you." I grabbed the spoon and put a hefty scoop of dip on my plate. "And by the way, this is a very special nacho dip. I make it with spicy sausage. I'd be willing to bet you've never had anything like it."

"Well then, forget what I said about not fighting with a girl." He snagged the spoon from my hand. "Out of my way, Southpaw."

"Southpaw?" I stared across the table, up into his eyes, feeling a little confused.

"Yeah. You're a leftie, right?" He pointed to my hand, the one he'd pulled the spoon from.

I chuckled and pulled my hand away. "Yeah, I'm a leftie. But don't hold it against me."

"Hey, some of the best players I know are southpaws." His face turned red. "Not that I'm calling you a player." Now he shook his head and grimaced. "I'm always putting my foot in my mouth." Derrick took a large scoop of my nacho dip and then stuck a chip into it. After shoving the chip into his mouth, a deliriously happy look came over his face. "Mmm."

Okay, I had to admit, he looked mighty cute — er, handsome — standing there with a dribble of nacho cheese dip on his lower lip. I fought the temptation to reach up and wipe it off with a fingertip. Instead I pointed, and he reached for the napkin I offered with my right hand.

"Here's something better you can put into your mouth." My father plopped a large platter of barbecue onto the table in front of Derrick, who practically drooled as he stared at the burgers, chicken, steak, and sausage.

"Oh. Wow." He wadded up the napkin I'd given him and reached for a fork. After loading his plate with enough meat to make a healthy carnivore swoon, he nodded and smiled at me before heading to the far side of the room to join the other guys.

Seconds later, the other bridesmaids joined me at the table, with Tyler tagging along behind them.

"Wow, Derrick talked to you." Cassie giggled. "Lucky duck."

I shrugged, still not understanding the swooning going on with the other girls. "Yeah. He seems really friendly. Normal."

"Trust me, there's nothing normal about Derrick Richardson." Sienna giggled. "Nothing at all."

"True. He's way out of my league." Brianna sighed and scooped some dip onto her plate.

"Not sure what we did to land him in this wedding party, but I could pinch myself. I get to walk down the aisle with him at the end of the ceremony!" Sienna pulled out her cell phone and snapped a photo of Derrick. From a distance, of course. Without his knowledge.

Crystal walked up, her eyes narrowing to slits as she glared at her best friend. "Don't you dare post that, Sienna. We need to give Derrick some privacy. He's just a normal guy, you know."

"So *that's* what normal looks like." Tyler looked up from his plate of tortilla chips and sighed. "Bummer." He stuck a chip into his mouth and walked away from the group, muttering something about how he'd never really wanted to be normal anyway.

Crystal gave us all a warning look. "I want you to treat Derrick the way you'd treat any of the other guys. Okay?"

As I nodded along with the others, my heart did that strange fluttering thing again. Try as I might, I couldn't really think about anything except the twinkle in Derrick Richardson's eyes as he'd stolen the spoon away from me. Treating him like any of the guys . . . well, that might be a little harder than I wanted to admit.

# CHAPTER THREE

I spent the next three weeks waiting for Crystal to come to her senses and ask me to help with the wedding. I could tell she was stressed, and it broke my heart. Finally, I could wait no longer. I would offer my services and pray she accepted.

"I hope you don't mind, Crystal, but I've done some research on the web. Wedding planning basics, that sort of thing."

"You have?" A look of sheer relief passed over her face. *Oh, good.*

"Sure. I know this wedding means a lot to you, and I want it to be perfect. So I put my research into a spreadsheet. Everything from the bridal shower to wedding guest list protocol — that kind of stuff. And Cassie and the other girls want to help too. Even Grandma Nellie, but you might not like some of her ideas. One of them involved a piñata."

That got a smile out of Crystal. For a

minute, anyway. "I've been so overwhelmed. I mean, Mrs. Frazier at the church is technically supposed to be my wedding coordinator, but she's so busy right now. Her daughter just had a baby."

"Right. I heard. A girl."

"Yes, but even when she's not distracted, we didn't quite agree at our first meeting. Her ideas are a little . . . outdated. I haven't decided how to handle that. And I've been so worried about things not getting done. We've only got three months left, you know? There's just so much to do. Almost nothing's been taken care of yet."

"Yes, it has." I laid my spreadsheet on the kitchen table in front of her. "I've put together a plan by date. Everything is listed in order, so you don't have to get overwhelmed. It's kind of a step-by-step process."

Crystal looked over my spreadsheet, and then looked at me. "Mari, what would I do without you? I mean, I've done what I could, and so has Phillip. We purchased some invitations we found online, but . . . ever since their engagement party for us, Mrs. Havenhurst has been asking questions —"

"What other things are left undone?" I glanced at my spreadsheet, spurred on by that revelation. "Be specific, so I can make sure they're covered on the spreadsheet."

"Well, things Sienna's supposed to be doing, for instance."

"Ah." I cringed as I heard the infamous maid of honor's name.

My sister sighed. "I mean, usually the maid of honor helps plan the bridal shower, but I talked to Sienna this morning and she seems a little, I don't know . . ."

"Out of it?"

"Yeah. Maybe I've asked too much of her. She's not terribly focused."

I reached for an apple from the fruit bowl in the center of the table and rolled it around in my palm. "Crystal, I hate to say this, but Sienna's never been focused."

She nodded. "Right. I guess I just thought she would take this wedding more seriously. I mean, a bride pictures her maid of honor being really excited. But Sienna's a little . . ."

"Disengaged?"

"Yeah." My sister's eyes took on a faraway look. Just as quickly, she snapped to attention. "Anyway, she'll pull it together. I know she will. It's only the middle of February, after all. We have until the middle of May. And to her credit, Sienna is going with me to look at flowers. Her aunt Catherine is a florist."

"That's nice."

"Yes, and I'm grateful. Her aunt is even giving me a discount. So I shouldn't be complaining. It just helps so much to know you're taking such an interest, and you're organized to boot." Crystal glanced back down at my spreadsheet. "You have no idea how much better I feel, just looking at this. It makes everything seem . . . doable."

"I love this kind of thing. And remember, I'm only working thirty hours a week at the bank right now and my schedule is pretty flexible." I took a bite of the apple and leaned back in my chair. For the first time since the conversation began, I noticed a hopeful look in Crystal's eyes.

"We are getting one thing done today. Are you busy this afternoon at four? Phillip and I have a cake tasting appointment set up at the bakery. We want to get more opinions than just ours. I mean, it's the guests and wedding party who actually eat the cake. The bride and groom are so busy at the reception, they barely get a nibble. Sienna and Derrick were supposed to come with us, but she's tied up at work and can't come."

"He's still coming?"

"Yes."

"Does Sienna know Derrick is going to be there?"

Crystal shook her head. "I don't remember if I told her that."

"Well, that's one way to get her to show up. Just saying."

"I guess. But she's not responding to my texts, so maybe I shouldn't bother, especially if you're willing. I'd love to have you there, Mari. If you're free, I mean."

"I'm free, and I'd love to go. I'm crazy about cake." And while I didn't share the same hero worship as the other girls, I didn't mind the fact that Derrick planned to be there. Not one bit.

At four o'clock that afternoon, after working several hours at the bank, I sat at a table across from a very nice woman at Crème de la Crème, Houston's most celebrated cake shop. Crystal, Phillip, and I chatted with the sales rep — if that's what one called a cake salesperson — until Derrick arrived. He rushed through the door, pulled off his sunglasses, and squinted, as if waiting for his eyes to adjust to the change in lighting.

Standing there, with the shimmer of sunlight beaming through the glass door behind him, Derrick looked a bit like one of those old church paintings of the apostles.

He had a heavenly glow about him. Fascinating.

Not that my gaze remained on his face. Those broad shoulders swept me in at once. Apparently I wasn't the only one to take notice of his tall, athletic physique. The minute the good-looking ballplayer took a couple of hesitant steps our direction, the sales rep could barely string two words together. Not that I blamed her. Something about the guy suddenly made me scatterbrained too. And hungry for nacho dip.

Just a few minutes into the taste testing, however, my jitters evaporated. It happened just about the time Derrick shoveled a big bite of white cake with raspberry filling and cream cheese frosting into his mouth.

"Ooh. Mmm." He closed his eyes and licked his lips before his eyes popped open again. "I'm gonna go with this one." The blissful expression on his face convinced me. We'd go with the white cake with raspberry filling, no doubt about it. Not that this was my wedding, of course.

"I like the chocolate cake, though." My sister looked at Phillip, and he nodded in agreement.

"We have a new dark chocolate hazelnut you might like to try, then. It will take just a few minutes for me to bring you a sample."

The sales rep left for the room in the back.

"How are we ever going to decide on just one?" Crystal shook her head. "This is too hard."

"You're right about that." Phillip looked just as confounded. "Who knew it would be this hard? I thought we'd just walk in, take a couple of bites, and order a cake."

Derrick took another bite, and this time a look of contentment came over him. "You don't have to settle on only one. Each tier can be a different flavor."

I nodded. "Sure. People do it all the time. How many tiers is your cake going to be, Crystal?"

"I don't know." My sister looked panicked. "Haven't even thought about it. Should I know that?"

"How many guests are you expecting?" Derrick asked. "The number of tiers depends on the number of guests." He went on to share details about how many people each tier could feed, depending on the overall size of the cake.

"How do you know all that?" Crystal looked as amazed as I was.

"I know my cakes." Derrick waggled his eyebrows. "My mom bakes wedding cakes."

"What? Your mom is a baker?" Crystal slapped herself on the forehead. "Then what are we doing here?"

Phillip cleared his throat. "My parents suggested Crème de la Crème because all their friends use it. I think it's more of a social thing. Their friends expect it."

"Right." Crystal nodded and sighed.

Derrick shrugged. "No biggie. I think a wedding cake for three hundred might be more than my mom could handle, anyway. She's up to her eyeballs in other events around that same time, I think. But if you need anything for a bridal shower, for instance, I'm sure she'd love to be involved. She's pretty amazing."

Hearing the man talk about his mom made me smile. So . . . he was easy on the eyes and a family guy as well.

My sister smiled too. Well, until her phone rang. She glanced down and sighed. "It's Sienna."

"Ah." I should've come up with a more enthusiastic response, but nothing came to mind. My gaze shifted to Derrick as I tried to gauge his reaction. He was too busy staring at the cake samples to notice.

As Crystal turned her attention to the phone call, Phillip engaged Derrick in a conversation about an upcoming ball game. I tried to pay attention, but I found myself distracted by a loose strand of hair on Derrick's forehead. I wanted to take my index finger and nudge it into place. Instead, I cleared my throat and focused on the plate of cake samples, which proved to be equally as tempting.

My sister continued her conversation with Sienna in hushed tones, but I couldn't help but overhear. "It's okay, Sienna. Really. I understand." A pause was followed by, "Oh, we're still sampling cakes." Another pause. "Who? Oh, me, Phillip, Mari, and Derrick."

I could hear the squeal come through the phone. Crystal pulled it away from her ear and made a face, then put it back. "You're hurting my ear, Sienna." A long pause on Crystal's end followed. "Okay, okay, I'll give him the phone." Crystal held out her cell to Derrick and sighed. "She wants to talk to you. Is that okay?"

He shrugged. "Guess so."

A lengthy conversation followed between best man and maid of honor. I couldn't tell from the expression on Derrick's face if he was just tolerating Sienna or if he actually enjoyed talking to her. Either way, he handled the back and forth bantering with grace and ease. My sister seemed more than a little put off by the distraction from the cake tasting, and I didn't blame her, though it certainly wasn't Derrick's fault.

When the sales rep returned with a large piece of the dark chocolate hazelnut cake, Derrick ended the call. He handed the phone back to Crystal, jabbed his fork into the new cake sample, and took a bite. Another look of near delirium appeared on his face. "Mmm. Okay, I've changed my mind. Forget the white with raspberry filling. I'm going with this one."

I laughed and then reached for my fork, ready for a taste. I took one bite. Then another. Then another. Derrick jabbed his fork into the cake sample once again, our forks battling it out for the last tidbit of yummy goodness.

"Out of the way, Southpaw." He gave me a wink as he nudged my hand away. "I let you win the first round with the nacho dip, but this one's all mine."

"First round?" Phillip seemed perplexed.

"Nacho dip?" My sister gave me a curious look.

I didn't take the time to explain. I was too busy looking at Derrick and trying not to giggle as I remembered that night we'd met over the nacho dip. "Oh yeah?" I gave him a playful "You'd better watch out" look, then pushed his hand away. "Over my dead body." I took another bite, then licked my fork clean. "Mmm."

Okay, so maybe I flirted . . . a little. Who would blame me?

Across the table, Crystal cleared her throat. "Mari?"

I glanced her way and realized she was glaring at me. "What?" I wiped my lips with a napkin.

She pointed at the empty plate. "Excuse me, but Phillip and I didn't even get one bite of the chocolate hazelnut. You two ate the whole thing."

"Oops." I laughed.

"Guess you'll just have to trust us that it's the best." Derrick flashed a boyish smile. "And if you can't trust your best man and maid of honor, then who can you trust?"

"I . . . I'm not the maid of honor, remember?" A little shrug followed as I fought the temptation to allow jealousy to surface. The look of compassion in Derrick's eyes brought comfort and wiped away any feelings of angst that might threaten to rise up. Was this guy great, or what?

It took him a moment, but he eventually nodded. "Oh, right. Well, you might as well be, Mari."

*Thank you!* I knew I liked him.

Crystal mumbled something under her breath about Sienna, but I didn't hear all of it. I was too busy staring at the smudge of chocolate frosting on Derrick's upper lip. I gave him a little nod and gestured to it. He reached for a napkin and wiped his mouth, then leaned back in his chair with a satisfied look on his face.

I felt pretty satisfied, too, but it had nothing in the world to do with cake. It had everything to do with the handsome guy smiling at me from across the table.

# CHAPTER FOUR

On the first Saturday in March, all the bridesmaids met Crystal at the All Things Wedding boutique. Finding her wedding gown was my sister's main goal, but selecting our bridesmaid dresses — in a lovely shade of pink — was also high on the agenda. I'd never cared much for pink, but I vowed to keep my opinions to myself, at least in my sister's presence.

We arrived promptly at ten. Well, all but Sienna, who was noticeably absent. She came meandering in several minutes later with a massive shopping bag in her hand.

"Sorry!" She giggled. "I just can't come to the mall without going to the shoe store. They have the best sale going on right now. Aren't these adorable?" She pulled out a shoe box and opened it to reveal some strappy sandals with high heels. Very, very high heels.

"Shoedipity." Cassie whispered the word

in my ear. When I turned to give her a curious look, she added, "Wearing ridiculously uncomfortable shoes just because they look good."

I bit my tongue to keep from laughing.

"They're cute shoes, Sienna," Crystal said. "But we really need to stay focused. Today's all about the wedding dress and bridesmaid dresses, remember? We can talk about shoes another time."

"Right, right." Sienna gave the shoes another glance and then closed the lid on the box and pressed it back into the shopping bag. "What did I miss?"

*You missed being on time,* I wanted to say. But didn't.

"We're just about to start the hunt for my dress," Crystal said. "Mama and Grandma are going to be here in a few minutes. This is a special day for all of us, and I really want to —"

"Oh, look!" Sienna squealed. "It's Derrick and the other guys!"

Through the opening between the bridal salon and the tuxedo shop, I could see all the groomsmen standing with Phillip.

Sienna let out a whoop and took off running in their direction.

"So much for telling her what's on the schedule." Crystal sighed. She walked over to Phillip and gave him a kiss on the cheek, then whispered something in his ear.

Phillip's gaze shifted to Sienna, who stood entirely too close to Derrick. Not that Sienna appeared to care. Her gaze never left the good-looking baseball player. On and on she rambled, her animated voice traveling the distance over tuxedos and bridal gowns.

Derrick's eye caught mine. He waved and called out, "Morning, Southpaw." I couldn't much tell what he said next because Sienna reached to touch his face — *Really? Who does that to someone she barely knows?* — and turned him, literally, back to her. I remained in the bridal shop, deliberately keeping my distance. Well that, and responding to the snide comments from the other bridesmaids, who all took aim at Sienna. I couldn't stop thinking about her hand on Derrick's face. A wave of jealousy washed over me, but I did my best to push it aside.

Minutes later Crystal dragged the reluctant maid of honor back into the dress shop, but the giddy young woman couldn't stop chattering. "Ooh, Derrick is going to look great in a tuxedo. Almost as good as he does in his uniform. Speaking of his uniform, he's got a game in just a few hours. I asked if he could get us tickets, but he didn't answer. Do you think I should text him and ask again? Of course, I'd have to ask Phillip for Derrick's number. Do you think he'd give it to me? Ooh, I hope so. Maybe Derrick will get me seats near the dugout. That would be amazing." Off she went, talking about her impending trip to the ballpark.

Crystal clapped her hands together, just a few feet in front of Sienna. "Sienna." When the chattering didn't stop, she did it again. "Sienna!"

Sienna startled to attention. "W-what? What, Crystal?"

"We're not here to talk about Derrick. We're not here to talk about baseball. We're not here to talk about shoes."

"My shoes!" Sienna looked around, her eyes widening. "What did I do with my new shoes?"

I pointed to the floor, where she had dropped the shopping bag before running to the tuxedo shop. She picked it up and hugged it to her chest. "Oh, thank goodness. I'd hate to lose these. They cost me a fortune, even on sale."

"Sienna." My sister crossed her arms at her own chest. "Do you even remember why we're here?"

"Well, duh. To try on dresses that are going to make us look fat." Sienna rolled her eyes.

Crystal's jaw clenched. "We're also here so you can help me choose my wedding dress. Remember?"

"Your dress? Isn't that why your mama and grandma are coming? I thought we were here to pick out bridesmaid dresses. And by the way, I can't stay long. I have to be at the tanning salon in an hour."

Crystal groaned. "Mom and Grandma are coming, yes. But I need other opinions too. You are my . . . Maid. Of. Honor. Sienna."

I loved the way my sister stressed those last few words.

"Right, right. But just so you know, it's not my shift. I'm working on my tan so I'll look good in my bridesmaid dress. So, really, it's all for you."

Crystal groaned again, this time with an added, "Ugh."

Sienna didn't seem to notice Crystal's distress. She appeared to be more than a little distracted by the guys. She turned to give Derrick a little wave, but he didn't respond. Instead, he and the other guys disappeared behind a group of mannequins. Thank goodness. Now maybe Sienna would pay attention.

My mother and grandmother arrived a

couple of minutes later. Crystal headed off with them to start looking at wedding gowns and left Sienna in charge of bridesmaid dresses. Great. Just what we needed — Sienna making the selections.

We looked at a variety of dresses in pink, but the irritated maid of honor turned up her nose at every one. "I don't want to look like a big ball of cotton candy." She groaned as she held up a floor-length gown in a soft shade of pink. "Ick."

"But that's the color Crystal wants." Why did I even have to argue this point?

"And the bride always gets her way." Cassie gave Sienna a stern look.

"Always." Gillian emphasized the word with a nod.

Sienna's eyes sparkled with mischief. "Unless some clever bridesmaids convince her otherwise. You know what I mean?"

"Um, what *do* you mean?" Brianna's gaze narrowed. "You're up to something, Sienna."

"Are you saying we need to somehow change her mind?" I shook my head. "That's not going to happen. She's wanted a pink wedding for as long as I can remember. We're not going to ruin this for her."

"Did I mention I look terrible in pink? It totally washes me out." Sienna rolled her eyes. "And anyone who's anyone knows this season's hot color is teal. You girls can talk her into that." Sienna launched into a lengthy dissertation about how great teal looked against her tanned skin, but she lost me a few words into it. I would not be sucked into this game, no matter how much manipulation she used.

"Nope. We're not going there." I glared at Sienna.

She stopped cold and stared at me. "Huh?"

"We're not going there. My sister's going to have what she wants. End of discussion." I pointed to the rack of pink dresses and pulled out a really cute mid-calf gown in a shade of pink that had suddenly grown on me. "I think Crystal will love this one. What do you girls think?"

With the exception of the cranky maid of honor, everyone agreed.

Soon we had plowed our way into the changing rooms and emerged, a quintet of — I admit — silly-looking, bubble-gum-pink bridesmaids. Well, not exactly a quintet. Sienna slugged her way out of the changing room with a scowl on her face.

Crystal loved the dresses and pronounced them, "Amazing! Perfect! Just what I always dreamed of!" Likely she didn't see the somber look on her maid of honor's face. Not that it would've mattered, anyway. My sister was far too busy narrowing her list of potential wedding gowns.

I slipped out of my bridesmaid dress and back into my jeans and T-shirt. Then I joined the other girls to watch as Crystal tried on dress after dress. Mama sat nearby, tissue in hand so she could dab her eyes, which she did repeatedly.

My grandmother, ever practical, shook her head a lot.

Until she saw *the* gown. From the minute my sister appeared in the gorgeous princess gown with full tulle skirt and Austrian crystal bodice, my mother and grandmother could scarcely speak a word. They were too busy wiping their eyes and sniffling. I found myself sniffling a little bit too.

So, I was surprised to see, was Sienna. In a moment of endearment, I slipped my arm around her shoulders and whispered, "It's perfect, isn't it?"

She shook her head and whispered back, "Perfect? Are you kidding me? It's the farthest thing from perfect. I look *awful* in pink." She rolled her eyes and then pulled out a tube of lipstick and smeared it across her pouty lips.

I pulled my arm away at once and did my

best not to groan aloud. If this girl didn't take her eyes off herself — and Derrick — this irritated southpaw might just have to throw her some fastballs and strike her out.

# CHAPTER FIVE

The first couple of weeks of March sailed by. I settled into a fun routine, working at the bank during the day and helping Crystal in the evenings. We pored through magazines, looking for ideas for everything from centerpieces to bridesmaids' gifts, and we had a blast putting wedding plans in motion. I even helped her address wedding invitations. Talk about exhausting. But I didn't care. Anything for my sister.

I felt closer to Crystal than I had in years, and I tried not to feel sad that she would soon be a married woman. Would we still get to share these precious sisterly moments we'd grown to love? I grabbed them while I could and hung on for dear life.

On the third Friday in March, I hosted a fun get-together for the bridesmaids to complete plans for the bridal shower, which would take place in April, a little less than a month before the wedding. We were also going to put together centerpieces for the event.

With Grandma Nellie's help, Mama made a great dinner for everyone — grilled chicken Caesar salad and fettuccini. The girls arrived at six thirty. Well, all but Sienna. She told Cassie and me she'd be late, but no one commented on her absence, and neither did we. Weird. Maybe we were all just getting used to it by now.

As we settled in around the table, Crystal popped in just long enough to say hello. I sent her away in a hurry with a bit of a scolding. After all, the plans for the shower were top secret. She gave us a little wave, then headed out the door to meet Phillip for dinner, with a promise that she would return in time for some cheesecake.

The bridesmaids were in good spirits. Even Dad seemed to be in a great frame of mind. On the other hand, he did head into the living room to get away from all the estrogen at our dining table after Mama and Grandma left for their ladies meeting at the church. I didn't blame him.

As we ate, I filled the girls in on the idea Cassie and I had come up with for the centerpieces.

"Each table will have three clear vases in different heights. We'll drop in marbles —

pink, of course — and then add a silk magnolia blossom. On the day of the bridal shower, we'll fill each vase with water and place a floating candle on top. Simple, right?"

"Simple but beautiful." My cousin jabbed her fork into her salad. "Best idea ever."

"Cheaper than those centerpieces I'm having to rent for the wedding reception." My father's voice rang out from the living room. "Those suckers are twenty-five dollars apiece, and we don't even get to keep them."

"Well, don't tell anyone, Dad, but we got all the supplies for these centerpieces at the dollar store. I've done my calculations, and it's going to cost less than six dollars per table."

Was that a happy grunt we heard?

As I shared some other ideas, the girls chimed in, and before long ideas flowed like water. I hadn't had this much fun since . . . wow, I couldn't remember when.

By seven fifteen we'd finished our meal and prepped the table to work on the centerpieces. I gave each girl a specific task, then put them to work.

Cassie seemed a little preoccupied. "Okay, I just have to say I can't get over the fact that Sienna's not here yet." She looked around the room, as if expecting the maid of honor to magically appear. "I mean, we knew she couldn't be here for dinner, but she promised she'd come by seven. She's really supposed to be in charge of the shower, you know?"

I knew, all right.

"She'd better get here quick." Brianna dumped a handful of marbles into one of the vases. "I've got to write a paper for my psych class."

"Write it about Sienna." Cassie rolled her eyes. "You won't have to go far to find your information."

That got a laugh out of everyone. Well, all but me. "We should probably stop taking aim at Sienna."

Cassie sighed. "She's just such an easy target."

"Maybe too easy. But she has her good points too. She's helping with the flowers. Did you know that? She even got Crystal a great discount through her aunt Catherine."

Cassie reached for some marbles and rolled them around in her palm. "Did you have to go and say that? I was enjoying being mad at her."

"I know. We all were." I glanced at the clock. Seven thirty. Hmm.

"The groomsmen are coming by at eight

for dessert," Cassie told the other girls. "All except Tyler because of some school event. Anyway, we thought it would be fun to hang out with them."

The moment she said the word *grooms-men* I thought of Derrick. I couldn't help but smile. Of course, he wasn't a grooms-man. He was the best man. And what a great man he was turning out to be. My face heated up as I thought about his nickname for me: Southpaw. I glanced down at the silk flower in my left hand and giggled.

"What's so funny, Mari?" Brianna looked my way.

I snapped back to attention. "Oh, nothing. I think we'd better get busy. We've got to settle on our final plans for the bridal shower before everyone else gets here. That's the point of our little meeting tonight — besides making these centerpieces."

My cousin kept looking at the clock on the dining room wall. I knew she was still fretting over Sienna's absence. By the time seven forty-five rolled around, we could deny reality no longer.

"Maybe I'd better check my messages." I dug around inside my purse and came up with my phone. A quick glance down, and I groaned. I'd missed a text from her, all right.

"Let me guess." Gillian rolled her eyes.

"She's not coming."

I shook my head. "She has a headache."

"She *is* a headache." Cassie laughed, but I still didn't join in. Not just because I was trying to set a good example, but because I realized just how painful her disinterest had become for Crystal.

I typed a response and then tossed the phone back into my purse. "Oh well. Her loss. She had no idea Derrick was coming tonight."

"She doesn't know?" Gillian asked.

"She does now. I just told her." I wanted to add that Sienna would no doubt have a miraculous recovery, but I had just advised we stop shooting arrows at her, hadn't I?

An awkward silence filled the room. I cleared my throat. "Let's go ahead and talk through our final plans for the shower. You all seemed to like the idea Cassie and I came up with for the tea party theme the best."

Gillian clasped her hands together. "Yes, we loved it!" All the girls nodded.

"In addition to the centerpieces we just made, each table would have its own teapot and teacups and finger sandwiches cut out like teacups. We could also have a variety of teas and even some ornate cookies shaped like teapots. How does that sound? I even saw the cutest mini cupcakes online with chocolate-covered pretzels on the side that looked like handles. Get it? They look like teacups."

Gillian gave me a hopeful look. "Sounds great, but who's going to make all that stuff?"

"We are." I swept a hand toward them all. "I've been researching like crazy. Even bought the cookie cutters, just in case you did like the idea."

"Have you ever made specialty cookies, Mari?" Brianna gave me an admiring look. "I hope so, because I'm not a baker."

"Me either." Gillian shook her head.

"You know I'm terrible in the kitchen," Cassie added. "So that leaves you to do the baking, Mari." She gave me a confident look. "I'm sure you'll figure it out."

"I'm willing to learn." I spoke the words with determination. How hard could it be to make a cookie that looked like a teacup, anyway? Surely I could go on the Internet and figure out how to paint the cookies to look delicate and pretty.

"Making them yourself is cheaper than hiring someone." My dad's voice sounded from the living room again. "Make the cookies, Mari."

Cassie laughed. "Okay, so you're in charge

341

of cookies. And the cupcakes."

"I'm great with sandwiches." Brianna dropped the last handful of pink marbles into a vase. "Put me in charge of food, okay?"

"And I love to decorate." Gillian set a silk magnolia on top of the marbles. "We're having the shower at the church, right?"

"Right." I nodded.

"I can take care of the invitations," Cassie said. "I love doing stuff like that. Have you put together a guest list, Mari?"

"Weeks ago. It's on a spreadsheet on my computer."

"Just like everything else for this wedding." Cassie laughed. "You girls should see how organized she is. She's been such a big help to Crystal."

"Your sister is blessed to have you." Gillian gave me a smile.

I paused to think that through. The past few weeks with Crystal had been so much fun, and I'd learned a lot. By the time my own wedding came around I'd know just what to do. Of course, I'd never have a reception at the country club, but at least I'd know how to take care of the details. And maybe — just maybe — I'd have a maid of honor who cared as much about me as I cared about my sister.

"Have we lost you?" Cassie nudged me with her elbow, and I startled to attention.

"Oh, just thinking."

"About Derrick?"

My face grew hot. "Why would you say that?"

"Just to see the expression on your face." She grinned. "Now, what were we talking about?"

"Cookies." I jumped right back into the shower plans. "And I saw the cutest teacup invitations online." I stood to gather our leftover supplies. "I'm going to order them later tonight now that we're all in agreement on the tea party theme."

Five minutes later I'd jotted down all the assignments. Gillian was particularly helpful when it came to shower games, which she'd done before.

The guys arrived just as we were boxing our creations. Derrick headed right for me, as if he had nothing better to do than be with me. Okay, maybe my imagination was running away with me, but how could I help myself with his gaze fixed on mine? I found myself drawn in by his confident stride, his engaging smile, and those gorgeous eyes.

"Hey, Southpaw." Derrick flashed a smile. "Am I late to the party?"

"Only if you planned to help make these

centerpieces."

"Um, no thank you. I think my skills are better served on the ball field, not with glass vases and marbles."

"I don't really know much about baseball."

"Seriously?" His eyes widened. "Well, we'll have to remedy that, and soon. We're early in the season. Want to come to a game or two and see if it grows on you?"

"Sure." I gave him a little shrug, feeling a little awkward for admitting I knew nothing about the sport he loved.

"Just hang around me, and I'm sure the love of the game will rub off on you." A boyish wink followed.

Oh boy. The love of something was rubbing off on me, but it had nothing to do with baseball. A warm, funny conversation with this guy felt completely comfortable.

Before we could continue the conversation, my sister and Phillip arrived. I could tell from the pained expression on her face that something had gone wrong. No doubt it had something to do with his mother. The woman really seemed to be pulling Crystal's strings these days. She sighed as she walked past me, but she didn't say a word.

I excused myself from the conversation with Derrick and caught up with her in the kitchen, standing at the counter and eating a jumbo-sized slice of cheesecake.

"You okay in here?" I gestured to the dessert, and Crystal sighed again.

"Yeah. A little stressed."

"Phillip's mom?" I whispered the words.

Crystal nodded. "Yeah. She called in the middle of our dinner to tell me that she talked to my florist. She's taken the liberty of changing the flowers in my wedding bouquet."

"W-what?" I couldn't believe I'd heard that right.

"Yep." My sister took another giant bite and spoke with a full mouth. "The woman actually said roses are cliché. Cliché. Can you believe it?"

"No." I shook my head. "I can't believe it. I sure hope you stood your ground."

"I didn't know what to say without crying, so I just handed the phone to Phillip." Crystal sighed yet again. "I only wish I was as thin as my patience right now."

I couldn't help but laugh at that one.

She plopped the fork onto her plate. "Of course, if I keep eating like this, I won't be. They'll have to let the seams out in my dress."

"It's not that bad, Crystal."

"Wedding. Planning. Is. Stressful." Just

that quick she picked up the fork again and took another bite, pinching her eyes shut.

*Tell. Me. About. It.*

Her eyes opened and she stared at her plate. "I shouldn't feel so intimidated, I guess. I should stand up for myself. And I should have a maid of honor I can count on, one who shows up for stuff and actually acts interested. Sienna's not here, is she?"

"It's going to be okay, Crystal. I know it is. Everything will come out fine in the end."

"I hope you're right. I only plan to get married once."

"I know."

She grew quiet for a moment, then looked into my eyes. "I made a mistake letting Mrs. Havenhurst talk me into choosing Sienna, didn't I?"

I paused to think through my response. "Sienna is Sienna. Nothing much ever changes with her. I'm sure you felt pressured, and no doubt Phillip's mom sang her praises."

"Yes, she did. And I wanted to believe every word. I really thought things would be different, that maybe she'd be able to focus on me. On the wedding." Crystal took another bite, then spoke around the cheesecake. "Guess I was wrong."

"Maybe she'll come around." I tried to

sound hopeful.

"Ooh, there's cheesecake in there?" Derrick's voice sounded from behind me.

"You girls are missing the party." I turned just in time to see Phillip enter the kitchen with Derrick on his heels. "What are you girls doing in here?"

Crystal slid her plate in front of me and handed me her fork. "Thanks for the nibble of your cheesecake, Mari, but I'm not really that hungry."

"W-what?"

She slipped her arm through Phillip's and changed the subject, talking about the weather.

Derrick watched as my sister and her fiancé left the room, then glanced down at the half-eaten cheesecake. "Um, that's not yours, is it." He spoke the words more as fact than question.

"Not even." I shook my head.

A smile lit his face. "Well, I hate to see good cheesecake go to waste. I say we split the rest of that piece."

I nodded, excited by that possibility. "Great idea. I'll get a couple of clean forks."

Derrick and I sat down at the kitchen table, and somehow he managed to turn my angst into laughter. The guy had a real knack for that. He shared the plans the guys had just made for Phillip's bachelor party. Then he shifted gears and started telling me about his recent trip to Haiti with an international mission team. I could see the passion in his eyes as he talked about a young man there he supported monthly, about how much he wanted to help him.

"I don't really talk about it much, but my parents' divorce really got to me. I was sixteen when it happened."

"I'm so sorry, Derrick." Seeing the pain in his expression, I longed to reach out and put my hand over his.

"I buried the pain in . . . bad behaviors." He shrugged.

"Bad behaviors?"

"Poor choices." He clenched his jaw. "I . . . well, I got involved in drugs, Mari. And drinking." He paused and stared into my eyes, as if waiting for me to respond in shock or disbelief.

"You're obviously not the same person now. Something must've happened to change all that."

"Yes, something definitely happened. It's been a long journey back from a tough place. And I never would've made it if Phillip hadn't been praying for me."

"Wow."

"Yeah, he was there through it all, good

and bad. Your sister's getting a great guy."
He paused and gave me a thoughtful look.
"I've done all the talking. Sorry about that.
What about you, Mari? What were you like
as a kid?"

My dad happened through at that very
moment and laughed. "I could tell you
some stories." And so, much to my embarrassment, he did. Talk about humiliating.
On the other hand, Derrick laughed in all
the right places, and even made me laugh a
time or two with his responses to Dad's
crazy tales.

After my dad left the room, I told Derrick
a couple of stories about my teen years,
including a funny one involving a family
vacation at a dude ranch when I was fourteen.

"Sounds like fun." Derrick leaned in close,
as if hanging on my every word. It felt good
to talk about something other than the wedding.

"Crystal and I had the time of our lives
on that trip." I paused as the memories
flooded over me. "You just haven't lived till
you've traveled with our family. Things get
crazy, trust me."

"Your dad seems like a real character."

"Oh, he is. He's perfect. Really. Best dad
a girl could ask for. I feel so blessed." As I

spoke the words I thought about what Derrick had said earlier, about his parents' breakup. Maybe we'd better change the subject.

Turned out, I didn't have to. Our private conversation was interrupted when Sienna arrived. She must've sniffed out Derrick's cologne, because she bounded into the kitchen, all giggles and smiles. It looked like she'd been miraculously healed from her headache. She grabbed Derrick by the arm. "C'mon, best man. We're needed in the living room. The bride and groom want to give us our marching orders." She seemed to narrow her gaze as she glanced my way. What was up with that? Surely Sienna didn't think I was treading on her turf . . . right?

Not that Derrick seemed pleased by Sienna's insistence that he leave me. In fact, he gave me a "Woe is me" look as Sienna pulled him out of the room. I just offered him an "Oh well" shrug. Still, from the smile he gave me as he rounded the corner, I had a feeling I'd be seeing more of this guy, and maybe not just at the wedding.

# CHAPTER SIX

Two days before the bridal shower and four failed attempts at making the intricately designed teacup-shaped cookies, I finally threw in the towel. Grandma Nellie offered to help, but quickly gave up when she got the consistency of the royal icing wrong.

"Not gonna happen, Mari." She waggled her finger at me. "We'll have to order some from a bakery."

No way, Jose. When I'd revealed our shower theme to my sister, I had promised home-baked, teacup-shaped cookies. I had to deliver them, even if it killed me. Which it might.

In a moment of clarity, I recalled that Derrick's mother was a baker. It took some doing to locate the best man's cell phone number. After all, I didn't want my sister to know I had failed in the baking department, so I couldn't ask her. Instead, I went straight to Phillip, who was happy to share Derrick's contact information with me.

I called Derrick late Thursday evening, my nerves a jumbled mess. He seemed a little surprised to hear from me, but from the pleasant tone in his voice, I could tell it was a happy surprise. When I explained my predicament, he offered to call his mother on my behalf. "She usually needs a couple of weeks' notice to fit in a new job. But she might make an exception if she's not already booked. I don't know if she has the ingredients, so she might need to make a run to the store."

"I'll bring the ingredients. She won't have to do a thing." I sighed. "Well, except the obvious. Teach me how to bake. And decorate."

Derrick laughed. "Okay. I see how it is. I'll have her call you, I promise."

Ten minutes later I received a phone call from Mrs. Richardson, who agreed to help me.

"How many people are you expecting at the shower, Mari?" she asked.

I swallowed hard. "Fifty to sixty."

"Ah. A lot of work, then."

"Yes, ma'am. If it's too much —"

"Nah, I do this all the time. You just come on over to my place tomorrow afternoon. And don't you dare bring any ingredients. I have plenty, trust me. We'll knock out those cookies. And if Derrick shows up, I'll boot that boy of mine right out the door. He wouldn't be caught baking, but he's notorious for eating the baked goods."

I couldn't help but laugh at the idea of Derrick eating our teacup cookies.

I thanked Mrs. Richardson — who insisted I call her Nadine — before ending the call.

The following day passed quickly at the bank. Around two thirty I looked up when I heard a familiar voice traveling across the lobby. Derrick?

All the female tellers clustered around him like ants around a piece of candy. I fought the temptation to hide under my desk. Why I felt so embarrassed, I could not say.

Derrick glanced my way, then confusion etched on that handsome face. After politely weaseling himself away from my coworkers, he walked toward me, smiling. "Mari?"

"Mari Hays, personal banker, at your service." I flashed a professional, over-the-top smile. "How can we help? Do you need a loan?"

He laughed. "No. I stopped by because I'm going to be filming a new commercial for your bank soon."

"Hey, it's not my bank. I just work here."

"You know what I mean." He gave me a

playful look. "It's the least I can do. Your manager, Bill Henderson, was my first Cub Scout leader. A boy never forgets his Cub Scout leader." Derrick saluted me. Well, I guess it was a salute. Must be a Cub Scout thing. Regardless, it caused my already skittering heart to go bouncing down to my stomach and then back up again.

"Ah, so it all makes sense now. That's why you do commercials for Accentuate Bank."

"Yes." He raised his hand, as if taking some sort of pledge. "I, Derrick Richardson, promise to do my best to do my duty to God and my country, to help other people — especially my scout leaders — and to obey the law of the pack."

"You have a pack?"

He laughed and put his hand on my shoulder. "You have a lot to learn, Mari Hays."

I sure did, and he made a fine teacher.

Derrick excused himself to talk to Mr. Henderson. I went back to work, waiting on a final customer before preparing to leave for the day. Still, I could barely keep my mind on my work.

My shift ended when the lobby closed at three. Derrick was still deeply engaged in conversation with our bank manager. Well, that, and fending off flirtatious interruptions from a couple of my female coworkers. About the same time I had gathered my belongings, he shook off the giddy females and met me at my desk. "So are you headed to my mom's place right now for the baking extravaganza?"

"I am. If I can figure out how to get there."

"I happen to know the way." He gave me a little wink. "Want to hitch a ride with me?"

My heart flip-flopped. From the cubicle next to mine I heard my coworker, Shawna, give a little cough. I could guess her thoughts: *Say yes, girl!*

And so I did. Five minutes later I was seated in the passenger side of his Dodge ram truck, headed to his mom's house in the Memorial area. Under normal circumstances I would've been a nervous wreck, but his carefree conversation kept me at ease, as always. In fact, I found myself so comfortable around Derrick that I started to wonder why I'd ever been nervous in the first place.

When we got to her house, he introduced me to his mother. Nadine didn't look a thing like her son. Where he was tall and solidly built, she was petite and almost as round as the cookies we were about to bake. She was also covered, nearly head to toe, in powdered sugar. I even saw bits of frosting in her hair. Not that she seemed to notice or care.

She wrapped her arms around me in a warm — albeit messy — hug. "Please forgive me," she said as she led the way to the kitchen. "I'd like to say I don't usually look like this, but I'd be lying." A funny little laugh followed.

"It's true." Derrick nodded and laughed too. "There's a white haze in the air all the time here, and it has nothing to do with the ozone layer."

Sounded yummy.

Nadine gestured to several trays of adorable, baseball-themed cupcakes. "I'm just wrapping up an order for a Little League team. Let me put them away, and we'll get this party going." She glanced at Derrick, her gaze narrowing. "You scoot on out of here. You're trouble in the kitchen."

"What?" He feigned offense. "What are you talking about? You know I'm the best baker in this family."

"Humph."

"I plan to stick around and help." He offered me a boyish grin. "Wouldn't miss this for the world."

"Fine. Then suit up."

"Mom, really?" He groaned.

"If you're gonna stick around, yes." She

pointed at a baker's rack with aprons hanging from the corner knobs. "You too, Mari."

I'd imagined what Derrick would look like in a tuxedo. I'd even taken the time to find photos of him in his uniform online. But I'd never — repeat, never — pictured the guy wearing an apron covered in powdered sugar and bits of cookie dough.

Turned out, he looked pretty great in that too. And I must've looked okay after I slipped a hot pink-and-white "Let Them Eat Cake!" apron over my head, because he leaned my way and whispered, "You look like a pro, Southpaw." All I could do was smile. Well, smile and listen as Nadine gave me instructions for the cookie dough.

Turned out, her recipe was a little different from mine — only one egg instead of two and baking powder instead of soda. Interesting. A bit more flour, too, so the cookies would hold their shape.

I mixed up three batches of the dough and then, at her instruction, put them into large zip-lock bags and placed them in the freezer to chill for a few minutes. While we waited, she prepped the royal icing. Or, rather, she had Derrick prep the royal icing. Turned out, the guy was pretty handy. Who knew? He kept a watchful eye on his whirring mixer, and I helped roll out the cookies and cut them to look like teacups.

A short time later, I rolled out more dough and filled a couple more trays while the first two baked in the oven. I couldn't believe how much better Nadine's recipe seemed to be working. If the woman had seen my attempts at home, she would've cringed. Or maybe not. Maybe she would've taken my mess, plopped it back into the mixing bowl, and reworked it with her magic fingers.

While we worked, Derrick and I kept a playful banter back and forth between us. Nadine joined in, her voice ringing with laughter as she told story after story about Derrick's childhood. I'd never had so much fun baking before. Of course, that might have a little something to do with the yummy-looking guy scraping the royal icing from the edges of the mixing bowl.

Nadine separated the white mounds of sweet, fluffy icing into several smaller bowls and began to add coloring gel. I watched as she worked to get the consistencies just right — thicker for the piping icing and thinner for the flooding icing. She passed off the bottles of icing to me just as the first two trays of cookies came out of the oven. They looked and smelled amazing. And they were shaped like perfect little teacups. The ones I'd made at home had looked more like little round blobs.

Derrick tried to snag one of the hot cookies from the tray, but his mother slapped his hand with an oven mitt. "Not on your life," she said. "These are for the bridal shower."

"But I'm the best man."

"If you want to live to be the best man, you'd better keep your fingers to yourself."

He grunted and waited until she'd turned toward me, then nabbed a cookie. I didn't let on that I had seen him do it, but from the pained expression on his face, I knew it must've been too hot to eat. Still, he didn't make a sound. Obviously, the boy didn't want to tip off his mama.

"Speaking of bridesmaids, I hear you're the maid of honor in this wedding." Nadine gave me an admiring nod. "Never got to play that role myself."

"Oh, no, ma'am." I put another tray of cookies into the oven. "I'm just a bridesmaid."

"No you're not." Derrick brushed the cookie crumbs from his hands and stared at me so intently I almost felt as if he could see my thoughts. "You're not *just* a bridesmaid. You're the one holding things together."

"I . . . I am?"

"Sure. And I know why. The person who cares the most does the most. You clearly care the most, and Crystal is lucky to have you, not just as a sister, but as her go-to person. She really needs that right now."

Well, now. If that didn't make a girl feel better about things, nothing would. I stood in complete silence for a moment, unable to think clearly, what with his flattery going straight to my head and all.

"Speaking of holding it all together, let's see if these cookies hold their shape once we get them onto the cooling racks, shall we?" Nadine dove right back into the baking project, never realizing that my heart was *thump-thump-thumping* after hearing her son's sweet words.

Out of the corner of my eye I saw Derrick take another cookie and pop it into his mouth.

"I have eyes in the back of my head, son." Nadine turned to face him, hands on hips. "And laser-sharp hearing. Now, quit eating the merchandise or this poor girl won't have a thing to take to that party tomorrow."

We didn't really have to worry about that. By the time the sun went down, we'd baked and decorated five dozen gorgeous teacup cookies. Nadine even took the time to help me with the cupcakes I'd left to the last minute. After feeding me dinner.

Derrick stayed put, all smiles and fuzzy conversation, as if working in the kitchen making teacup cookies with a discombobulated bridesmaid was something he did every day.

Maybe he did, in between innings. Or maybe, just maybe, this handsome best man was up to something else altogether. Yep. The cute little signature wink he gave me over the cupcake tray was a dead giveaway. Looked like Derrick Richardson was stirring up something a little sweeter than cookies and cupcakes. Maybe he was tossing me a pass. Hopefully my catching skills were a little better than my baking skills.

# CHAPTER SEVEN

I could barely sleep that night. My thoughts ping-ponged between the upcoming shower and the amazing time I'd had with Derrick and his mom during our bake-a-thon. Still, I needed my beauty sleep. I finally dozed off around one in the morning, but the oddest dream kept my imagination going.

In the dream, Crystal and Phillip got married on home plate on a baseball field. Derrick stood on the pitcher's mound, tossing teacup-shaped cookies at them. Nadine served as umpire, critiquing my swing when I came up to bat. And Sienna — ditzy, curvaceous Sienna — coached the whole thing from the sidelines while having her nails done. No wonder the game was so wonky.

I awoke around seven, my head pounding. Still, I had to get busy. All the bridesmaids would be at the church early enough to set up for the noontime tea party. I could hardly wait to get started. With my sister's happiness at the forefront of my mind, I pressed any daydreams about Derrick aside and got out of bed.

By ten, the bridesmaids, Sienna included, were gathered in the fellowship hall of our church, Grace Chapel. I couldn't quite believe the maid of honor had actually shown up — and on time, no less — until I learned Derrick planned to swing by the church at eleven to drop off tickets for an upcoming game. Ugh. No wonder Sienna had made the extra effort.

My sweetheart of a baking partner came into the fellowship hall, walked right past the maid of honor, and headed straight for me.

"Hey, you." A broad smile lit his face. "Long time no see."

"I know, right?" I didn't even try to hide a smile as I stared into his twinkling eyes. "You never call, you never write, you never bake me cookies . . ."

He laughed. "Well, I'm here now. Speaking of which, this room looks great."

"Thanks. It took a village, but we got it done."

He gestured toward the tables, all decked out with teapots and teacups. "I get it now. It all makes sense. The cookies, the cupcakes, all of it. This is themed from *A* to *Z*."

"From *T* to *T*." I laughed. "Do you really like it?"

He smiled. "Well, I've never actually been to a tea party before, but if I had to go to one, I guess this would be it." A playful laugh followed.

Apparently Sienna noticed our interaction. If looks could kill, she would've taken me down with her hateful glare. I did my best to ignore her. Still, as Derrick launched into a jovial conversation about all the fun we'd had baking together, she and the other girls hung on his every word. I could see Cassie glance my way as if to ask, "Really? You baked with this guy?" I would explain later. Right now, we needed to get back to work before the guests started arriving.

Derrick hung around long enough to hand out the tickets, not just to Sienna but to all of us. Then he headed out, giving me his best Cub Scout salute, which I returned. Actually, I think I returned it with a Girl Scout salute, but I couldn't be sure. I'd only lasted in the scouts one year.

As soon as he left, the girls swarmed me, asking question after question. I did my best to answer them as we finished decorating and setting out the sandwiches. Sienna kept her distance, but the penetrating glare continued.

My sister arrived at eleven forty-five. She ooh'd and ah'd when she saw what we'd done, and she greeted the guests with great enthusiasm as they came into the room, but the strained smile I saw as she hugged her friends told me something wasn't right. I did my best to push any concerns aside and focus on the task at hand. I had a party to host, after all. Clearly, Sienna didn't plan to take charge. She'd disappeared into the kitchen to make a call. Go figure. So, as the guests arrived, ready for an afternoon of tea-party delight, I dove in, playing the role of hostess. And I didn't mind a bit. My sister was definitely worth it.

The shower — *Thank you, Lord!* — came off without a hitch. Even the ladies of Grace Chapel declared it the most glorious tea party they had ever attended. And boy, did Crystal ever rake in the goods. I'd never seen so many shower gifts. Still, as we loaded her car later, I could tell she wasn't herself.

I pressed the last gift box into the backseat and shut the door, then turned to face her. "Did you enjoy the shower?" I felt a little sad that I had to ask, but the somber expression on her face made me wonder.

"It was beautiful, Mari. You did an amazing job." She climbed into the driver's seat and put the key in the ignition, but never looked my way. Very strange.

I had no choice but to press the issue. "Crystal? What's going on?"

She shook her head, then started the engine and pulled on her seat belt.

I know my sister pretty well. Something was very, very wrong here. "Crystal?"

"You were amazing, Mari. I mean that. You always are. But the gifts?" She gestured to her backseat. "It's pointless to load them in my car. Pointless to take them home. They all have to be returned."

"I'm sorry . . . what?"

"They have to be returned."

"Are you saying you already have all these things? These are duplicates? If so, I had no idea. I —"

"No. I'm saying that I've changed my mind."

My stomach felt like my heart had dropped straight into it. "Changed your mind about what? The things you registered for?"

"No. The wedding. I've changed my mind about the wedding." A lone tear trickled down her cheek.

"W-what?" Surely I'd misunderstood.

"Are you saying you're not getting married?"

She looked over at me, her eyes brimming.
"I don't know. Maybe. I'm just saying that
I've had what Mama calls a 'Come to Jesus'
meeting."

"With who? Phillip?"

"No." She sniffled. "With myself."

"You had a 'Come to Jesus' meeting with
yourself?"

"Yes. About what I want, I mean."

"In a husband?"

"No, not that." Crystal brought her hand
down on the steering wheel with a thud. "I
know what I want in a husband. I adore
Phillip. It's just . . . the wedding."

"What about it?"

"It's not what I want. I mean, I don't want
a big fancy wedding reception at a country
club. I don't want a thousand-dollar, five-
tiered Crème de la Crème cake. I don't
want Dad to spend his life's savings paying
fifty-five dollars a head for guests to eat
some chicken dish they won't even remember the next day."

"Um, sixty-five."

"Sixty-five." She paused. "I want something normal. Something I'll want to tell
my kids and grandkids about."

"Are you saying you're changing the plan

for the reception? Changing the venue?" Surely not. "The wedding is in less than a month."

She sighed and turned off the engine. "I know. It doesn't make any sense, does it? But Mari, I just don't think I can justify a show-offish wedding. I've never been that sort of girl. I'm the 'Let's go to a third-world country and take care of orphans' kind of girl, you know?"

"True."

"When I went to Haiti last summer, I saw all those kids living in poverty, and it broke my heart. I promised myself I'd come back a different person. I don't like being a spoiled-rotten brat."

"You're not. That's not you."

She sighed. "I know. I'm just weak. I can't say no to Phillip's parents. But I need to get past that. I need to be who I really am, on the inside. And I'm not the kind of girl who throws away money on a ridiculously expensive reception just because she feels pressured."

"So, you're changing . . . everything? You do know your wedding is in three weeks, right? And the guests already have their invitations with the address for the country club."

"I know, I know." She groaned. "It's too

late, isn't it?"

"Maybe." I glanced around to make sure no one else was listening in. Off in the distance, Gillian gave me a wave as she got into her car. I waved back, doing my best to look nonchalant, and then turned to my sister. "So let's talk about this. What's really troubling you?"

She leaned forward and put her head on the steering wheel. I could barely make out her words as she said, "I feel like I'm trapped, Mari. I have to do what his parents say. Mostly his mom. She's so forceful." Crystal's eyes narrowed to slits. "Oh, it's all couched in Southern sweetness — honey this and sweetie that. I even heard it at the shower today. 'Crystal, dear girl, don't you think the bridesmaids' shoes should be dyed pink to match their dresses?' But it's still manipulation, just the same. And I'm afraid it's just the first of a thousand times that's going to happen in the next thirty or forty years."

"So what you're really worried about is not being able to stand up for yourself."

"Yeah." She sighed and lifted her head.

"Have you told Phillip that?"

She shook her head. "Ever since our breakup — and his mom was the one who put doubts in his head, by the way — I've been scared to tell him what I'm really thinking or feeling."

"Because you're afraid of losing him?"

It took her a moment, but she finally nodded. "And because I don't want to stir up animosity between him and his mom. She's so strong willed." Crystal rolled her eyes. "You get my point."

"Then it's more important than ever to have a heart-to-heart with him. Maybe it's not really his parents you're upset with. Maybe it's him. You're trying to please him because you're scared your relationship will fall apart if you don't."

My sister released a sob so quickly that it startled me. Seconds later, she was crumpled over the steering wheel, tears flowing. I knelt down next to the open door and let her cry it out. Then I gave her the best advice I could by whispering, "I'll be praying, Crystal. I promise I will. But don't do anything rash, okay? Maybe the wedding is just the tipping point. You know?"

Crystal nodded just as her cell phone rang. She fished it out of her purse and looked at the screen, her eyes growing wide. "It's Phillip. I . . . I can't talk to him now." She pulled down the visor and checked her appearance. As if he could see her.

"You don't have to talk to him right now.

Wait until you're calmer. Pray, and then call him back."

She nodded just as the phone stopped ringing. "Okay. I will."

"It won't hurt him to wait an hour or two, Crystal. Send him a text and tell him that you'll call him back in a while."

She blew out a slow breath and then did just that. I stood and gave her an encouraging smile. "I'm going to pray that God gives you a peace in your heart when you come to the right decision about the wedding. Until then, just rest. Don't over think it. Don't worry about Dad or the venue or anything. Just pray."

"I will." She gave me a woeful smile. "Thank you, Mari. It helped so much to get that off my chest. You have no idea." A little pause followed as she glanced up at me. "You're my go-to person once again."

"I like being your go-to person. I hope I can still play that role, even after you're an old married woman."

That got a chuckle out of her, the first I'd seen in a while. Still, I knew my sister had a lot to think and pray about. I would keep my promise and pray too. Surely the Lord would calm troubled waters and this wedding could move forward as planned. I hoped.

# CHAPTER EIGHT

I climbed into my car, my thoughts reeling. Would my sister really go through with this? Would she change the venue for the reception? If so, would there be time to pull together a new plan? I sat with the car in park, deep in thought.

Until my phone rang. I recognized Derrick's number right away and did my best to steady my breathing before answering. He greeted me with a carefree, "Hey," followed by, "How did the shower go?"

"It was . . ." I paused as I thought through the events of the day. "Really nice."

"You hesitated."

"Did I?"

"You did." Now he paused. "She didn't like the cookies?"

"Oh, she loved them. Everyone did. And the cupcakes too. Please tell your mom thank you from all the guests. They were thrilled."

"Then why don't you sound thrilled?"

"I . . ."

The intensity of his voice grew. "C'mon, Mari. What aren't you telling me? Was Sienna up to her tricks at the shower?"

"No. Sienna was okay, actually. She even helped clear the tables afterward. It's more my sister this time."

"Crystal?" Derrick sounded worried. "Is she sick?"

Oh boy. I'd painted myself into a corner, hadn't I? How could I answer his questions without giving away too much personal information? "Not really sick, exactly."

"What, then?" I could hear the concern in his voice. "She's not getting cold feet, is she?"

Did he have to come out and ask that? I couldn't lie to him, now could I?

"Mari?"

"I think she's just going through a weird phase. She'll snap out of it." My next words had a pleading tone. "Promise me you won't say anything to Phillip. I'm sure she'll wake up tomorrow and everything will be perfect again. She's just having an off day, maybe." I paused and then sighed. "Or maybe she's still reeling from what they went through a few months ago. Maybe that whole breakup thing shook her confidence more than we realized."

"Well, about that . . ." Derrick's voice faded away mid-sentence.

"She mentioned that it had something to do with his mom. Did you know that?"

Derrick sighed. "Yeah. Phillip's mother thought he should slow things down — don't ask me why, I never could figure it out — but Phillip adores your sister."

"Are you sure?"

"Are you kidding me? The guy can't hold a conversation without talking about her. He notices every little thing she does. You wouldn't believe how many times I've heard that story about her trip to Haiti. He loves that she's so soft-hearted and cares so much about underprivileged kids. I've never known a guy so infatuated with a girl before, and I can definitely see why. She's great."

Hearing all of that made me feel better, but I still had my doubts about my sister's current state of mind.

"I think Phillip's mother is worried about losing her son. You know?" Derrick cleared his throat.

"To a girl who doesn't have a lot of money?" I voiced the words I'd rolled around in my brain over the past few months. "Someone who's not from the country club set?"

374

"Maybe." Derrick paused, and I wondered if I'd lost him. "She can be a little bit of a snob, I suppose, but I think there's more going on this time. I think she's really just going through that empty nest thing. My mom went through that right after I moved out. I'm sure your mom is going to experience some of those feelings after your sister's wedding."

"If there is a wedding."

"There will be. Trust me. If Phillip and Crystal could survive Mrs. Havenhurst's interference a few months back, they can make it through this. Their love is strong, Mari. It's tough, enough to overcome obstacles."

"You know just what to say to calm me down, Derrick. Thank you. I only wish Crystal had heard all that. You would've won her over, for sure."

"Do you think it would help if I called her? I'd be happy to do that."

"She'd kill me if she found out I said anything to you or anyone else."

"Ah. Well, if there's anything I can do . . ." His voice drifted away.

"There is." I paused for a moment and then whispered, "Would you pray? Please?"

"Well, of course." He must've thought I meant, "Right here, right now," because the guy dove into a passionate conversation with the Lord about my sister's upcoming wedding. On and on he went, asking God to lead, guide, and bring peace to Crystal's heart. By the time he finished, I felt completely at peace myself. Wow.

For a few moments neither of us said a word. I finally broke the silence. "Thank you so much for praying, Derrick. That means a lot."

"I've been the one in need of prayer a lot over the years. Remember the story about how I let my parents' breakup send me reeling?"

"Yes."

"Trust me, if God could bring me through that, he can see your sister through all this. He loves her even more than you do, and I know you love her a lot."

"I . . . I do." A lump rose in my throat.

"I've said it before, but I'll say it again. She's blessed to have you." He paused, then cleared his throat. "And I . . . I feel pretty blessed too. Glad I'm getting to know you, Southpaw."

"I feel the same way."

"Let's make a pact to stick together. I have a feeling the bride and groom are going to need us, okay?"

"Sounds good."

We ended the call, and I leaned back against my seat, thoughts spinning. Somehow, knowing Derrick Richardson was on my team brought great comfort. Together, we would get this wedding back on track. Somehow.

# CHAPTER NINE

On the Monday after the shower, Crystal was all smiles again. "I talked to Phillip." She took a nibble of a leftover teacup cookie and her eyes widened. "Mmm. These are great. I didn't get any at the shower. I was too preoccupied."

"Thanks. Derrick did most of the baking."

"I heard all about that from Phillip."

"Oh?"

"Yeah. I hear Derrick is quite a whiz in the kitchen." She took another bite, a look of complete satisfaction on her face.

"So what happened with Phillip? You talked to him, and . . ."

"And" — Crystal grinned and set the cookie down on a napkin — "it went well."

"Are you saying we don't have to return the presents after all?"

"Return the presents?" Grandma Nellie's voice came from behind me. "And why would she have to return the presents?"

Oh, yikes. Man, our grandmother was sneaky, listening in on our conversation. She started firing questions, but finally stopped when she saw my sister putting her finger to her lips.

"Grandma Nellie, don't. You'll scare Mama."

"You're scaring me." Our grandmother's gaze narrowed. "The wedding is still on, right?"

"Right. The wedding is still on." Crystal nodded, then gave me a comforting smile. "Thanks to Mari."

"Mari needs a man." My grandmother rolled her eyes.

"Wait . . . what?" How had we shifted from Crystal's wedding to my love life?

"I said, 'Mari needs a man.'" Grandma Nellie waggled her index finger in my sister's face. "And you, Crystal? You marry that boy. And keep the presents too." Then she headed into the living room, mumbling all the way. I couldn't make out much of it, but got the part about pre-wedding jitters.

"Crystal, you don't think she'll say anything to Mama, do you?"

"No." My sister shook her head. "She knows it would hurt me, so I'm sure she won't." A pause followed, and then her eyes brimmed with tears. "Mari, thank you so much."

"For what?"

"For talking me down from the ledge the other day. And for giving me the courage to have a heart-to-heart with Phillip."

"Tell me about it."

"I told him just what you said, that I've been scared of losing him if I dared to disagree with his mother, especially about any of her ideas for the wedding. He promised me it's not going to happen, no matter what. He even said we could get married at the justice of the peace if I wanted." She giggled and then took another nibble of her cookie.

"The justice of the peace?" Grandma Nellie's voice boomed from the living room. "Over my chubby dead body!"

I shuddered. "Please tell me that's not an option. Mama would have a meltdown."

"No, of course not. But I got his point. He wants me to be happy. And you know what? I am."

"So what did you decide?"

"I'm going to go through with the plans as they are. I've settled the issue in my heart. I'm not going to do it to please Phillip — or his parents — anymore. I'm going to do it because it's going to be the easiest for everyone involved at this point. The work is mostly done." She dropped the cookie and grabbed my hands. "And you, Mari, don't need any more on your plate. You and Derrick have already worked so hard to make everything amazing for us. Why would I do that to you? Or to Mom and Dad?"

"So everything moves forward as planned."

"Yes." She smiled. "And just for the record, my wedding bouquet will be loaded with very clichéd white roses."

"Amen!" I laughed. "Perfect."

"Exactly. Everything will be." Crystal sighed. "I feel good about the whole thing now. In fact, I don't know when I've ever felt better. Talking to Phillip made me feel like I'd lost twenty pounds." She took another bite of the cookie and spoke with a full mouth. "After all the sweets I've consumed, I need to lose twenty pounds." She chased down the cookie with a swig of milk from my glass. "I should start exercising."

"My favorite exercise is a combination of a lunge and a crunch." I took a little nibble of a cookie. "It's called lunch."

She laughed so hard I thought she might choke. "You're perfect just the way you are, Mari."

"Puh-leeze." I laughed. "You're the one

who's perfect, even if you do steal my food like you did when we were little."

"Was I ever little?" She rubbed her tummy and grinned. "And trust me, I'm far from perfect. Though Phillip did say the same thing."

"He's right."

"Oh, he also said something else." Crystal quirked an eyebrow. "He said Derrick told him all about your cookie-baking date."

"Oh?" I tried to act nonchalant. "What did he say?"

"That his mom adores you. And that it was the best four hours he'd ever spent in a kitchen."

"Ha." I giggled. "Well, maybe he's had some bad experiences in a kitchen."

"No, there's more to it than that. He really likes you, Mari. Phillip heard all about it."

I felt the corners of my lips curl up in a smile. No one could blame me, after all. "I really like him, too, Crystal. He's a great guy. Such a big heart."

"Big enough to include a petite little thing like you." She gave me a wink. "Even if you are at the end of the bridesmaid line."

"He'll have to travel farther to get to me."

"Pretty sure he's willing to make the journey, at least from what I gather." She shook her head, and I noticed a bit of an eye roll. "Is it wrong to say that I'm having way too much fun trying to picture the look on Sienna's face when she finds out you two are a couple?"

I shrugged and reached for my milk glass. "Sienna's not around enough to realize it's anything more than an attraction."

"You're right. She's not around much. That's the problem." Crystal shrugged. "But you know what? I love her anyway. And if I'm being totally honest with myself, I have to admit that she's always been like this, so I get what's coming to me for choosing her in the first place. Do you remember what she did to me in sixth grade?"

"Joey O'Shea." We spoke the name in unison.

"Yeah." Crystal smiled. "Best favor anyone ever did me. Joey was a piece of work."

"Whatever happened to him?"

"He sent me a friend request on Facebook. Let's just say he's not what anyone would necessarily call a catch."

"Wow. So I guess we should be thanking Sienna for stealing him away from you all those years ago, right?"

"Guess so. Anyway, I'm happy to be marrying my real Prince Charming. And as for you" — she gave me a knowing look — "I would like to think that, maybe, just maybe, the Lord brought the best man directly into your path. Well, the best man for you, anyway. You can thank me for that later."

"Thank Phillip, you mean."

"Whatever." She finished off her cookie and stood up, then hollered into the living room. "Grandma Nellie, you might as well come back in here. I know you're still eavesdropping."

"I don't eavesdrop." Our grandmother popped her head into the room. "But I like that part about the best man falling in love with Mari."

"See?" My sister laughed. "You were eavesdropping."

Grandma Nellie crossed her arms at her chest and stared at me. "Who could blame me? I worry about this girl."

"Worry? Why are you worried about me?"

"You've waited for a boyfriend so long, I'm tempted to staple a lost dog flyer to your blouse."

"Grandma Nellie!"

"It's true. But now, praise the Lord, I can stop fretting." On and on she went about my reignited love life. Not that I really had a love life . . . yet.

I put my hand up to stop her. "It's not love. I barely know the guy. It's just been a couple of months, you know?"

"Your grandfather and I eloped after six weeks. We were married for thirty years and had four babies." She narrowed her gaze. "Sometimes, the Lord, he works quick."

"True." My sister nodded. "Sometimes, the Lord, he works quick." She gave me another wink.

My cell phone rang, thank goodness. I was ready to be done with this conversation. Still, when I saw Derrick's number, I couldn't help but grin.

"Prince Charming calling?" Our grandmother reached for the broom and pretended to dance with it.

I bit back the smile and nodded. "It's Derrick."

"Mm-hmm. You see?" Grandma Nellie danced back into the living room, still clutching the broom. I reached to press the button, greeted Derrick with a cheerful, "Hello," and then felt my heart skip-skip-skip as he asked me to a picnic.

I agreed, of course. And as I ended the call, I also agreed that my grandmother had been right about one thing. Sometimes, the Lord . . . he works quick.

# CHAPTER TEN

"We couldn't have picked a better day for a picnic."

I looked on, all smiles, as Derrick unfolded a colorful quilt and spread it on the ground. Any day at Memorial Park was a good day, but spending an afternoon in this glorious weather with Derrick . . . blissful!

Of course, I found myself more than a little distracted by the muscles rippling beneath his white T-shirt as he worked. For a moment I felt like a heroine in one of those romance novels Grandma Nellie read — all swoony. Maybe it had something to do with the heat.

"There. Perfect." He finished with the quilt and then gestured toward it as if waiting for my approval.

"Yes." Everything was perfect, all right. He gestured again for me to take a seat, and then he settled in next to me. Our hands brushed as I reached for the basket that held our lunch. For a moment I paused, loving the idea of being so close. He seemed to enjoy it, too, if I could gauge from the contented expression on his face.

Derrick reached to brush a lock of hair off my face with his fingertip, and then he smiled. I froze in place, unable to remember what I needed to do next. Oh yes. Unpack the food.

To our right a family with four young children laughed and talked as they ate at a picnic table. Well, most of them. One of the boys rushed our way, eyes wide. "You're Derrick Richardson."

"I am." Derrick gave him a welcoming smile.

"I . . . I . . ." The boy seemed stuck. "I play too."

"Position?" Derrick looked genuinely in- terested.

"Pitcher." His eyes sparkled with pride. Seconds later his dad joined us, and I lost Derrick to a lengthy conversation about the Astros. Not that I minded at all. In fact, I rather enjoyed it.

Afterward, when the boy and his father left us to ourselves, Derrick turned my way, an apologetic expression on his face. "Sorry about that."

I shook my head. "I'm not, Derrick. It

shows me so much about who you are. You always take time for others. You don't make people feel like they're out of line for approaching you. I love that about you."

"Oh?" His eyes twinkled with mischief. "You love something about me, eh?"

"Well, I, uh . . ." I felt my cheeks grow warm.

"I'm kidding, Southpaw. But I'm glad to know you see more in me than just my so-called talent on the field. It's good, for once, to just be me." He gave me that signature wink of his. "With you."

A little giggle followed on my end. I couldn't help myself. To avoid showing him my embarrassment, I turned my attention to the basket of food. Minutes later, I had our little picnic laid out before us. It looked pretty good, if I did say so myself.

He gave me an admiring look. "I can't believe you pulled this off, Mari. Are you a gourmet chef as well as a cookie baker?"

"No." I laughed as I opened the container of fruit salad. "But I know how to shop at the local deli, and I'm a whiz with paper plates and plastic forks."

"Then you're the girl for me. I happen to be a pro with a paper plate myself."

His right eyebrow elevated, and I could tell he was teasing. Still, he'd lost me at "you're the girl for me." Did he really mean it?

I got my answer fifteen minutes later, after we'd finished eating.

"Want to go for a walk on the trails?"

"Sure."

Derrick rose and extended his hand. I took it and stood up, then smiled when I realized he wasn't letting go. In fact, he didn't let go . . . at all. Instead, we walked at a leisurely pace under the canopy of walnut trees, hand in hand. Derrick stopped when we reached a pretty little pond. I saw why at once. The sunlight shimmered down on the water, creating the most exquisite colors.

"Beautiful," I said after a moment of quiet reflection.

"Yes. Definitely beautiful." Only he wasn't looking at the water, was he? No, Derrick had turned to face me. The tips of his fingers brushed my cheek and a delicious shiver wriggled its way down my spine. I peered up into his face and saw the depth of emotion in his eyes. He slipped his other arm around my waist, and I instinctively leaned in to him, resting my head against his shoulder. In that moment, with the sound of the water rippling nearby and the glow of sunlight on our faces, I felt my heart burst into song.

Okay, not burst into song exactly, but I certainly felt like singing, and all the more as Derrick cupped my chin with his palm. I tilted my head to gaze into his eyes and felt myself captivated by the sweetness as his lips met mine for the most delicious kiss ever.

"You're the most wonderful girl I know, Mari Hays." He whispered soft in my ear.

If any other man had spoken those words, I might not have believed him. But hearing them from Derrick — seeing the sincerity in his eyes — I found myself completely and totally convinced.

And if his words didn't do the trick, the kiss that followed certainly did.

# CHAPTER ELEVEN

The first two weeks of May buzzed by. A sense of anticipation filled everyone in our home as the big day approached, and that excitement spilled over onto the wedding party. I'd never seen the bridesmaids so worked up.

Well, most of them. Our maid of honor — if one was willing to still call her that — had completely checked out from the moment she got the news that Derrick and I were dating. Not that she'd ever checked in, of course. She'd skated along the fringes of this wedding from the get-go, so most of us were used to it by now. We forged ahead without her help, each of us looking forward to the big day.

I found myself celebrating more than just the wedding. With each passing day, my budding relationship with Derrick gave me more to smile about. That wonderful first date at the park had bonded us and propelled us into a "Hey, what do you want to do today?" relationship. And much to the shock of my friends and family, I'd even fallen in love with baseball. Go figure. Perhaps it had a little something to do with the handsome right fielder, who discreetly gave me a special Cub Scout salute every time a new inning started.

As the wedding day approached, I did my best to make every moment with my sister count. More than once Crystal dissolved into tears over seemingly small, insignificant things. Like a greeting card in the mail. Or an unexpected wedding gift from a relative. She blubbered with each bit of news, good or bad. I'd never seen her so emotional. Probably pre-wedding jitters, just like my grandmother had predicted.

On the day before the wedding, I took the day off from work to devote myself completely to my sister. I chauffeured her to a day spa on Friday morning, where we'd arranged to meet the other bridesmaids.

We had planned to get a mani/pedi all together, and then the bride to be would enjoy a massage — a special treat on this very special day. I knew it would cost a pretty penny — we'd chosen the most popular spa in town — but with all the bridesmaids chipping in, we'd cover it, no problem. Besides, Crystal was worth it. She deserved the very best.

During the mani/pedi time, Cassie had us laughing nearly every minute as she told story after story about her ninth-grade boyfriend, a guy named Caleb who was socially awkward.

Thinking about Caleb reminded me of Tyler. In all the wedding excitement I'd almost forgotten that we'd be walking the aisle together. Interesting. Suddenly I didn't mind anymore. In fact, I looked forward to it. I no longer saw Tyler as someone I had to spend time with; I saw him as one of the guys. The wedding had morphed all of us into one big happy family.

Well, most of us. Sienna spent most of the time at the salon texting — once her fingernails were dry. Instead of being angry, I felt a little sorry for her. What kind of person completely ignored those she was with to communicate with someone she wasn't with? On a day this important, she needed to be focused on my sister.

Not that Crystal seemed bothered. As she headed in for her hot stone massage, she gave us all a relaxed smile and thanked us for treating her to such a special day. Once she disappeared, the rest of us gathered to settle up her account. Forty-five dollars for the mani/pedi, plus a five-dollar tip. Seventy-five dollars for the hot stone massage, plus a ten-dollar tip. I quickly divided the total — one hundred and thirty-five dollars — by five, since there were five bridesmaids. It looked like we would each be chipping in twenty-seven dollars. Brianna, Cassie, and Gillian handed over cash. In fact, Cassie threw in a couple of extra dollars.

But when it came time to fetch the funds from Sienna, she seemed confused at best. "Huh?" She gave me a blank stare. "What are you talking about, Mari?"

"Today's outing was a gift for Crystal," I reminded her. "We all decided, remember?"

She shrugged. "I'm pretty sure I would've remembered that. I'm not forking over any more money. I've already paid for that ugly bridesmaid dress, and it's cost me a fortune for my shoes and jewelry for this stupid wedding."

"Stupid wedding?" I stopped cold at those words. "Stupid wedding?" The other three bridesmaids stood beside me, fortifying me and giving me courage to speak my mind. "Are. You. Serious?"

"Yes, I'm serious. And this ridiculous bachelorette party tonight is going to bankrupt me. Do you have any idea how much I had to pay to get the private party room at

Valentino's? It's crazy."

Valentino's? The most exclusive club in Houston? What was she thinking? "So, let's go someplace else," I said. "It doesn't have to be that fancy."

"And have people say I didn't give my friend the best bachelorette party ever? No way. I know what people think already, trust me." Sienna's eyes narrowed. "Besides, I've already ordered the bachelorette package — cake, drinks, everything."

"There aren't really a lot of drinkers in our group anyway, Sienna, so maybe we should just go someplace else?" Cassie cleared her throat.

"Nothing I do is right, is it?" Sienna slung her purse over her shoulder, and I could read the anger in her eyes.

"I . . . I didn't say that." For a moment I almost felt sorry for her. She'd gone to a lot of trouble to get a private room at Valentino's, after all.

"I just want to get this whole stupid thing over with." For a moment, pain flashed in Sienna's eyes.

"The wedding?" I asked.

"The rehearsal. The rehearsal dinner. The bachelorette party. And the wedding. I can't believe I have to walk down the aisle with Derrick Richardson. He's so full of himself."

"Derrick? Arrogant?"

"Yes." Sienna rolled her eyes. "I've never met anyone so stuck up. He hardly gives me the time of day."

"So because he doesn't fawn over you like the other guys do, you think he's arrogant?" Cassie's voice trembled, a sure sign she was angry. "Maybe you need to look in a mirror, Sienna. There's only one arrogant person here, and it's not the best man."

"I'm going to be the bigger person and pretend I didn't hear that ugly remark." Sienna reached into her purse and came out with a tube of lipstick. She smeared it across her lips and smacked them. Loudly.

I fought the temptation to say more. Instead, I paid the balance of the bill myself, and Cassie, Gillian, Brianna, and I opted to walk next door to the frozen yogurt shop to cool down. Sienna obviously didn't care to be with us, anyway.

Gillian remained quiet until we all took a seat at a table. Then she looked at us with a troubled expression. "Did you know that Sienna paid for a private room at Valentino's?"

I shook my head. "No. I mean, I knew she had someplace special in mind, but every time I asked her about plans for the bachelorette party, she said she wanted it to be a surprise."

"But . . . Valentino's?" Brianna looked concerned. "That place is over-the-top expensive. And the cover charge is ridiculous."

"Right." I paused to think through my response. "But I guess it debunks the theory that Sienna has completely fallen down on the job."

"Still . . . Valentino's?" Cassie pinched her eyes shut and shook her head. "I can't imagine even walking in there. Definitely not my sort of place."

"Mine either," I said. "But it won't kill us to go. We can eat cake and drink diet soda."

"I guess." Gillian gave me an impish smile. "Just one more thing I can knock off my bucket list. A night at Houston's most exclusive club."

"Yippee skippy." Brianna laughed. "Can't wait to tell my grandchildren about that."

When we walked back to the spa, we found Sienna on her phone — of course — talking in an over-the-top voice to someone on the other end about "this ridiculous wedding."

When she saw us, she stopped talking long enough to glare.

My sister emerged from the massage room just about the time I thought Cassie was going to knock Sienna's lights out. The cranky maid of honor ended her call and shoved her phone into her purse, then plastered on the fakest smile I'd ever seen.

Crystal had a blissful look on her face. Her eyes filled with tears when she saw the five of us standing together. "Ooh, what a perfect picture. Do you mind?" She fished around in her purse and came out with her phone, then took a photo. "Thank you. I always want to remember the five ladies who gave me such a beautiful gift the day before my wedding."

Another fake smile followed from Sienna.

"That was so relaxing." Crystal hadn't noticed the deception. "It was the perfect way to take a little breather before the rehearsal dinner tonight. I can't thank you enough." She reached to give each of us a warm hug. When she got to Sienna, I wanted to say something. Ooh, did I ever want to say something. From the look on Cassie's face, I could tell she did too.

But we didn't. We just smiled and watched as the bride hugged her maid of honor and proclaimed this day the best ever. If we kept the peace, it would be the best day ever. I made up my mind right then and there to do whatever it took to keep that radiant smile on the bride's face. Even if it killed me.

# CHAPTER TWELVE

Later that evening we at tended the wedding rehearsal at the church, followed by a relaxing BBQ at our house, hosted by my parents. My father was in rare form, joking with everyone as he filled their plates with meat straight off the grill. I could tell Mama was a little stressed at first, what with the Havenhursts being in our home for the first time and all, but everyone seemed to have a great time.

When the rehearsal dinner ended, I headed out with the bridesmaids to the bachelorette party at Valentino's. We ended up having a great time, eating cake, sipping on diet sodas, and listening to the band. Sienna pulled Crystal out onto the dance floor and we all giggled as they did a silly dance. For the first time in ages, the wayward maid of honor looked comfortable in her role.

After a few more goofy dance moves, they

returned to the table, where Sienna made a toast to the bride to be. I found the whole thing rather endearing. Maybe I'd been wrong about her. She'd waited till the eleventh hour to come through for my sister, but Crystal seemed deliriously happy, and that was all that mattered to me.

By eleven o'clock we had all fizzled out. Crystal and I said our good-byes to the other girls and headed home. I dozed off just minutes after my head hit the pillow.

The following morning I awoke, raring to go. Just before my feet hit the floor, however, I paused to pray. This was the most important day in my sister's life and I wanted to start it off right. A few minutes later I found Crystal in the kitchen, at the table with Mama and Grandma Nellie. All three of them were drinking coffee. I poured a cup and joined them.

"I can't believe it." Crystal's voice trembled as she looked from person to person.

"What, honey?" Mama asked.

"This is going to be the last time we all sit here together at the breakfast table. It's just . . . bittersweet." A few tears trickled down her cheeks.

Mama and Grandma both started crying at this point. Oh boy. What a mess. Seconds later, tears stung my eyes, but I brushed them away before my sister could see them.

We sat until we'd each finished a second cup, laughing and talking over old times. Dad joined us moments later, still dressed in his boxers and undershirt. No doubt Crystal wouldn't miss this part of our morning routine.

By the time the clock chimed nine, however, we realized the party had to come to an end. Though the wedding wasn't scheduled to begin until two, the bridesmaids would meet at the church at eleven to begin the process of fixing hair and putting on makeup. I could hardly wait.

After showering and dressing in capris and a button-down shirt, Crystal made a phone call to her wedding coordinator to check on the progress in the sanctuary and at the country club. From what I could gather, Mrs. Frazier seemed a bit discombobulated but still confident the day would come off without a hitch.

I helped my sister pack her car with everything we would need — my dress and her gown, shoes, hair clips, jewelry, and the biggest makeup bag in the history of weddings. With Crystal's nerves a jumbled mess, I offered to drive. She nodded and climbed into the passenger seat.

Her cell phone rang just as we pulled into

the church's parking lot.

"It's Sienna."

"Ah." I didn't want to speculate, so I kept my mouth shut.

A couple of minutes later, however, I didn't have to speculate.

Crystal ended the call and shoved the phone into her purse. "I don't believe it."

"What?"

"She's getting her hair done."

"But I thought we were doing that here. Helping each other, I mean."

"Right?" My sister shook her head. "She said she didn't trust the girls to get her hair right, so she's paying top dollar to have it done at The Strand."

"The Strand?" I couldn't help but gasp. Who could afford to have their hair done at The Strand? Maybe folks like Mrs. Havenhurst, but not girls like Sienna, who worked at the tanning salon for minimal pay.

"Apparently Sienna's had the appointment all along. She never planned to be with me on my wedding day. She said she's been saving for weeks. Can you believe that?"

"Wow." We spoke the word in unison.

My sister opened her car door and stepped out. "Don't. Even. Get. Me. Started."

"O-okay." I plastered on a smile and

climbed out of the car. The other brides-maids greeted us seconds later. We worked in tandem to carry all our gear into the church, where we quickly set up camp in the small bride's room. Mrs. Frazier had placed a full-length mirror in the corner. It would come in handy later, once we put on our gowns, but for now we headed to the ladies' room to work on hair and makeup. At noon, Mama and Grandma Nellie appeared with a tray of meats and cheeses from a local deli.

"Eat." My grandmother pulled the lid off the tray. "And don't forget to drink plenty of water. We don't need any of you fainting at the altar."

"Yes, ma'am." I gave her the same little salute Derrick always gave me, then giggled.

After a few bites, we got distracted with the bride's hair and makeup. She looked like a cover model, a true princess.

By twelve thirty the rest of us had every hair in place and had turned our attention to makeup. With the photographer snapping pictures at every turn, I found myself making quite a production out of the wedding prep process. What fun!

Of course, we were still missing the maid of honor. She was noticeably absent from every photo. Ugh. When twelve forty-five rolled around and Sienna still hadn't arrived, I found my anger mounting. I headed out to the hallway to use my cell phone to call her. I stumbled into Derrick, who was walking down the hall, tuxedo bag slung over his shoulder. He let out a whistle as he saw me.

"Wow. Mari, you look gorgeous."

"Really?" I gestured to my jeans and sleeveless shirt. "In this?"

"Doesn't matter. You look amazing, and I can only imagine what you'll look like in that bridesmaid dress. Can't wait to see." He hung his tuxedo bag on a nearby door handle and walked toward me. My anger dissipated as he pulled me into his arms and gave me a kiss on the cheek. "Sorry, don't want to mess up that perfect makeup job."

"It's the only thing that's perfect right now."

"Oh?" He stepped back. "Something's gone wrong?"

"Just a missing maid of honor. Sienna isn't here yet."

"You're kidding." His eyes reflected the same concern I felt.

"I wish I was kidding. She's at The Strand, having her hair done. Don't even get me started, or I'll tell you what I think about that."

"Wow."

"I'm. Just. So. Mad. At. Her." As the words were spoken, I began to tremble. How dare Sienna ruin my sister's big day?

"Deep breath, Mari." Derrick rested his hands on my shoulders and gazed into my eyes. "Crystal is taking her cues from you. They all are."

"They are? Why?"

"Because you've been the natural leader all along. You're the real maid of honor, whether you hold the title or not. And it's time to step onto the mound and pitch a winning game."

"Huh?"

"Do what comes naturally. Put the biggest smile on your face and give your sister the best day of her life, free from worries and stresses." He pulled me into his arms. "You can do it, Southpaw." He whispered the words soft into my ear. "I know you can. You're a pro player."

He groaned and slapped himself on the forehead. "Sorry. I called you a player again. But you know what I mean."

I sure did. I gazed up into his eyes and felt my cares slip away. He gave me a kiss on the tip of my nose, then loosened his hold on me and took a step back. "Guess I'd better get into this tux. We're scheduled to have our photos done at one, I think."

"Right. The bridesmaids are supposed to be ready for pictures at ten after. That's one of the reasons I'm so stressed about Sienna not showing up on time."

"Do your best to relax. If you get nervous, just look my way and I'll give you a little salute."

"Don't you dare! Not in the middle of the ceremony."

"Just kidding." He pulled me close one last time. "The next time you see me, I'll be standing at the front of the church holding up the groom. I've never seen Phillip so nervous."

"The next time you see me, I'll be standing at the end of the line —"

"You'll be at the front of the line, in my book." He paused. "And just so you know, I might have to walk up the aisle with Sienna — if she shows up, I mean — but I'll be focused on someone else. There's only one girl here who's caught my eye. And I hope she'll save the first dance for me."

"Oh, she'll save you a dance, for sure." I gave him a light kiss on the lips, doing my best not to mess up my lipstick. Just as quickly, I changed my mind. To heck with the lipstick. I gave the best man a kiss he wouldn't soon forget.

Afterward I walked back to the bride's room, my thoughts now shifting from Sienna to Derrick. I slipped on my pink gown and checked my appearance in the full-length mirror. Cassie, Brianna, and Gillian joined me, and we sighed in unison.

"We look pretty in pink." Gillian giggled. "Don't you think?"

"You're a poet, Gillian." Cassie laughed. "But yes, I think we look amazing in pink."

"I knew you would!" My sister, still dressed in a shirt and capris, joined us. We stood, a deliriously happy group of giddy females, staring at our reflections until Crystal startled to attention. "I need to get into my gown. Will you help me?"

"Of course!" I flew into action, heading straight for the bag that held her wedding gown. I knew the photographer would be looking for us soon, so we'd better get this show on the road.

Before I could even unzip the bag, Sienna came rushing in. The frazzled maid of honor was dressed in short-shorts and a snug shirt, but her hair and makeup were impeccable. She greeted us with a squeal, followed by, "I'm so sorry, Crystal! It took forever at the salon. Would you believe they gave someone else my appointment time?" On and on she went, griping about what a rough morning she'd had. Ugh.

"Sienna, I cannot believe you went to a salon to have your hair and makeup done on your best friend's wedding day." Cassie folded her arms at her chest and glared at the maid of honor. "Seriously?"

"Well, of course. I wanted to look perfect for Crystal." Sienna looked absolutely devastated that we didn't get it.

"I wanted you to be here for me, Sienna. I couldn't care less whether you look perfect." Crystal squared her shoulders and stepped into place directly in front of Sienna. I noticed my sister's hands trembling. I didn't blame her for being angry. "We spent the morning together. We helped each other with hair and makeup. That was half the fun. But you missed all of it."

"I'm here now." Sienna gave her a little pouting look. "I can help you put on your gown."

"You're not even dressed yet. We're supposed to be ready for pictures at ten after one."

"I can do it. I'm fast. I left my dress hanging in the ladies' room. I'll go put it on there." Sienna took off running.

Cassie shook her head. "Wow. Well, I guess

we should be glad she showed up at all, right?"

"Whatever." My sister rolled her eyes, then looked at me.

"Don't let it get to you, Crystal. At least she wanted to look great for your big day. There is that."

"Probably still hoping Derrick will look her way." Crystal groaned. "I'm sorry, Mari. That was rude. And hurtful. Will you forgive me?"

I shrugged. "Nothing to forgive. You're probably right."

"I have it on good authority he's only got eyes for you now." Crystal gave me a reassuring nod.

About ten minutes later, we gave up waiting on Sienna and helped Crystal into her wedding gown. I'd never seen a more radiant bride. The gown fit just right, accentuating her tiny waistline. The beading on the bodice took my breath away, but the full skirt sent me over the moon.

"Oh, Crystal!" Brianna clasped her hands to her chest. "You're picture perfect."

"Exquisite!" Cassie added.

Crystal gazed at her reflection in the full-length mirror, tears brimming.

"Oh no you don't!" Gillian reached for a tissue. "Don't you dare ruin that beautiful makeup job. No tears. Promise?"

Crystal had just nodded when Sienna came rushing into the room wearing her dress. Only it wasn't her dress, at least not the one she'd purchased that day at the bridal shop. The one she wore today was shorter and a different shade of pink. Worst of all, the shoulder straps were missing, definitely not an appropriate look for someone as buxom as Sienna.

"Sienna?" My sister turned away from the mirror and gave her a blank stare. "What in the world are you wearing?"

"What do you mean?" Sienna checked her appearance in the full-length mirror. "It's my maid of honor dress, silly."

"That's not the same dress. It looks nothing like the one you bought." Crystal pointed at all the rest of us bridesmaids. "You look nothing like them."

"Well, I'm the maid of honor. I'm supposed to look different. A little fancier. You know." She nudged her way in front of the bride to look at her reflection in the full-length mirror.

"Wouldn't that be my decision?" My sister balled up her fists and placed them on her hips. "What did you do, go back and get another dress?"

"Nope. Just had that pink thing altered a little."

"A little?" We all asked in unison.

"Well, I had them raise the hemline. That mid-calf look is not good on me. And I think I look better in a strapless dress, too, so I had the straps removed."

Double-D's with no straps. Oh dear. I sensed the whole top could come tumbling down at a moment's notice.

"That's not even the same shade of pink." Crystal's complexion was looking mighty pink too.

"Well, I meant to talk to you about that." Sienna wrinkled her nose and gave my sister a little shrug. "I've never looked good in cotton-candy pink, so I asked the alterations lady to dye it a darker shade. Since I forgot to tell you, I was hoping you wouldn't notice."

"Wouldn't notice a hot-pink mini-skirted maid of honor with a strapless dress? Are you kidding me?"

"Everyone will notice I'm different from the others and know for sure I'm the maid of honor. So that's a good thing, right? Isn't that the point? I need to be different."

"She's different, all right." Gillian sighed and went back to work on my sister's wedding gown, fixing the bustle.

Crystal closed her eyes, and I could see her counting silently. Her lips moved as she mouthed out, "One, two, three, four . . ."

Not that Sienna seemed to notice. On and on she went, talking about herself. Not a word about how beautiful Crystal looked in her wedding gown. All conversation was focused squarely on herself.

Just about the time I felt my temper mounting to a new high, the photographer knocked on the door. I gestured for her to come inside for a couple of photos in the changing room before heading into the sanctuary for the group photos. My parents entered the room seconds later, both erupting into tears when they saw Crystal in her gown. They gushed with all sorts of flattering words, hugs, and well wishes, and the bridesmaids joined in, all smiles.

Finally. The focus had shifted to the proper person. Now, if we could just keep it that way, all would be well.

# CHAPTER THIRTEEN

At five minutes after two, with the sanctuary filled to the brim with guests, the long-anticipated wedding ceremony began. The bridesmaids had gathered in the foyer, doors to the sanctuary closed until the appropriate moment. When Mrs. Frazier gave the go-ahead, the processional got underway. She swung the door open and the bridesmaids entered, one by one.

I led the way, my heart in my throat as I took one calculated step after another. To think I'd once fretted over being the last in line. It had never occurred to me that I'd be the first to make an entrance. What was it the Bible said about the first being last and the last being first? I almost giggled now, thinking of the irony.

Next came Brianna. Then Gillian. Then Cassie. Finally Sienna stepped into the sanctuary. Of course, her low-cut gown caused quite a stir among wide-eyed guests.

I turned my focus to Phillip and his groomsmen, who stood in a perfect row at the front
of the church.

Okay, so the groom looked a little wobbly.
Nauseated, in fact. But when the back doors
of the sanctuary opened a second time to
reveal his beautiful bride, Phillip's expression shifted from fear to deep, pure love.
And joy. I could see the excitement behind
the tears in his eyes as he watched my gorgeous, wonderful sister make her way down
the aisle on our father's arm.

Looked like my dad was a little misty too.
As they neared the front of the church and
the pastor asked, "Who gives this woman to
be married to this man?" my father could
barely spit out the words, "Her mother and
I." He managed, and then took a seat on
the front row next to Mom and Grandma
Nellie. Mama once again dabbed her eyes
with a tissue. I glanced at Mr. and Mrs. Havenhurst on the other side of the aisle.
Phillip's mother appeared to be smiling
through her tears, too — a sincere smile.
Perhaps she finally realized just how happy
her son was to be marrying my sister. The
look of sheer bliss on Phillip's face was all
the proof anyone could ever need, after all.

Our pastor welcomed the guests and the
ceremony got underway, but I found myself

distracted as the best man gave me his signature wink. I felt my cheeks grow warm. I gave him a warning look, but it didn't stop him. This time I shook my head and nodded slightly toward the bride and groom. Derrick finally focused on them . . . thank goodness.

My gaze shifted from Derrick to the other groomsmen standing in line behind him. Like me, Tyler was at the end of his row. Wow. He looked pretty spiffy in a tuxedo. With his face clearing up and his hair neatly combed, I almost didn't recognize him. Then again, he looked a little uncomfortable in the bow tie. He tugged at it, a pained expression on his face.

I tried to focus on the happy couple, but found myself completely distracted. Memories of my sister flooded over me as they said their "I do's." The two of us swimming at the neighborhood pool. Vacationing at Disneyworld with our parents. Mission trips with our youth group. These images planted themselves in me, but I did my best to push away the tears.

The tears could not be held back, however, as Crystal and Phillip had their first kiss as a married couple. And the emotions only intensified when the pastor introduced them as husband and wife. The congregation gave a cheer as the new Mr. and Mrs. Havenhurst turned to face them, then headed up the aisle.

Sienna and Derrick linked arms and headed up the aisle after them. Sienna seemed a little subdued, and I briefly wondered why. Then Gillian and her partner, followed by Brianna and hers. Tyler and I met in the middle. He gave me his arm, flashed a comforting smile, and we walked up the aisle last. I didn't have a care in the world, nor did I feel less than any of the others. In fact, thoughts about me didn't enter into it. I was far too busy focusing on my sister and Phillip, who were standing in the foyer, kissing.

A few minutes later the foyer filled with happy wedding guests, who offered their congratulations. I allowed myself to be pushed to the edge of the crowd, pressed away by the ever-growing throng. Fortunately, I wasn't alone. I found myself standing right next to Derrick, who slipped his arm around my waist.

"That went well." He drew me close.

"Mm-hmm." I snuggled up to him, loving the scent of his cologne. "Loved every minute."

"Oh, but the fun is just beginning. Remember, you promised me a dance."

"I did. I hope your feet are ready for the pain I'm going to cause."

He laughed and then turned his attention to Tyler, who called out to us to join the rest of the wedding party. We still had a handful of pictures to take before leaving for the reception. The photos would forever mark my spot as the end-of-the-line bridesmaid, but I didn't care. Not one bit. All that mattered now was celebrating the happily ever after of my sister and her new husband.

But, I admit, I was pondering the possibilities for a happily ever after of my own. Just as soon as we wrapped up the photoshoot.

The photographer had obviously done this a time or two. She corralled us into position after position, taking one photo after the next. I couldn't help but notice that she angled Sienna to hide the Double-D's. Mostly, anyway. Oh well. We would laugh about them later. Maybe.

When the photo shoot ended, I rode with the other attendants to the River Oaks Country Club. Phillip's father had rented limos for the whole wedding party and, despite my earlier reservations about feeling out of place in a hoity-toity world, I enjoyed the ride immensely.

"A girl could get used to this." Cassie

giggled as she leaned back against the seat. "Don't you think?"

"I do." Brianna opened a can of soda and poured it into a glass of ice. "They can chauffer me around any day."

I glanced over at Sienna, who remained quiet, gazing out the window. Her silence threw me a little. "Didn't you think the wedding was gorgeous, Sienna?"

"Hmm?" She looked away from the window. "What?"

"The wedding," I repeated. "It was beautiful."

She shrugged. "Yes. It was great. I'm sure even Phillip's mother would agree. I know she's given Crystal kind of a hard time."

"Well, I thought it was great." My heart flooded with emotion as I glanced from one bridesmaid to another. "I've loved every minute of getting to know you all better. I don't want this to end."

"Interesting." Sienna turned back to the window. "Because I can't wait for it to be over."

"You don't mean that. I think maybe you're just sad and a little confused right now."

She shrugged again and continued to stare out the window. When we arrived at the country club, we were all staring out the window.

I'd heard about the River Oaks Country Club for years but had never seen it for myself. Now, as the driver swung the door of the limo open and offered me his hand, I stepped into a whole new world. The gorgeous front doors were majestic in size. Gorgeous. I could barely breathe as I took it all in.

A man in a tuxedo greeted us, and we took a few cautious steps into the grand foyer. "Are you here for the Havenhurst reception?"

I nodded, unable to speak as I gazed upward at the massive chandeliers, in all of their crystallized beauty.

"This way, please." He gestured down the hallway to our right and we walked as a group until we came to the reception hall. There simply were no words to describe its beauty.

"Wow." Cassie's eyes widened. "This is . . . wow."

"Wow is right." I stood completely dumbfounded by the place.

Off in the distance a band played country tunes, my sister's favorite. The heavenly aroma of food emanated from the buffet table to our right. I pushed away the "sixty-five dollars a head" speech rolling around in my brain and made up my mind to relax and enjoy myself.

A few minutes later my parents arrived with Grandma Nellie close behind. As they were seated, she carried on and on about the beautiful room. "This place!" She gestured to the hall chandeliers, also dripping with crystals. "I've never seen anything like it."

"Me either. But I think Crystal is going to have the time of her life. This is perfect for her."

"She deserves this." My grandmother's eyes flooded with tears. "You, too, precious girl. You deserve this, and so much more."

"Aw, thank you, Grandma Nellie. Maybe someday."

"Maybe someday . . . soon." She nodded toward Derrick, who stood nearby, talking to one of the groomsmen. "Remember, sometimes the Lord —"

I put up my hand and laughed. "Don't say it. Don't say it."

At that moment, the deejay announced the arrival of the bride and groom. The guests rose and greeted them with applause, and then the band began to play.

I stepped away from my family's table as Crystal and Phillip took to the floor to share their first dance as husband and wife. In that moment, as I saw the two of them together, all concerns about my sister's happiness faded away. Phillip couldn't take his eyes off her, and she returned his gaze, a blissful expression on her face.

"They're a perfect match."

I turned when I heard Derrick's voice and then nodded, a lump rising in my throat. I managed to speak above it as I said, "Yes, they are."

Derrick slipped his arm around my shoulders and pulled me close. "I'm just waiting for all the designated dances to end so I can spin you around the dance floor."

"Did I forget to mention that I'm a terrible dancer?"

"Sure you are."

"No, really. I'm terrible."

"You said you were terrible at baking, too, and you made some pretty amazing cookies."

"Your mom made those."

"Well, sometimes all it takes is someone leading the way." He gave me a knowing look. "You can follow and learn the steps."

"So you're good at dancing?"

"No." He laughed. "I was kind of hoping you were so you could teach me. But I know enough to fake it." He leaned close, his voice lowering. "And honestly? I won't be thinking about my feet. If you'll dance with me, I'll just be thinking about how lucky I am."

Okay, someone had better pinch me, and quick. What had I done to deserve a guy like this?

Before I could give it another thought, one of the wedding guests approached Derrick. "Dude, you're Derrick Richardson."

"I am."

"Could I have your autograph?"

"Of course." He signed the guy's wedding program. This started a group of fans gathering around him, just as my father took to the floor for the father-daughter dance. Derrick continued to sign autographs as Phillip and his mom shared a dance, but he finally managed to turn everyone's attention back to the bride and groom, who opened the dance floor to all of their guests.

"Finally!" Derrick slipped his arm around my waist again. "I thought this moment would never come. Let's hit the floor, Southpaw."

I took a couple of steps, but a troubling thought caused me to stop just short of the dance floor. "I'd love to dance with you, Derrick, but before I do, I think I need to take a spin with a different partner. Do you mind?"

"A different partner?" For a moment Derrick looked offended — until I pointed to Tyler, who stood against the wall, looking lost and a little overwhelmed. "Ah. Great move, Southpaw. Show the guy how to trip the light fantastic."

"I'll show him how to trip, all right. Over my feet, is more like it." The belly laugh that followed must've startled the prim and proper woman to my right. She turned to give me a stare, straight down her nose. Oops. Almost forgot where I was. People probably didn't belly laugh at the River Oaks Country Club.

"Promise you'll save the next dance for me?" Derrick asked.

I nodded and then stood on tiptoes to give him a kiss on the cheek. "I promise." Then, with a song in my heart, I headed over to Tyler, extended my hand, and offered him the first dance.

# CHAPTER FOURTEEN

My sister's reception turned out to be the party of the century. I'd never seen so many people have such fun. Turned out the country club set knew how to celebrate, especially when it came to the dance floor, where they boot-scoot'n boogied the night away. Go figure.

The sixty-five-dollar-per-head dinner was scrum-diddly-umptious. Even Grandma Nellie agreed. My dad loved the Chicken Cordon Bleu so much that he almost forgot about the price tag attached. Almost.

And me? I almost forgot there was no nacho cheese dip to be found anywhere.

After Crystal and Phillip cut the cake, the time arrived for the maid of honor and best man to give their speeches. Derrick went first. My heart went out to him as he held the microphone in hand. I'd seen him perform on the ball field, but how would he do with a speech? Turned out, pretty good.

He told stories about Phillip that made us laugh . . . and sigh. I had to give it to him.

His job as best man now complete, he passed the microphone to Sienna. Poor girl. Her social skills obviously didn't extend to public speaking. She stumble-bumbled her way through the speech, pretty much making a goober of herself. In fact, she got so flustered at one point that I thought she might run from the room crying.

Derrick gave me that same knowing look he'd given me before. As Sienna ended her speech, he took the microphone and handed it to me. I put my hand over it and mouthed the words, "What are you doing?"

"You know." He nodded. "Go for it. Give your sister a maid of honor speech she'll never forget."

And so I did. I shared a funny story about the time we'd shared an upper bunk at camp, and she'd knocked me out of it in the middle of the night. I also told the story about the night she'd decided to go on the mission trip to Haiti, how she'd cried as she talked about the children she wanted to help.

When I finished, the whole crowd cheered. Crystal threw her arms around my neck and squeezed me so tight she almost crushed my windpipe. Next in line to give me a power hug was Phillip. After that, strangely, Sienna. She gave me a quick hug and mumbled, "Thank you for saving my neck." I hadn't really saved her, of course, but hugged her in response. Maybe, with time, this goofy girl would win me over. And she did, when she added, "You know I love her. Do you think she'll forgive me for falling down on the job?"

"Of course. My sister loves you too, you know."

In a surprise move, Sienna threw her arms around my neck and gave me a warm hug. Though stunned, I couldn't help but hug her back. Afterward, she gave me a cute little wave and then headed across the room to visit with some of the other bridesmaids. Go figure.

I headed to the cake table for a second slice of the dark chocolate groom's cake. I found my father standing nearby with a large slice from the almond-flavored wedding tier. He took a big bite and sighed, then spoke with a full mouth. "Good stuff. Almost worth the fifteen-hundred-dollar price tag."

"It is pretty good. Wonder what that breaks down to per slice?"

"I'd rather not think about it, thank you very much." He took another huge bite.

I laughed and then continued to eat my cake. Mmm.

Just about that time, the deejay announced it was time for the bouquet toss. I hadn't planned to join the festivities, but my father insisted. "Go ahead, Mari. I'll slip over there and tell your sister to aim it your direction. I paid a hundred and twenty-five dollars for that throw-away bouquet. I'd like to keep it in the family."

I put my cake plate down. "You'll do no such thing. But, are you serious? Don't you know what it means if I catch it?" I stared at him, not quite believing it. "You're already wanting to do this wedding thing all over again? Don't you think you'd better give your wallet a rest?"

"Yeah, probably. But I know you. When you do get married, it won't be here. It'll be a simple wedding at the church with a reception in the fellowship hall. I'll toss a couple of briskets on the grill and we'll invite folks to wear their cowboy boots. And you won't be paying fifteen hundred dollars for a high-end wedding cake."

"You're right about that last part. I happen to know someone who's great at baking, and she would probably be open to the idea of making my cake. But why are we talking about weddings, Dad? Derrick and I have only been dating a while."

"I know that, but a father can hope, can't he? You know how cool it would be if I could tell people my daughter was going to marry a pro baseball player? I'd be a celebrity at the office."

"So this isn't really about me?" I shook my head. "You want me to marry a pro ballplayer because it'll make you more popular at work?"

"Hey, just saying it wouldn't hurt. And maybe we'd get season tickets to the Astros games. I'm not asking him to fork them over right now, of course, but maybe one day. And who knows? You and Derrick might fall head over heels in a hurry and decide you can't wait to tie the knot. Stranger things have happened."

The deejay called for single women to line up behind the bride and, at my father's insistence, I walked over to join the other bridesmaids. My sister counted down — "three, two, one . . ." — and then the bouquet flew up in the air, over her head, headed straight for me. I almost had it in my hands when Sienna took a flying leap and attempted to grab it away.

*Really?*

*Oh. No. You. Don't.*

Thank goodness, I grabbed it first. The

bouquet was mine, all hundred and twenty-five dollars' worth of it.

The crowd cheered, especially my father, who must've taken it as a sign straight from above. He walked over to Derrick, patted him on the back, and then said something that made my fella laugh.

Derrick looked my way and shrugged. I returned the gesture and then held the bouquet close, concerned that Sienna might still try to nab it. Behind me, I heard my grandmother's voice ring out. "I told you, precious girl."

I turned to face her. "Told me what?"

"Sometimes, the Lord, he —"

"I know, I know." Laughter followed on my end. "Don't say it, Grandma Nellie."

Derrick stepped into the spot beside me, his brow wrinkled in obvious confusion. "Don't say what?"

"Oh, nothing." I tried not to giggle when my grandmother jabbed me with her elbow.

Derrick extended his hand and then gave me a little nod. "Could I interest you in another dance, Ms. Hays?"

"Absolutely." I pressed the bouquet into Grandma Nellie's hands and then took his arm. "You certainly may, Mr. Richardson."

I couldn't help but notice the photographer snap our picture as we headed out to the dance floor. I didn't mind, as long as it didn't end up on the front page of the sports section. Or, heaven forbid, the society column. I cringed just thinking about that one.

Then again, dating a guy as famous as Derrick probably meant my whole life would change, once the tabloids caught on. Maybe I'd better prepare for life in the spotlight. And while I was at it, I'd prepare for a lot of baseball games in my future. Knowing this wonderful fella was on my team suddenly made the sport much more appealing.

And, as he took me for a spin around the dance floor, I had to admit one other thing as well. I might not be the maid of honor at this shindig, but this guy — this awesome, Godly guy — was certainly the best man for me.

# ACKNOWLEDGMENTS

A huge "Thank you" to my editors, Becky Monds and Karli Jackson. I'm grateful you gals took a chance on me. Working for HarperCollins has been pure delight!

To my copy editor, Jean Bloom: You put a lovely Texas spit-shine on this story and I'm tickled to have your input. Mari's tale is in much finer shape, thanks to you.

To my wonderful agent, Chip MacGregor: you are my biggest cheerleader and faithful guide. How wonderful to walk alongside you.

To my prayer team: Kathleen, Dannelle, Sharen, and Linda: you've been a God-send. Thank you for walking me through the ups and downs of this past year.

To all of the girls out there who've ever walked a mile in Mari's shoes: You know what it's like to be overlooked and to feel left out. Don't let that stop you from responding with grace and ease. You might be the last bridesmaid in the lineup but you're still #1 in God's eyes.

And last, but certainly not least: to my Lord and Savior Jesus Christ. Every word is for You.

# DISCUSSION QUESTIONS

1. Mari feels slighted when she's overlooked for the maid of honor position. Have you ever felt offended as a result of being overlooked? If so, how did you respond?
2. Crystal's future mother-in-law is the overbearing sort. If you were in Crystal's shoes, how would you handle Mrs. Hayvenhurst's demands?
3. Sienna falls down on the job as maid of honor and Mari has to fill in the gap. Have you ever had to step up for someone who didn't do his/her job properly? If so, how did you handle it?
4. Derrick is well known and loved for his abilities as a right fielder. Why do you suppose he enjoyed the fact that Mari saw more in him that just his talent?
5. There's a fairly large socioeconomic gap between Crystal's family and Phillip's. How would a typical upper/middle class father-of-the-bride react to the news that

he had to pay for such an expensive event?

6. Mari and Derrick's first "date" takes place as they bake for the bridal shower. What do you learn about his character as he nabs cookies behind his mother's back?

7. In the end, Mari gives the first dance to Tyler, not Derrick. What did you think of this gesture? Would you have done the same?

8. Do you agree with Grandma Nellie? Does the Lord really "work quick" sometimes? Has He ever done so in your life?

# ABOUT THE AUTHOR

Award-winning author **Janice Thompson** also writes under the pseudonym Janice Hanna. She got her start in the industry writing screenplays and musical comedies for the stage. Janice has published over 100 books for the Christian market, crossing genre lines to write cozy mysteries, historicals, romances, nonfiction books, devotionals, children's books, and more. She particularly enjoys writing light-hearted, comedic tales because she enjoys making readers laugh.

Janice was named the 2008 Mentor of the year for ACFW (American Christian Fiction Writers). She currently serves as president of her local ACFW chapter (Writers on the Storm), where she regularly teaches on the craft of writing.

Janice is passionate about her faith and does all she can to share the joy of the Lord with others, which is why she particularly enjoys writing. Her tagline, "Love, Laughter, and Happily Ever Afters!" sums up her take on life.

She lives in Spring, Texas, where she leads a rich life with her family, a host of writing friends, and two mischievous dachshunds. When she's not busy writing or playing with her eight grandchildren, Janice can be found in the kitchen, baking specialty cakes and cookies for friends and loved ones. No matter what she's cooking up — books, cakes, cookies or mischief — she does her best to keep the Lord at the center of it all. You can find out more about Janice at www .janiceathompson.com.